the six loves of ebony jones

THE HOLIDAY SISTERS

TERREECE M CLARKE

LIFESLICE MEDIA

"To those who have given up on love: I say, 'Trust life a little bit'."

MAYA ANGELOU

contents

Author's Note ix
Playlist xi

1. No Scrubs 1
2. Still Blocked 14
3. Vacation Hookups Don't Count 26
4. Clear the Air 39
5. A Can of Worms 52
6. The First Love. 65
7. Decompress and Debrief 76
8. Trauma Bonding 84
9. The Crazy Love. 91
10. Debrief Part Deux 100
11. We're A Team 110
12. Whatever You Need 121
13. Copper Smile 130
14. You Told Me to Sit on Your Face! 144
15. My Teddy-Weddy 154
16. Uncomplicated 166
17. Happy Birthday to Me 178
18. Respect me 195
19. Young Hoes 202
20. Dead Chickens 214
21. The Safe Love. 220
22. Butt Play 226
23. What I Do 228
24. Real Villain 239
25. The Love That Almost Broke Me 241
26. What If... 252
27. The Almost Forever Love. 261
28. Tender Parts 276
29. Perfect 278
30. One 285

31. I'm Glad It Was You — 291
32. Group Therapy — 295
33. Good Shot — 297
34. Stop Bleeding — 306
35. New Balance — 308
36. Vegas — 322
One Year Later — 332

Acknowledgments — 339
Also by Terreece M Clarke — 340
About the Author — 341

Thank you for picking up The Six Loves of Ebony Jones. This book was a labor of love and fun in the midst of difficult times in my personal life and in the world. While it is a romcom, if you're familiar with my work, you know I don't shy away from the real.

As a heads up, this book contains discussions of people of larger size, the death of a friend, and open door sexual shenanigans.

Enjoy!

Download The Six Loves of Ebony Jones Playlist today and listen along with the book for a more immersive experience.

Non- Apple Music Users:

https://bit.ly/4qM29P6

https://apple.co/4fzz5Zb

1. NO SCRUBS

Sock It To Me (featuring Da Brat) - Missy Elliot

5. A CAN OF WORMS

"WHERE IS MY HUSBAND" - RAYE

Doves in the Wind (featuring Kendrick Lamar) - SZA

7. DECOMPRESS AND DEBRIEF

I Want You Around by Snoh Aalegra

9. THE CRAZY LOVE.

Could've Been (feat. Bryson Tiller) by H.E.R.

12. WHATEVER YOU NEED

Let 'Em Know - T.I.

13. COPPER SMILE

I Found My Smile Again (Radio Edit) by D'Angelo

Plan B - Megan Thee Stallion

15. MY TEDDY-WEDDY

Thinkin Bout You by Frank Ocean

16. UNCOMPLICATED

That's Why I Love You (feat. Sabrina Claudio) by SiR Chasing Summer

Tell Me by Groove Theory

17. HAPPY BIRTHDAY TO ME

All I by Jill Scott

18. RESPECT ME

Fool's Gold by Jill Scott

19. YOUNG HOES

That's Why I Love You (feat. Sabrina Claudio) - SiR Chasing

23. WHAT I DO

open by Joy Rhodes

25. THE LOVE THAT ALMOST BROKE ME

Oscar Winning Tears by RAYE

27. COURTESY OF MISS PUSSY

If Only for One Night - Luther Vandross

29. PERFECT

Floating (featuring Hope Tala) by Raveena

30. ONE

I Love You, I'm Sorry by Gracie Abrams

35. NEW BALANCE

We Can't Be Friends (with RL) by Deborah Cox

What Am I Gonna Do On Sundays? by Olivia Dean

36. VEGAS

i. open by Joy Rhodes

"THIS ALL YOU? ALRIGHT, BIG MONEY!"

Marcus Montgomery peered around her living room with deep appreciation and set off alarm bells. He'd just dropped two red-flag phrases that sent chills down Ebony Jones' single, childless, and successful spine.

Shit. I waxed for nothing.

"Are you going to give me a tour, beautiful?" He grinned over his shoulder at her, and she hesitated.

His dark beard glistened, his bright white smile beckoned, and he smelled fantastic. She *had* been plotting to get to know him and his inches ever since they met at the gym. She'd needed a spot and he'd been wearing gray sweatpants. It was fate. Or pheromones.

Whatever.

After two coffee dates, a home-cooked meal date, and an evening with friends at a jazz club, it was the perfect time to explore the rest of what this Fred Warner lookalike had to offer. She was a Cleveland Browns girlie, but Fred could *get it* and by proxy so could Marcus.

Relax, don't be so judgmental. Maybe he was joking.

She looked down at his very large, dress-socked feet, and her kitty purred a little louder in agreement. With a slight shrug, she threw off her reservations and showed him around the first floor. After all, it had been a long week, and she needed this. A cute little date with a fine man and consensual coitus was just the antidote for writer's block and family group chat drama.

Maybe he didn't know how he sounded. Maybe he was just nervous.

Maybe he should let the anaconda in his pants do the talking for him.

By the time she showed him the backyard and they took in the lightning bugs doing their mating dance, the conversation was flowing again, and her mind was at ease. He talked about his tough decision on whether to rent out his condo or sell it completely as he looked for a place closer to his job. She gave him the business card of her realtor and shared the humorous story of the money pit she fell in love with before purchasing her current home.

"My dad drove past it twice because he just knew he had the address wrong. To this day, he calls it 'The Dollhouse' because the back wall had separated from the rest of the house!"

Marcus laughed with her and politely offered to open the bottle of red wine she pulled out for them. His pecs did a little jump move underneath his snug merlot-colored sweater as he maneuvered. Outside she was calm, adjusting her favorite plum blouse with practiced ease to ensure he was distracted by and lingered on her décolletage. Inside? She was licking her lips in anticipation.

[1]*I'm no better than a man.*

---

1. Sock It To Me (featuring Da Brat) - Missy Elliot

While the wine breathed, they stood at the kitchen island discussing new builds versus renovating older homes; established neighborhoods versus up-and-coming ones, and in general, had a grand time.

During a natural lull in the conversation, Marcus leaned in and kissed her. Slow and sensual, his hand cupped her neck and tipped her face back for better access. When his tongue met her lips, she opened up and relaxed into his body. From languid exploring to devouring, their chemistry exploded in the bedroom where he gave and gave. Her leather skirt bunched around her waist; he feasted on her. Her moans mixed with his approving groans, and seeing him - beard wet, locs flowing across her thigh - turned her on more.

The cunnilingus was top-tier, but his stroke? Masterful. Long lasting. Energetic.

In fact... it was too energetic. And too long-lasting.

She had an important meeting with an editor in the morning, and he was giving her Friday night, long weekend dick on a Sunday before the work week. And while she didn't want to be ungrateful, she had to beg off after the second round.

Seven a.m. would arrive in — she checked her phone — three short hours, and she needed to come up with a slate of article ideas before her nine o'clock meeting. Right now she had nothing but four orgasms and a blank computer screen. Her worries about work must be why she slipped up, fell asleep, and let Marcus sleep over. A huge no-no.

THE STARTUP BEEP OF A GAMING CONSOLE WOKE HER AT SIX.

She didn't own a gaming console, but she'd had plenty of friends, cousins, and former partners who did. And before she could dismiss it as a fluke, the rapid clicking of buttons confirmed it. This man was playing video games in the sitting room off her bedroom.

How the hell?

It didn't matter how; what mattered was the audacity. Ebony threw her legs over the edge of the bed and reached for her green satin robe with its sexy peekaboo lace and dramatic flared and feathered sleeves.

Nah.

This was a possible Grandma Holiday housecoat moment, and Ebony grabbed her completely unsexy pink cotton muumuu instead. Grumbling all the grumbles of sleep and peace disturbed, she shoved her feet into a pair of slippers and set off... but not before she clocked two pairs of men's shoes beside her vanity. Neither of which were the shoes Marcus had worn on their date.

Oh, hell no. Tell me this mutha...

"Girl, you know you look good," Marcus said, licking his lips in appreciation as she stepped through the door. "Come sit on Daddy's lap and let me say good morning."

Ebony was stunned stupid. This fool was lounging, *comfy* on her settee, headphones on, cords strung from his gaming machine to her TV, a sandwich and the wine they hadn't had time to drink last night ace deuce to the side. The entire bottle. At 6 a.m.

And Daddy? *Nah. Randolph Jones would never.*

"Boy, are you crazy? Where did that come from?" she pointed toward the PlayStation, irritation rising. "Why are you — wait, is that my washing machine?"

Overwhelming curiosity - the thing that made her good at her job, but also subject to embarrassing, dangerous, and/or complicated scrapes - got the better of her, and she stepped out to her upstairs laundry room which sat just off the sitting room. Ebony briefly watched clothes - large, lumpy, and stupid - tumble around merrily in her machine. Another load sat on the floor. Not in a basket. On the floor.

That felt *extra* disrespectful. She couldn't explain it, but luckily for her, it was her house, and she didn't have to explain shit.

Marcus dropped his controller with a clatter and rushed over to her. "I've crossed a line... I'm sorry, I just had so much... ENERGY... I couldn't sleep. I didn't want to wake you...because you have work...and I...had hoped to take you to breakfast—"

"Why are you talking like you're reading from a teleprompter?"

Ebony's irritation flipped over to rage as she reached out and hit the "Off" button on his headphones. Voices blared out of her television in the next room, accompanied by gunshots and explosions.

"He's going to have to take her out to eat again to recover. My dating AI says tell her you'd like to make it up to her with breakfast. You gotta feed a fat bitch plenty before you move in."

Loud guffaws, more gunshots, and combat orders followed the pronouncement. Her eyes narrowed as Marcus' widened.

"I'm just sayin'," another voice chimed in. "He moved too quick. You gotta work slow over a solid, like, four to eight weeks. Break some shit, let her find it, and then you fix it. Make yourself useful. Pretend to care about her day that *whole* time. *'Babe, how was your day?' 'Babe, let me take care of that for you.'* Simp shit like that. If she got kids, you gotta bring them toys and do some family activities before she gone be like, 'You might as well stay the night.' Rent free take work, bruh, for real."

"His moms is fed up, he ain't got that kinda time," another voice chimed in.

Ebony jabbed her finger at the power button on the

washing machine. Embarrassment, anger, and what the fuck-ism coursed through her, but she'd be damned if she let Marcus see it. Holding his gaze steady the entire time, she waited until the load stopped and the unlocking mechanism clicked. She took her eyes off him long enough to snatch the load of clothes out and toss his shit on top of the soiled clothes on the floor. Silently she pointed toward the door, now fully in Granny Holiday mode. The only thing she was missing were curlers and the smell of Estee Lauder 'toilet water.'

The gamers continued shooting things up and talking shit while Marcus gathered his sopping lot. She marched to the bathroom where she found - yep, a goddamn toothbrush - and snatched it out of her rose gold toothbrush stand.

What kind of grown man travels with an uncovered toothbrush?

Disgusted, the devil on her shoulder told her to wipe her ass with it, the angel on the other side reminded her that while it would be funny, she was an adult and one of her new year goals was to be more grounded and less rash.

Fine.

After taking a deep breath, she patted herself on the back for her restraint and moved back into the sitting room to supervise as Malcolm zipped up his *TWO* weekend bags. She marveled again at the sheer audacity while chastising herself for her slip up.

Doggone it, he got me. I brought home a...

"Hobo-sexual."

A groan rolled through the crowd of mostly women.

Saturday brunch at Armello's was a decidedly femme-leaning affair with its limitless mimosas, to die for buffet, hidden garden-style decor, and judgment-free, tipsy karaoke.

"Exactly!" Ebony yelped into the mic, then blinked at the feedback noise. "It was a classic dick and switch! I should've known. He put it down like he didn't have to go to work the next day. Like it was getting cold out, and put my ass - excuse me, Miss Mabeline," she nodded to the septuagenarian holding court in her corner booth, "right to sleep. And *while* I was dreaming of deadlines, he brought in his PlayStation, two big-ass weekend bags, and was doing laundry!"

The crowd gasped appropriately.

Ebony nodded and took another sip of her mimosa.

"Are we going to stop this?" January, her best friend and cousin, asked Faith, her other bestie slash cousin. Both were standing on stage with Ebony, waiting for their collective turn at karaoke to begin.

"She's been holding this in for a week. I think we let her lance the boil," Faith said with a shrug. January laughed and shook her head.

"Let this stand as a reminder to all those who date men - she, her, gays, and theys - there is not a penis worth your peace. Not a stroke worth your stride. Not a cunnilingus worth your nearly paid-off rehabbed Victorian." Ebony hiccuped and giggled. "That alliteration didn't work, but you get my point."

The crowd of women laughed and whooped in response. Ebony tossed back the last of her truly bottomless mimosa, pulled the mic close and crooned, "Hit it, DJ."

Ebony, January, and Faith launched into their energetic version of "No Scrubs" by TLC, goaded on by the crowd. By the time they stepped down from the small raised stage, Ebony was sweating, January had the giggles, and Faith was holding a stitch in her side from laughing so much.

The women plopped onto their seats and promptly began fanning themselves. The crowd and the summer heat had the air conditioning working overtime in the popular establishment. Ebony's pink, wide-leg slacks and cream off the shoulder blouse were sticking to her. She pulled her goddess braids up off the back of her neck and hoped for a breeze.

"I brought over your favorites," Armello said as several members of his family set plates in front of them.

"Armello, you are sent from heaven," January said as she batted her long eyelashes and tucked her bone-straight, chin-length bob behind her ear. "I *really* didn't want to get into the line for the buffet after all that dancing."

Armello smiled, his black eyes twinkling behind gold wire rim glasses. "I didn't want Ebony passing out drunk before she got her French toast."

"Hey! I am not drunk… much." Ebony protested as she swirled her fork in the air.

"When you're sober I have a cousin," he said, ducking Ebony's swat with her napkin. "He owns his own business, is good to his mom, AND has a home."

"With his momma?" Ebony squinted her eyes with suspicion.

"No, I promise," Armello said as he eyed the crowd around the restaurant and redirected staff with a nod.

"Welp, too bad. I've decided I'm not dating anymore. I'm no good at it," Ebony grumped. "I've loved, lost, and tossed enough men at this point to realize there's something wrong with *me*. I am the common denominator, so I will gracefully bow out of the dating scene. No husband or partner and no Holiday Baby for me."

She popped more French toast topped with Armello's signature Ohio maple syrup into her mouth and signaled for another mimosa. January raised her eyebrows and shook her head at Lilian, the bartender, while Faith kicked Ebony under the table. Her pointy pumps made direct contact, and Ebony's eyes crossed in pain.

"Well, maybe you should try dating a woman," Armello said with a shrug. "Exhaust all options? And what's a holiday baby? Is that like when girls plan their weddings when they're five?"

Faith cleared her throat. "Er, yeah, something like that—"

Ebony hiccuped loudly again and rubbed her shin, giving Faith the stink eye. "I'm hopelessly hetero, Armie. Plus, what if I find out I pick the wrong girls too?" She shook her head with a slight wobble. "My ego won't allow it."

"You're also a hopeless romantic, cousin," January soothed. "No way you're giving up on that 'forever love' you always talk about."

"Boooo. Forget dating, forget forever love. At least for me, anyway. You guys, on the other hand…Armie-dillo, tell January about this cousin of yours."

That earned her another kick from Faith in the same spot. *Gah!*

Ebony pulled her head out of her ass and looked from January's deer in headlights expression to Armello's open mouth glitch and got the instant yikes. Armello and January had been doing the "I like you dance" for a good two years now. Kicking herself at her faux pas, she threw herself on a goofy grenade.

"PENIS!" she yelped out of nowhere, causing January to choke on her Eggs Benedict and Faith to snort water up her nose.

"Smooth," Faith murmured as she shook her head and delicately dabbed her nose with a napkin.

"French toast shaped penises with little pancake balls," she said to Armello and the nearby table. "For, like… you know, bachelorette and divorce parties…"

She mouthed a quick 'Sorry' to January as Armello excused himself with a quick "I'll think about it."

"Yeah," Lilian said with a wink as she brought over a seltzer water. "You are cut off, girl."

ARM IN ARM, THE THREE WOMEN WALKED ONE OF THE WINDING PATHS through Franklin Park near Ebony's home in a half-hearted attempt to burn off brunch calories. It really was a continuation of their weekly gab session.

"So why is this really bothering you, cuzzo?" Faith asked. "I thought this was just a little gray sweatpants fling."

Ebony observed a gaggle of elegant geese glide along the small pond in the park and let out a tired sigh. "It's not that complicated; this just isn't fun anymore. Ok, parts are - a good dick down is always nice - but everything before and after is annoying or boring or more hassle than it's worth. It feels like... work."

"Relationships *are* work, girl, nothing just falls into place," January said.

"I know that, but now it feels like I'm clocking out as an investigator at work, then clocking back in as an investigative dater. What's their background? What's their angle? What is their health like? Who did they vote for, and what game are they trying to run on me? Before Marcus hard-launched his toothbrush in my bathroom, I actually enjoyed our dates. I relaxed a little and BAM, video game beeps."

"You're tired of keeping your guard up," Faith nodded, deep in thought.

"Mmm...I feel that," January leaned in and touched her head to Ebony's. "Now, are you tired of keeping your guard up *and* are you really ready to share your life? Those are two different things."

"Both," Ebony said with the certainty she felt. "I want to be free with the right person, have adventures together, get tied up and spanked sometimes, then relax in peace alongside someone who feels the same."

"Jilly from Philly said something like, 'she wants to close her eyes while her man drives,' kind of peace," Faith said wistfully.

"Now that *is* peace," Ebony agreed.

January stopped short, jerking Ebony with her halt. Faith's heels clacked loudly beside her. "Girl, what are you talking about?! You go to sleep on every road trip," January said, laughing. "We don't even make it to the Outerbelt before you are OUT."

"HA! That's right," Faith yelped with a snicker. "The only way to guarantee you stay awake is to make you drive, and then we're getting a ticket because of your lead foot."

"One, my Holiday Sisters are a platinum source of peace; two, we always make good time when I drive; and three..." Ebony trailed off.

"And three," Jan nudged her after a few moments.

"And three, I've never been able to sleep while any man outside of family drives. Not since Eric."

"Jesus," Faith muttered as they started walking again. "That man... And to think we were almost rid of him last year."

"Faith, the man had a heart attack; he almost died," January admonished. "And don't let Joy hear you imply he's not family."

Ebony sucked her teeth. "Joy is never around to hear a damn thing. And just because he's *her* husband doesn't mean he's *my* family. Family wouldn't have left me outside, at night, asleep in a car in February. He doesn't think about anyone else but himself, and he never takes responsibility for anything."

She shook her head, irritated. "You've got to stick up for your twin Jan, I get it, but that man—"

"Ain't shit," Faith finished for her. "God, I hope she's still on birth control."

"For real."

"Fingers crossed."

The one thing January and Ebony agreed on when it came to Joy's shitty husband is that he'd make a shittier father. Sometimes Ebony wondered if he wasn't with Joy *just* for the prize of a Holiday Baby. He was the kind of man their Aunt Easter - Faith's mom - warned them about.

"A man of little accomplishment will eventually co-opt or resent yours," Faith said quietly.

"Auntie Easter stay droppin' wisdom," January acknowledged. "Joy was right there with us. I wonder why..." She cut herself off with a shake of her head. "Well, she's in it now. Though... there's always tomorrow."

Ebony smiled. Gentle January was an optimist's optimist and though most of the time she kept her thoughts on the Joy and Eric situation close to the vest, Jan hoped Joy found it in herself to break free of her punk ass husband just as much as the rest of them did.

The cousins walked a little while longer before Jan's head popped up like a meerkat and she skedaddled up the path. "Oooh! Can I jump?" she asked a group of preteens gathered playing Double Dutch.

Surprised, the kids gave her an enthusiastic yes, and Jan kicked off her Crocs before she jumped into the ropes with a laugh.

"Ooh!" Faith exclaimed before she slipped out of her pumps, pulled up her pencil skirt a bit, and got ready to join Jan. They jumped in tandem, and the sight transported Ebony back to their childhood.

Long summers of Double Dutch, running the neighborhood until the streetlights came on, slumber parties, and fights over the last piece of Grandma Holiday's pound cake. The memories were bittersweet. Beautiful moments they wouldn't get back as life and physical distance split the bonds the second generation of Holiday Sisters shared.

Gone were Faith's natural honey-blonde puffs that contrasted beautifully with her deep brown skin, replaced by a trendy, super short, platinum taper fade and January's sleek blunt cut was far from the matching beaded cornrows she and Joy sported most of childhood.

"Jump in, Eb-bon-nee," Faith called out in a singsong way that bounced in time with her jump beats.

Ebony shook her head no. She was still a lil' tipsy from brunch and wearing a bra built for style, not momentum. Her girls clocked in at a 40G and were *dense*. She could black an eye if one got loose. Plus, she was happy to just watch because the longer they jumped, the more she could see the little girls they once were.

Yep, just underneath the style and curves they were all guilty of rushing Mother Nature to bestow were two of her lifelong playmates. And if she closed her eyes for a moment, she could hear the rest of the Holiday Sisters. A sweet echo of girlish joy on the wind.

"Come on, E!" Jan hollered in between heavy puffs. "I don't have much gas left!"

Dangit. Ebony could never resist a "Come on, E!" Shaking her head, she crossed an arm over her chest and jumped.

still blocked

*"NOT A CUNNILINGUS WORTH your nearly paid off rehabbed Victorian. *Hiccup.* That alliteration didn't work, but you get my point."*

Malcolm Knight rolled his eyes as the latest nonsensical viral clip played loudly on Beatrice Lang's laptop. His knock interrupted her rapt attention, and she tapped a button as she waved him in, silencing the whoops and off-key voices.

"And here I thought you were a serious journalist," he chided as he sat down in the chair in front of her desk and gestured toward her prestigious Prater Prize for Journalism on the shelf behind her. "Don't tell me you're on the 'all men suck' train."

Beatrice crooked a half-smile. "And I thought you had vision." She nodded toward his camera gear that never left his side.

"The gender wars are tired, Bea. Something content creators trot out for clicks and politicians mine to keep their bases enraged. There are more serious things going on."

Bea leveled him with a look. "Ah. Yes, the all important 'more serious things.'" She tapped a few buttons on her laptop, and the photo essay he submitted came up on the enormous flat screen to his right. She clicked through the photos.

"Authoritarianism breathing down our necks. Technocrats spending billions to curtail freedoms, surveil, and control the population while unleashing untested and uncontrolled technology on the world at the expense of drinking water and vulnerable communities. The nation's laws and institutions breaking down, public education under attack, the climate collapsing, multiple genocides happening around the world, and journalists targeted and dying at rates we haven't seen since the last world war."

She stopped at that photograph. The one that he could see on his worst days without closing his eyes. Justin's cold, still eyes looked back at him, frozen on screen and forever in his mind.

"The more important things," she said quietly, "don't exist in a vacuum." Bea hit another key, and the viral video clip played alongside the embedded video of Justin with their other friends singing to his new wife at their wedding, about three weeks before he died.

With the videos muted, they were remarkably similar. Three women singing with their arms around each other, laughing with ease, surrounded by community; Justin and his own community in a moment of joy...

"I get it. It's part of the human condition, and you're right, we need both, but too much of one over the other is why we are in the mess we are in."

"Oh, I can think of several people and reasons that have nothing to do with frivolity to explain all of this," Bea said as she tapped her knuckles on the desk and stood, coming around the desk to sit on the edge. "How are you sleeping?"

"Bea, I'm fine. When is the essay going to run?"

She studied him a moment longer, then sighed and looked at her shoes - never a good sign. "Maybe never, Mal."

She put up her hands to quiet him before he even got started. "You could use a slice. Let's go grab some lunch."

He'd seen that look on Bea's face before and knew when she made a benign, yet out-of-place suggestion, he needed to go along because the story was getting hot. "Yeah, I could eat," he said as he grabbed his gear.

"I don't have to tell you things are…uncomfortable right now. There is no privacy. Anywhere," Bea said once they were walking among the teeming masses of New York. "Your work is phenomenal and five years ago? It would be the lead with a full push behind it. Now?"

"Don't tell me you're scared to run it? It's the truth of what's happening out there, Bea!"

"Truth is not the point. Money is. Shareholders and mergers are. Clicks and views are. And right now I can't publish the piece as it is."

"The people need to see—"

"One can argue that the *people* are tired, overstimulated, and at the same time numb," she said, cutting him off. "One cheese, please... Malcolm?"

Looking from her to the vendor, he gave a half-shrug of apology. "Pep, ma'am, thanks." He slipped out his phone and tapped to pay for their meal, then dropped a heavy cash tip in the jar while the woman prepped their slices.

Malcolm watched with longing as Bea shook a generous amount of red pepper flakes onto her slice and forced himself to shake his head no when she offered the shaker to him.

"I get heartburn now." He shook Parmesan cheese onto his slice and took a big bite, sucking in air to cool the hot cheese.

"Oh my god, you're getting old," she scolded as she folded and bit into her own slice. "I'm supposed to be the wizened one."

Other than an attractive graying at her temples and a slight crinkle at the corners of her eyes, Bea Lang looked exactly as she did when he started as her intern way back in the day. Her sharp, dark eyes scanned the area as they continued their walk. He mirrored her vigilance. Together and apart, they'd covered enough stories where good instincts and grandma's grace were the only things that kept them alive. Both of them had a wary relationship with the world around them.

"I'm an old-school journalist, but my MBA is what has kept me where I am," Bea said after a moment of thoughtful chewing. "I can find and pitch the ROI of almost any article, column or beat while sliding in the actual work. Lately, it's getting tougher to slide. I need a big win that isn't something everyone is already doing. I get that win, you get your feature. Without it, I am on my ass and you are out of luck with legacy media. No one is going to touch an essay on the cost of journalism. Not in this country, not right now."

Malcolm swallowed, his pizza going to lead in his belly. He owed this to Justin and his family. He brutally crushed the paper plate into a tiny ball and slammed it into the nearest trash can as they passed. "I'll sell it to an online mag then."

"And it'll get 2.3 seconds of notice before people swipe. This piece is important, built for the moment Malcolm; it deserves more than that. I need a little quid pro quo...get that woman to work with us and I'll grease up your story and slide it in."

"Why do I feel dirty? And why do you need me to do it? I take pictures, not interview people. I'm sure this lady would jump at the chance for a solid seven and a half minutes of fame if the editor of the venerable Metropolitan Times called."

Bea shook her head as she carefully wiped grease on her paper napkin, chewing her last bite slowly. "I already tried that, she told me, professionally, to get lost."

"I agree with her on that," he scoffed, their trek slowing as they looped the block back to Bea's office. "Who do you have in mind to write it?"

Bea smiled, and Malcolm felt the hairs on the back of his neck stand up. "Why would anyone but Ebony Jones write her own story?"

MALCOLM SETTLED INTO HIS SEAT AND POPPED HIS HEADPHONES IN. Reluctantly, but with more curiosity than was good for him, he flipped over his phone and typed in "cunnilingus rehabbed vic —." He hadn't typed the whole search phrase before the app auto filled in the rest and pulled up the video and a thousand different hot takes on it.

Twenty million views?

He scrolled through the comments. Some were laugh-out-loud funny, and he had to put a squash on his reactions so as not to disturb the surrounding passengers.

There were also many people, including men in comments, siding with Ebony. Many others were offended by and offensive toward her. Shaking his head, he sighed at the predictability of the comments devolving to the lowest common denominator. He rewound the video and zoomed in.

Yep, that was Ebony Jones. Her hair was like how she wore it in Cabo, except this time it had attractive little tendrils of curls throughout the braids. He hadn't seen her in two years. They'd gone from crossing paths every so often at media events to spending a very nice long weekend together in Cabo following a conference, then unfortunately, nothing.

That was a great weekend.

A tap on his arm brought his attention back to the present. He took out an earpod and was slightly embarrassed when the passenger next to him gestured to his phone.

"The same thing happened to me too," the woman said, "before I met my current partner. One minute this dashing man was wining and dining me, the next he was sleeping on my couch because it was too late to drive back to his place. Next thing I knew he was chatting up my mother about *his* mother's heirloom engagement ring. I wish I'd been as smart as her," she said, pointing to his phone.

"It took discovering he'd been opening up credit cards in my name for me to kick him to the curb. Turns out everything he ever said was a lie, from his apartment renovations to his job. And his mother's engagement ring? Glass. And on the finger of the next victim."

"*I* stopped dating last year," the sistah in the window seat chimed in. "It's exhausting. All of my friends turned forty and started getting married, finding these suddenly available, wonderful men. Turns out half of them were in debt up to their eyeballs; the rest were at death's door."

"Nurse or purse," the airline attendant nodded sagely. "That woman gave a service to men and women both. Now, what would you like to drink?"

Malcolm double-blinked at her and the random sharing taking place. Knowing excellent sources when he saw them, he placed an order for a ginger ale and leaned in.

"YOU SEEM MORE ON EDGE SINCE YOUR TRIP, HONEY," HIS MOTHER said, as he drew down her dose of Heparin. Not wanting to meet her eyes, he shrugged and prepared the second syringe with slightly less for mid-treatment.

"Things stateside are different now; I'm making the adjustments."

"Now you want to set out your 16-gauge needles and today is an iron day," the dialysis tech said.

Nodding, Malcolm concentrated on getting all the black liquid iron into the syringe and tapping out the air bubbles.

"Perfect, Mr. Knight," Dwayne encouraged. "The one thing you want to watch for is make sure you put the cap back on the needle the way I showed you. You don't want to stab yourself with it, and with the Heparin, it'll keep bleeding."

"Right, right," he shook his head to clear his focus. He finished prepping the table with everything he would need. After double-checking the list they'd tacked to the wall, he took a deep breath. "Ok Mom, ready?"

She gave him a wobbly grin, the lines around her mouth deeper than he remembered, and turned her attention to wiping the numbing cream off her arm. They both hated this part. He hated stabbing her with big ass needles, and she sure as hell hated to get poked. Taking his time, he made sure the needle was at the right angle and lined it up with the previous puncture hole. "Deep breath, Ma."

She turned her head away, and he got that uncomfortable flip-flop feeling in his stomach as the needle moved through her flesh. Once it was in position and there was a flash of blood in the tube beating in time with her heart, he taped it down and drew down the blood, flushed the tube, and prepared for the second poke.

"You're doing great," Dwayne said, "both of you. It will continue to get easier the more you do it, and when Mrs.

Knight's buttonholes are set up, then you're just going into the same channel over and over again. It should hurt less; the needle is blunt instead of sharp."

Nodding, he locked eyes with his mom, and they gave each other reassuring, if not a bit watery, smiles.

Malcolm continued with the rest of the process of getting his mother's home dialysis treatment started, and once she was safely on the machine and tucked into a nice warm blanket, he exhaled a long-held breath. She slipped on her headphones and rocked her head slightly to what he assumed was her gospel playlist.

"You know, you don't really need us coming back out," Dwayne said with a reassuring pat on Malcolm's back as he gathered his things to head out. "You both are doing great, and I know it's a heavy expense."

Malcolm walked Dwayne to the door. "I think both of us would feel more comfortable with another couple weeks of support." If he were honest, he wished he could hire full time in-home care for his mother, but it just wasn't in the cards. He needed to be mindful of their expenses from now on.

Dwayne nodded. "I'll see you next week."

Ebee, this is Malcolm Knight. Are you available for a chat?

No response...

After a moment, his call went straight to voicemail.

Hmmmm... Still blocked ...

Malcolm occasionally wondered what he might have done to make Ebony block him after that weekend, but ultimately work got busy and before he realized it, weeks had passed. In a way, he was grateful. Ebony Jones had that certain something that made you want to forget everything and stay hugged up on the couch with her.

That shit was dangerous. Plus, after Dad and Justin died... Malcolm barely kept in contact with anyone. Shaking off those thoughts, he reached for a burner phone to call her again, but his personal phone lit up, and he smiled.

> cuz! when you get back hit me up i got this
> fire shrimp recipe you gotta try

> aye man just got back in, at mom's house
> now doing her treatment

> how is she? Cat went by the other day and sat
> with her a bit

> she's ok, just trying to get used our new
> normal

> I hear that, when you're finished come
> through for dinner I'll have Auntie Bell a snack
> that's ok for her renal diet

Malcolm hesitated, checking the numbers on the medical tablet as his mother gently snored.

"Stop staring at me, boy, you're giving me the heebee jeebees," she grumped without opening an eye. "Don't you have something better to do than stare at me for the next three hours?"

"I was checking, not staring." And to prove it, he swept his gaze over the entire setup again.

"Mmm hmm. I'm not an invalid, you know. Go edit some photos. If anything happens, the machine alarms are loud enough to wake the dead."

"Ma."

"Boy, it's just kidney disease; I ain't dead yet. I can joke about it. Our joy is good medicine. Now, while I appreciate you going on this journey with me, realize that while we are on it, I'm the one driving." She popped open one eye that clearly warned against any argument.

"It's not just—"

Her eye narrowed.

"Fine. I'll be in the dining room, Your Highness," he muttered as he kissed her on the cheek and propped the tablet up for her to see from her brand new medical chair. It was large, covered in that peculiar medical tan pleather that reminded him of examination room tables and had the magical ability to make his mother - the magnificent Mabeline Knight - a woman who was nearly as tall as him, look so damn small and fragile.

He hated that chair. He hated that it threw off the aesthetic of her carefully arranged sun porch, where she liked to sip hot tea and watch the deer in the yard.

He hated that they moved the chair his dad used to sit in to the garage in order to make room.

He hated that the chair was a necessity because it made it easy to clean off blood and could lie flat with the quick pull of a lever in case his mom's blood pressure dropped too low. It was a beige, ugly, shitty reminder that without a transplant, his mom could leave him sooner than either of them wanted.

Swallowing a deep sigh, he retreated to the dining room before his mom accused him of hovering again.

> seriously cuz, come through after her
> treatment the vibes are chill on friday nights
>
> we can't keep only seeing each other at
> weddings and funerals man

...

you right

Malcolm pulled into the lot behind his cousin's restaurant and double tapped his horn when he saw him transferring boxes from a delivery van into the backdoor.

"Hey, I got it," he called out. Parking next to the van, he quickly hopped out and grabbed a box from Armello before his cousin could do anything but smile.

"Mal! Man, perfect timing, but I didn't call you to come help me move boxes, cuzzo..."

Malcolm shook that off. "The faster you get this in, the faster you can personally cook me that shrimp dish. I'm starvin.'"

Armello laughed. "Mal 'Many Stomachs' in the house, just like old times. Every time I see you, you look like you've been training for the Combine."

"The camera's heavy," Malcolm joked.

In no time they'd moved cases of champagne in place, locked up the van and Armello pulled Malcolm into a bear hug.

"Glad to see you safe, man, for real. We worry when you're on the road."

Malcolm let his cousin love on him and beat the shit out of his back with his heavy-handed version of soothing pats. Armello had kept his college linebacker build and still hit like one too. "I'm glad too. Thank you for keeping an eye on Ma when I'm gone."

"You know we got you, but Auntie Bell only lets us get so far before she's over it and kicks us out the house."

Malcolm laughed deeply. "Right... Now, about that shrimp."

Armello gave him one last backbreaker and led him

through the back area of the building, past the champagne, and into the kitchen. Malcolm stood in the doorway, out of the way, and watched his cousin clean his hands, change his apron, and get to work. The big man moved about the kitchen like the principal dancer in a complicated routine that only he and his staff knew. Malcolm took over a dozen shots before Armello noticed.

"Bruh. Do you ever stop workin'?"

"When was the last time *you* took the weekend off?"

"That's different," Armello said with a shrug. "People eat every day."

"And people exist every day," he retorted as he zoomed in on his cousin's careful plating.

"Camera down or no food."

Reluctantly, he put his camera back into his bag and followed Armello out into the restaurant. It was as if he'd stepped back outside, but instead of the bustling, gray streets and beige, muraled buildings of Columbus's Short North District, he was in a beautiful garden that happened to serve food. He weaved between the mostly full tables of guests enjoying their meals when Armello stopped at a table near the far corner of the restaurant with three women in deep conversation.

"Cuz before you sit down I'd like to introduce you to some of my most loyal customers. Everyone, this is my cousin Malcolm Knight, that is Faith Holiday-Johnson, January Holiday and —"

"The elusive Ebony Jones," Malcolm interrupted.

vacation hookups don't count

"THE UNEXPECTED MALCOLM KNIGHT."

She gave him a smile she didn't quite feel because this was the third time she had encountered someone who'd seen her naked this week. Ever since that video went viral, various jump-offs, ex-boyfriends, and wannabes have been reaching out either to confirm it was her in the video, to protest her stance, or to make overtures that they could cure what ails her. Now Malcolm Knight.

Here.

In Columbus.

All snug t-shirted up, his full sleeve of tattoos adding to his attractive, devil-may-care vibe perfectly. He looked the part of the dashing, globe-trotting photojournalist, complete with a camera bag permanently attached to his person. His eyes, however, held all the intensity of a life lived documenting the depth, breadth, resilience, and depravity of human existence. He surveyed her with acute interest and an underlying hunger that shifted the temperature of the evening. Just like that first night.

Anyothertime. ANY. OTHER. TIME.

She would have been delighted to be the focus of his gaze, but today? After the week she'd had?

She was exhausted from all the attention.

Armello looked between the two of them. "It didn't occur to me that you two would know each other. Small world!"

"The industry is smaller," Malcolm said, smiling slow. It was the same slow grin he'd given her when he peeled her swimsuit off in Cabo. The thought made her clench her thighs together tightly. As vacation flings go, Malcolm had been one of the best. She could still feel his low, springy curls under her fingers and the rough tingle of his facial hair against her exposed collarbone.

Nothing I can or want to do about that now.

"Well, enjoy your meal, Malcolm. Your cousin is a gifted chef."

January's eyebrows reached for the sky; Faith cleared her throat, and Ebony felt bad for being so dismissive. Grabbing hold of the better manners her momma Noel Holiday-Jones instilled in her, she pasted another smile on her face and gestured to the fourth open seat. It was Joy's seat, but she hadn't joined them in months.

"Forgive me, I'm a bit distracted. Would you like to join us?"

Armello grinned big and slapped Malcolm on the back. It looked like it hurt.

"Here, I'll put this down—" and he moved to place the dish he held with one hand on the table, but before he could finish, Malcolm stilled his movements.

"Thank you for the offer, but I couldn't interrupt your evening. I've been looking forward to catching up with my cousin since I moved back home—"

"Home?" Ebony interrupted, startled.

"My mom is originally from here. My parents were nomads

for a long time and moved back permanently when Dad got sick. So here I am."

"I'm sorry to hear about your father. Has he recovered?"

Malcolm looked away for a moment, and Ebony's heart sank. Without thinking, she reached out, grabbed his hand, and squeezed it gently. "I'm sorry."

"May his memory be a blessing," January said quietly.

"Amen," Faith agreed.

"Thank you," he said as he squeezed her hand back, then, with a lingering hesitation, let go. Strangely, she noticed the absence of warmth when his hand was gone.

"Uncle Jet had the best puzzles," Armie said with a grin. "Ten thousand pieces of nothing, but Oreos and a glass of milk. It took us weeks and somehow three pieces were missing in the end. We were beat up about it and looked everywhere."

"What did you do? I hate puzzles, but that would have driven me crazy," Jan asked, riveted.

"After a couple weeks, I was ready to pack it in. We had looked everywhere, but Malcolm took that old tank of a camera Auntie Bell gave him and started taking pictures of Oreos until he got just the right shots. I got to glue them on to spare pieces of cardboard and Unc cut them out just right. There was a piece for each one of us, and when I tell you it was the ultimate satisfaction for a kid."

"How old were you all?" Faith asked, laughing, as she took another bite of her red velvet cake. Her gold bangle caught the light merrily as she moved.

"What, ten?"

"Yep, ten because that was right before we moved that first time," Malcolm answered with a chuckle.

"Do you still have it?" Ebony could see them as young boys spending quiet nights poring over a table, celebrating perfect finds.

"Aunt Bell had it framed along with a photo of us. It's in my mom's living room now. We've been passing it back and forth for decades at this point."

"Are you sure you don't want to sit?" Faith asked, a mischievous smile on her lips.

"I couldn't possibly interrupt you any further. It was great meeting all of you. Good seeing you again, Ebee."

Malcolm slipped off to the table furthest in the corner and moved the seat to give him a view of the whole restaurant. Armie winked at her and followed.

Even though the men were nowhere near a safe enough distance away, Jan leaned in expectantly. Ebony sighed, but didn't make her wait or play dumb; there was no point with her cousins, they could sniff out a lie like bloodhounds.

"Cabo."

"Vacation Boo?!"

"Shhhhh…" Faith waved at Jan and leaned in further, rolling her eyes. "You blocked *that* man?!"

"You told me too!"

"I told you to stop seeing the Precious Moments versions of these dudes you find and start seeing them Right Now."

"Yes, well, he said he'd call me when he got to his next assignment later that week and didn't. I blocked him, and that was that. Plus, you're the one who always says vacation hookups don't count."

Faith sat back in consideration. "This is true."

Ebony nodded once in triumph.

"Although…"

"There is no although, Jan," Ebony dug into her tiramisu and her eyes rolled back in her head. *My god, Armie's pastry chef is amazing.*

"He's *here* now."

Ebony's eyes popped open in annoyance and did a side-eye

to make sure Malcolm wasn't listening. "Have you forgotten what has been happening for the last week? I'm avoiding the world right now. Even my parents, thanks to Aunt Easter."

"Sorry about that," Faith said, cringing. "She's taking her self-appointed position as family archivist seriously."

"We used to program the microwave clock for her; now she's uploading videos to the group chat?"

Jan snorted, tucked a piece of hair behind her ears and swiped a piece of Ebony's treat. "I had to turn off my notifications for, like, two days. Between the Bible verses, confusion, dating advice from the aunts, and offers of different personal protection devices from the uncles for 'that man without a pot to piss in or a window to throw it out of,' I couldn't concentrate on anything important."

"And the international and different time zone cousins," Faith grumped. "Pumpkin's Australian ass woke me up with that full-throated feminist 'right to her body' essay. You can always count on her to throw herself in front of a bullet on your behalf."

Ebony cackled. "I appreciated that, but it's easy to avoid a Holiday Family projectile halfway around the world; also, I think she's in South Korea now. I wish she could take a bullet for me with work. I'm avoiding my editors because I don't have a single idea. Colleagues from various news outlets are calling me nonstop for the scoop on the video, and now look - we have to come to Armello's on Friday night instead of Saturday brunch to avoid lookie loos."

Faith leaned over and patted her hand. "This will blow over soon, the internet, the family. As far as work goes, you're bored. We can tell. You don't get the same excited glow when you're talking about your articles. E, I think you are a woman in the midst of revolution." She whirled her hands around like a magician.

"That's a nice way of saying I'm a mess."

She shrugged. "Revolutions are messy, but out of the ashes of deconstruction and the pain of rebirth is something free and lovely."

"Well damn. On that note—" Ebony rolled her eyes at her phone vibrating across the stable, her inspiration stopping before it could get going good.

Jan leaned in and stared at the nickname on Ebony's phone. "When did you start talking to Professor again?"

"I haven't. He saw the video and has been reaching out. It's weird."

"Is it?" Faith asked, and Ebony got a sinking feeling in her stomach because Faith had her thinking face on. Faith's thinking face meant she would either say something genius or diabolical. "What if you spun the block, journo-style?"

"Wha—"

"Just listen. Use all of your skills as a journalist - statistics, researched questions, sources, and go all Barbara Walters, Oprah Winfrey on your ex-boyfriends."

Ebony and Jan both sat back incredulously.

"That sounds horrible," January said as she stared at Faith in disbelief.

"I'd rather scratch my ass with Marcus' toothbrush."

"No, listen — wait, that is specific as hell. Ebony, tell me you didn't?"

"I thought about it..." Ebony popped another forkful of tiramisu into her mouth.

Faith shook her head, but would not be deterred. "Joy always says the keys to the future can be found in studying the past."

"No—"

"AND," she spoke over Ebony, "you can make it an article. The audience is already there, AND it will build your platform, allowing you to transition into whatever you want to do next."

"ABSOLUTELY NOT—"

"What if you discover *why* you've been 'picking wrong' this whole time—"

"No."

"And next time pick Mr. Riiiight!" Jan said, one finger on her nose and the other pointing at Faith like her life was a game of charades.

"NO!"

"What if you set the rules, the budget, wrote it for the most prestigious publication in the country as a multimedia series?" A deep, rich, and definitely amused voice spoke from the corner table.

As one, the Holiday Sisters turned in Malcolm's direction. Faith was nodding slowly. Jan's hand patted Faith on the knee because, apparently, collectively, they were on to something. And that something? Was some bullshit.

Her eyes narrowed as he took a swig of beer.

"Real convenient that you just so happen to stumble into this restaurant with nearly an identical pitch as Bea's."

He grinned. "Mine is better. Bea offered you digital, I'm offering print as well, plus a right to refuse deal from their publishing arm and other things."

"You don't have the power to offer that."

"I have the knowledge to tell you to negotiate that, and they will agree to it." He sat back, his eyes challenging her.

"What other things," Faith cut in. The woman had pulled out her tablet and was taking notes!

What world was she in?!

Malcolm slid his napkin from his lap and placed it next to his plate, and locked eyes with Ebony.

"Me... shooting the entire thing."

Ebony thought her head was about to explode. This whole thing was...was...

She pointed at Jan as she stood. "No."

She pointed at Faith. "No."

She pointed at Malcolm. "Fuck no."

"Goodnight," she called as she strode without pause through the front door of the restaurant.

Ebony woke with a start. Sitting at the edge of her bed, arms crossed, was her mother. Her dad was casually eating a peach in the doorway, clad in the retired Black man's uniform of coordinating athleisure gear, his bald head shining.

"Jeez, y'all scared me!" Ebony flopped back in the bed, her hand clutching her chest.

"Oh, so we scared you? *We* scared *you?*" Ebony's mother looked around at the invisible audience in her bedroom. "It's not like we were the ones avoiding phone calls for the past week. As a matter of fact, you knew we were alive every single day this week and chose not to answer the phone or call." Her mother sucked her teeth and got up from the bed.

Her dad took another bite of his peach. "For all we knew, that random boy you hooked up with came back, chopped you up, and put you in the basement. Only reason we knew you were alive is because Faith told us. Why I gotta ask Faith what is going on in my daughter's house? I didn't have to ask Faith what was going on in my daughter's house when I was here spending my golden years repairing your parquet floors, now did I?"

Not the tag team double guilt combo on a Saturday morning.

"Come on, y'all, I just needed a little bit of space. Auntie Easter told all my business in the family group chat and—"

"This is not about the family group chat. This is about why you felt the need to hide from us of all people," her mother said quietly as she folded the towels Ebony hadn't gotten to yet. The silver streaks in her hair caught the morning light. And while her beautiful mahogany skin was smooth and unfussed, the lines of her pursed lips showed her true feelings. She was hurt.

Shoot.

"I was embarrassed," Ebony admitted flopping back into her pillows. "And frustrated, and I didn't want to hear I was a disappointment to the Holiday family line. I am one of the oldest of this branch and have no Holiday Babies in sight. Plus, who wants to talk to their parents about a hookup gone wrong?"

"Oh, Little Bit," her mom said, dropping a folded towel back into the basket. "You know...this Holiday Baby issue has gone too far. There's no guarantee that any of you girls will have the same...luck."

"Grandma always said it was a blessing, and I don't want to be the one to break the magic."

"Dammit Ebony Elizabeth, you are a Holiday, yes, but you are also a Jones, and the Joneses are the ones everyone's trying to keep up with." He pointed at her with his peach. "If you don't want to have kids, fine. If you have boys born on a Thursday that is NOT a holiday, that's going to be just as great. There's no need to swing booty willy-nilly trying to catch a man for some stupid family legend."

"Stupid family legend?" Her mother repeated, her eyebrow arched.

"Swinging booty willy-nilly?" Ebony asked, because really?

"The magic of my birth is not some stupid legend. Overemphasized? Yes. But not stupid."

"And I don't 'swing booty willy-nilly,' Daddy. Especially to get a man. Getting a man is easy. Getting the right one has been hard, but frankly, sometimes I just want to have sex."

Her dad's face screwed up in displeasure and shook his head roughly to get the thought out of his head, but she knew he was going to dig in when he crossed his arms and planted his feet.

"You, woman," he pointed to her mother, "are a miracle in every way and one of the best things to ever happen to me. You and my baby girl right here."

Her mother batted her eyelashes and gave him gooey eyes.

"That doesn't mean that all of you women born on a holiday hasn't put undo pressure on these girls coming up. Joy is stuck catering to that asshole she married, and my baby girl who is a phenomenon onto herself, and yes, born on the great day of liberation, is worried about disappointing us because she hasn't popped out a kid on the right calendar date."

Ebony was relieved he got it. But she was still stuck on him saying 'swingin' booty willy-nilly.' Wait 'til she told the cousins.

"Now both of you are missing the good things I'm sayin' to fuss about some bull and I ain't going for it today. Y'all are spoiled... And fussy and need to eat. You," he pointed at Ebony, "are going to get out of that bed and stop hiding from us and the rest of the world. You are the daughter of a Texan-born Black man whose grandparents couldn't read or write, and you grew up to write articles people around the world enjoy. You were born on Juneteenth; you are liberation and strength. You want a good man? Stop settling and focus."

He turned and stomped out of the room.

"Where's he going?" Ebony whispered.

Her mom shrugged. "He's right, you know."

"Yeah, but don't tell 'im or he'll start giving these pep talks more often."

"GET OUT OF BED, EBONY!"

Ebony jumped up and flew to the bathroom to shower, her mom tossed her a towel with a laugh.

A HALF HOUR LATER EBONY SAT AT HER DINING ROOM TABLE EATING strawberry-covered pancakes her dad made her while her mom scoped out her wine selection.

"Oooh, I don't have this one!" her mom exclaimed. And after checking to make sure Ebony had two bottles, she snatched one up and dropped it into her tote bag.

"So... Faith and January think I should turn this media maelstrom into something," Ebony said as she pushed a bit of strawberry back and forth on her plate.

"Well, if you can make good come from all of this..." her mom called over her shoulder as she loaded the dishwasher.

"Noel. Come sit down and sit still, love," her dad called and pulled out a chair next to him, shaking his head. "What are you looking for, Lil Bit? Advice, approval, or a listening ear?"

Ebony scrunched up her nose in thought. "I'm not sure yet." She explained the rough idea as she sat out her vitamins for the day and put her dirty dishes in the dishwasher.

"Here," her mom placed a scratch pad of paper and a pen in front of her and sat in the seat Randolph had waiting for her with a slight wince. "Make three lists: one - your goals, two - your rules for the project and yourself, and three - the pros, cons, anticipated problems and workable solutions. You don't need our approval, Baby, you are grown. My only advice is don't violate your boundaries, don't compromise your integrity, or your vocation."

After her parents left, heavy a couple bottles of wine and the reassurance that she was done hiding, Ebony hit the neighborhood sidewalks to turn everything over in her mind. On her third lap around the neighborhood, she accepted that the viral video wasn't that big of a deal. One of those unexpected, silly things that happen sometimes. Sitting down on her porch swing, she took the scratch pad out of her pocket and got to work.

<u>Goals / Wanted Outcomes:</u>

1. Identify past healthy + unhealthy patterns of partnership for future forever love. (Am I the drama?)
2. Book deal.
3. Wrap this shit up so I can get back to Saturday brunches w/mimosas.

"Easy," Ebony said outloud to no one.

She snatched that sheet off the top, set it to the side and started on her pros and cons. That list took longer, but she felt pretty confident she'd covered both sides of the argument of the project, but instead of feeling solid on a decision, she felt even more unsure. A lot of shit could go wrong...but... a lot could go right.

She set a decorative rock she'd had since she was six on top of the paper and pulled her earbuds out of her pocket. Once she selected her playlist, she walked to the shed to grab some garden gloves and put in some some dirt equity to clear her mind.

Three hours and a spotless flower bed later she was ready to tackle the third list of rules and moved on to a fourth list:

<u>Great Loves</u>
1. The first love.
2. The crazy love.
3. The safe love.
4. The love that almost broke me.
5. The almost forever love.

"Shit...This could get soo complicated..." She tapped her pen a while longer, lost in thought and memories. Many good ones and several bad ones. Was she strong enough to wade into those waters?

Ebony blew out a breath and flipped through her phone unblocking numbers. Swiping to the key party in all of this, she hesitated a moment before calling. She was prepared to leave a voicemail and set up a time to meet, instead the deep and deeply amused voice answered on the second ring.

"Ms. Jones. You've unblocked me, does this mean you are ready to take me up on my offer?"

clear the air

"THE OFFER WAS NOT yours to give. You're just talking out your ass like you did in Cabo. I'm calling to see what you know and why Bea sent you before I call and talk to her myself."

Malcolm chuckled despite the mild irritation he felt. Vacation Ebony was nicer. He continued to flip over puzzle pieces on his dining room table.

"Maybe we need to clear the air about Cabo."

"No thank you, it was a million years ago. Why did Bea send you after me? What's in it for you?"

Malcolm's eyes narrowed and he paused flipping over pieces. "It was two years and clearly I did something to piss you off. You don't trust me."

"It was, obviously, nothing. And I don't need to trust you, I simply like to know all the players before I jump into anything."

He wouldn't say it was nothing...

"So you're going to take the gig?"

"I'm considering it, however, this is my life and career. I

won't jeopardize either. The video was a silly thing, but this project, if I take it on, is not a joke to me. Now, are you going to answer my question?"

Malcolm turned over his answer in his head. He hit the button for video chat and waited for her to connect.

When she finally did, he noticed she was outside and annoyed. There was a dewy glow to her sunkissed skin and despite her serious face, she look absolutely edible.

Focus.

"I'm one of the best at what I do. You want this to be a serious project, you need a serious team that can execute. I had no idea you'd be at Armello's. I actually tried calling you earlier, but you know... blocked. The stars just lined up for us to connect. What did I do wrong in Cabo?"

She rocked in her green porch swing a second or two, her brown eyes focused somewhere off camera. "This isn't your usual assignment. It's not politics, a war, or natural disaster. This is a puff piece compared to what you normally do. Why are you even interested?"

He could tell her about his own work hanging in the balance, hell it might make it easier to get her to say yes. But...he didn't want to guilt her into this. She was right, this was her life and silly video aside, this meant something to her.

Plus, she was perceptive. If he told her about the piece, she would sense it was more than an assignment. She had a way of asking questions... no, she had a way of *listening* that made it easy to spill your guts. He'd caught himself more than once sharing more than he should during that weekend together. *Was that it? That he overshared?*

Still, outside of his therapist office, he probably would never talk about Justin, about that day ever again. So he chose a different truth.

"I'm taking assignments closer to home now. It keeps me near my mom, so I can be more hands on in her care."

Her eyes zeroed back in on her phone, on him, and she cocked her head ever so slightly. "That's a big adjustment."

He nodded, "You know it will happen someday and you think you're prepared for it, but this was sooner than either one of us was ready for. I don't know if I'll do as good of a job as she did taking care of me but I—" Malcolm caught himself.

Damn. She did it again.

"You what?"

"I'll figure it out."

Her brow dipped ever so slightly, but she didn't say anything. She broke eye contact with him and he sighed inwardly in relief. He'd have to be careful or this woman will have him sucking his thumb while telling her his darkest secrets and alarm passcodes.

"Look Ebony, you already have a solid offer from Bea. And my instinct says you can get everything I shared last night. This thing has success written all over it, but you're going to have to trust your team."

She nibbled at the side of her lip. "I don't want this sensationalized."

"I only shoot what I see. I don't create caricatures and I don't shoot for vanity."

She sucked her teeth and rolled her eyes. They caught the summer sun on their journey, brightening the amber spokes within the deep brown depths. "If this was a vanity project I wouldn't be trotting my love life out for the world to see. The bad decisions..."

The anxiety was all over her. From the nibbling, to her reflexive swallows, to the tightness in her shoulder... He had the overwhelming urge to soothe her.

"You want to learn and grow, that's what people will focus

on. Anyone who wants to think the worst of you will, no matter what you do. Let that shit roll right off of you. Plus, you should be more worried about my requirements in a partner."

Ebony jerked in confusion. "In a partner? Wh—"

"That I *work* with," he said with a chuckle. She visibly relaxed and her eyebrow quirked up in challenge.

"I require trust and communication," he continued. "I always need to know what we are walking into and if I say let's go, we go. The same goes for you. We come together and leave together, and we need to have a couple of signals as well."

Ebony's eyes crinkled in the corner as she grinned. "Exactly what do you expect to happen here in lil' ol' Columbus?"

"The same thing I expect to happen everywhere: anything."

MALCOLM GLANCED DOWN AT HIS NOTES. FIVE POSSIBLE INTERVIEWS, three in town, one in an unknown location and one halfway across the country.

But no names.

"I still think you need an objective look at your list of interviewees. Let me do some digging."

Ebony's eyes narrowed. "Do you think I'm incapable of doing my own research?"

He could smooth it over, avoid ticking her off after she had finally relaxed and they'd spent the last half hour collaborating pleasantly, but, nah. "I think you could be compromised by the nature of the assignment. These are people you've been in intimate, committed relationships with, sometimes we don't always see the dangers."

Ebony grinned ruefully and shook her head in disbelief. "Typical male nearsightedness. I've been navigating the dangers of being a woman well before puberty. We learn what danger feels like and who is dangerous before we even understand what those feelings really mean. And I grew up *protected* and still learned."

He nodded. "Don't you think I deserve to have my safety considered?"

She glitched. "I—I—"

"I fear no man," he interrupted, "but I do fear the unknown. I lived this long because I've made it my business to understand as much as I can about every situation I put myself in. I have your back out there and I hope you would have mine."

Ebony nodded, then shook her head. "No, you're absolutely right. I was blinded by the muscles."

"Were you now?" He pulled up an arm where she could see it and flexed it a bit.

She rolled her eyes. "Not like that, you goofball. You just look like you can break... humans. I didn't consider that you'd be worried about— No excuses. I apologize. Here's the thing," she pulled herself into a straight sitting position and adjusted the camera, "I am very strict about my sources in general. I know these men. They have reputations, families, some have honor, in other cases a lot of ego, and the only way to get them to participate openly, honestly is to guarantee anonymity. Let me think over how I can protect my sources *and* give you the security you need, okay?"

He nodded then his eyes narrowed as he brought the phone closer. "Hey did you know you have a slug on your shirt?"

"What? A what?!" And Ebony proceeded to slap at herself while screaming and hopping across her porch. "Is it gone is it gone?!"

Malcolm held in his laugh as best he could, but it was

tough. Her wiggle and shimmy was the cutest thing. "You gotta stand still long enough for me to see."

She tried. Poor thing, she stood there with her fists clenched, eyes squeezed shut, teeth clamped tightly with a tiny little "eeeeeeeeeeeeeeekkkkkkkk" coming out under her breath as she waited.

"It's right there on your should—"

Swoosh.

In one swoop Ebony yanked off her shirt and swiped at every inch of herself, yelping. Malcolm averted his eyes at the first flash of black lace and luscious skin he knew was soft and and sweet smelling.

"Ah! I touched it!"

"Ebony chile, you alright?" someone called from nearby.

"Slugs, Mrs. Roberts," she yelped. "Can you help?"

Malcolm waited patiently as Ebony's neighbor commented on how nice her bra was, how bowls of beer will drown the slugs, asked when she was going to get married while simultaneously telling her to stay single and keep everything in her name.

"Malcolm I'mma let you go. I gotta go set fire to myself."

She clicked off before before he could say anything else. Chuckling he looked down at the puzzle and realized he no longer had the mind for it.

Stateside Ebony was not as nice, but she was definitely more interesting. On their own, memories from Cabo came flooding back.

The conference room at the resort was too cold, outpacing the tropical heat people paid thousands to experience. Rows of journalists were half-engaged in conversation, half-checking their phones. Beyond the tall glass windows, the ocean stretched out toward forever in the kind of blue that called to the soul.

He hadn't planned to come to this session. It was wedged

between a panel he cared about and a networking session he didn't. **After the Newsroom: How Journalists Build Power Outside Broken Systems** was a last minute add he received a push notification about and it seemed as good enough a place as any to sit for a moment. Then she started speaking.

"No one grows up dreaming of becoming an exhausted indie journalist with shit healthcare and ring light."

A ripple of laughter moved through the room at her unexpected, real opening and he glanced up.

She was a breath of fresh air wearing a soft orange pantsuit in a sea of business black, gray, and beige. Her long braids were pulled up and back from her face as she stood relaxed at the front of the room, not hiding behind the podium. One hand rested lightly against it like she dropped by to share a little update then go on about her day. No over-rehearsed cadence or panel voice despite the conference being one of the largest for Black media professionals in the U.S.

He pulled up the conference app and located the session info. Ebony Jones - Two Time Ryan Award Winner, Independent Journalist

"But here we are," she continued, clicking to the first slide. "Carving out careers outside of salaried legacy media, because the jobs we were told to aim for are either disappearing... or asking us to do three roles for one paycheck."

More and louder laughter this time. A few people straightened in their chairs.

He did too.

On the screen: a simple graph—ownership consolidation over time rose in a way that was jarring.

"We've all watched it happen or felt the sting," she said. "Local newsrooms shrinking. Stations getting bought, merged, restructured into something unrecognizable. AI language models centered. Fewer reporters and even less representation. The drive for more content without concern to context."

She paced once across the front of the room. "And we're expected to treat this like a natural evolution of industry and technology instead of what it is—consolidation that strips power out of communities and replaces it with centralized, corporate held perspective lauded as progress and efficiency."

She let that thought land and linger. Malcolm leaned forward slightly, his forearms on his thighs.

She clicked again.

"So the question isn't, 'How do we get those jobs back?'" she said. "They're not coming back in the same way. The question is—what do we build instead?"

- Ownership ≠ community
- Access ≠ sustainability
- Independence ≠ instability

She smiled slightly. "We've been trained to think independence is risky, less prestigious, less reputable" she said. "But for a lot of us, it's becoming the only honest option. And yes, anyone can hop online, pay for a checkmark and say, 'Breaking News.' Very few people have the skillset to tell the story beyond the headline, how it affects specific communities, have the data and sources to back it up and the training to maintain integrity and focus when the rest of the world is chasing the next viral clip. Anyone can stream music at a party. That doesn't mean DJs stop spinnin'."

A few heads nodded. "I know that's right," someone murmured agreement.

"I left salaried media because I wanted more control over my work," she continued. "What I didn't expect was how much infrastructure I'd have to build just to replace what used to be... automatic."

Soft rang out laughter again.

"Editors, legal review, distribution, audience development—

turns out, when you leave the system, you don't just lose constraints. You lose support." She shrugged. "But—" a small lift of her hand, "you no longer have to ask permission."

He exhaled quietly, almost a laugh, but it stayed in his chest. It was getting tougher to get shit through. He spent hours on the phone with Bea trying to get an angle that worked on a pitch just last week.

"So if independence is the direction —then we have to be strategic about it. And no, that doesn't mean you all have to become influencers. I know that's the fear."

A few people laughed—relieved.

"You can be completely indie or a hybrid of freelance and indie, but you're going to want to have: diversified income streams, direct audience relationships, and place the emphasis on owning your content and platform instead of only renting space on someone else's. Cultivate your team. Create standards that outlast trends. Get more involved in the community, not retreat from it. Those relationships are integral and belong to you - no matter who you work for."

She stopped ticking items off her fingers and settled her gaze on them, serious. "Your work has value beyond the institutions that used to validate it."

Ebony wasn't placating them or trying to stroke their ego, she was telling the truth and it was... empowering.

Ebony had the room fully engaged for the rest of her presentation. She gave practical advice, resources, hell, she even had supply lists and promo codes for discounted gear.

"I'm not saying this is easy," she said. "It's not. There are trade-offs. There can be some uncertainty. There's a lot of figuring things out in real time."

Then she smiled fully and compared to her smile, the ocean was a dull afterthought. He realized he was smiling back at her.

"But there's also ownership. And, for me, it's so worth it. Thank you."

The applause was steady and enthusiastic and as she stepped away she was already being approached by a few attendees. Grabbing his camera, he captured how she leaned in slightly when someone spoke, listening fully, not scanning for the next person, not rushing to disengage.

As the rest of the room started moving—chairs shifting, people standing, conversations starting up again, he made his way toward the front of the room.

"Ms. Jones, I'm Malcolm Knight."

They had lunch poolside, the warm bright sun danced across her skin. She was polite, warm, but distracted. He hadn't expected the conversation to go anywhere and it didn't until after the conference when it became an invitation for a drink in her room.

***

The balcony open to the still warm air and her lush, thick thighs open to him. Her needy little pants competing with the ocean waves in the night.

***

Her heels abandoned near the door of his room, her mouth wrapped around him mindful of his piercing and diligent in giving him pleasure.

***

The morning light too bright for his tired eyes and Ebony with her braids hastily tied back, naked, typing at the small table as she chewed a piece of candy.

"Do you always wake up this early and type naked?" he'd asked.

She glanced up at him, a smirk peeking out around the candy. "Do you always sleep in this late when you could be in me?"

***

Her feet topped with plum colored polish swishing absentmindedly in the pool, the low sun casting everything, including her, in gold. She listened intently as he confessed that covering back to back genocides was taking its toll. She didn't judge him or make him feel like he'd be abandoning his moral obligation if he took on different work. She asked quiet questions and listened to every word.

Thankfully or regrettably, a text notification interrupted his trip down memory lane.

> Ebony: Interviews -The first love. The crazy love. The safe love. The love that almost broke me. The almost forever love.
>
> I'll send a dossier w/in 24 hours after they agree and you'll have a location list as soon as I get out of the bath, NDAs all around, do not contact them in advance

> You're in the bath? 🐱

> Thank you Ebony for being flexible and considerate of my needs. Thank you for stopping what you're doing as slugs fall from trees all around you in a nightmare of slimy, wet grossness

> Thank you Ebony for being flexible and considerate of my needs. Thank you for oversharing that you're in the middle of a flying slug orgy

> OMG stop! 🙈

> In all seriousness they sometimes hang from their own slime threads. It's been raining a lot it should clear up on their own.

> That is actually worse. One was in my hair. I gotta take down these braids. Bye

Pleased with himself and tickled with her, Malcolm glanced at his notes.

THE FIVE LOVES OF EBONY JONES
1. FIRST
2. CRAZY
3. SAFE
4. ASSHOLE
5. ALMOST DOESN'T COUNT.

He frowned. "Might as well get it over with...." He flipped through his contacts and waited for her to pick up.

"Bea. I've got good news and bad news. I think Ebony is a go, but I gave her everything she's worth..."

In the solid six in the half minutes of swear words streaming out of his phone, Malcolm had completed a good amount of the border to his puzzle.

"Are you even listening?"

"Just waiting for you to take a breath, Bea. You're going to make it back in traffic, buzz, and all the other metrics ten times over. Plus, you know you love me."

"Don't get cute with me. I knew you when your camera case weighed more than you did. That velvet voice charm may apparently work on Ebony, but I am immune. Especially when I'm looking at my budget."

"What if I cut my rate?"

"What? No. Why would you do that?"

"I'm getting what I want - it's not about the money." *Well, not completely.*

Bea spoke after a moment, her voice softer. "Mal, Rick's transplant recovery needs almost bankrupted us and that was ten years ago. You need to save—"

"Mom has great insurance, Dad's pension, and dual citizenship in a country with universal healthcare. I've got savings. We are good."

We're ok, I'm still working on fine, and eventually trying to get to good. But he wasn't going to tell her that.

"How IS your saintly husband?"

"Hmmph. He's as healthy as an ox and a pain in my ass. Don't change the subject. I don't know about moving your mother halfway around the world to get meds... Are you sure?"

Malcolm slipped another puzzle piece into place.

"Give Ebony what she deserves."

a can of worms

"IT'S DECENT," Faith said as she listened to Ebony read off her lists.

"But?"

"Well, your goals seem shallow." Faith focused on Ebony a moment on their video chat, holding aloft the applicator brush she was using to mix bleach for her hair. "You'll reap some benefits, but what about all the people watching? What's in it for them? Entertainment?"

"Gosh no, I hope it's informative," Ebony said, tapping her pen against her lip. "I don't want people to take me for a joke."

"Right," Faith said as she started applying the product to her roots. "If it's serious for you, make it serious for them. Make it applicable like you do any other article you work on."

Ebony nodded, "I've been researching things to ask already, based on different therapy models and relationship experts... I could put the questions I ask in a supplement to the article and in the comments on social media. And maybe key takeaways and resources from each interview for people to make their own journey?"

"*That* sounds worthwhile and more in line with your work. Now," Faith gazed back into the camera, "what about sex?"

"What about it?"

"Is it on the table?"

"No!"

"E. Long talks, reminiscing, and all that? What if you feel a connection? What if you find forever love while you're circling the block? Be honest."

"I don't have sex with sources. It's completely unethical."

"What about *after* the interview? And remember this isn't a typical situation. You ARE the story."

"The idea of anything happening before the entire thing is complete feels wrong. That's going to be a hard no." Ebony said as she added notes.

"Good. That keeps you clear headed, especially with the Green Eye Bandit."

Ebony snorted at their nickname for her ex, Jordan. That man had a smolder that used to make her panties disappear. *Used to.* Breaking free of him almost broke her.

"I think I need to coordinate therapy sessions with this project."

Faith snorted as she snapped on a clear plastic shower cap and took a towel to wipe away some of the bleach smeared on her ears. "Duh. You're going out in the rain to open a can of worms. You're gonna need an umbrella."

Ebony paused her pen and looked at the camera. Faith paused as well, a puzzled expression on her face, then her eyes dropped to the camera. They stared at each other a moment in confusion.

"What the fuck does that even mean?" Ebony asked as she busted out laughing.

"I have no clue," Faith cackled. "I should've just stuck with opening a can of worms, I didn't need the umbrella and rain for razzle dazzle. Girl, I just be making shit up trying to sound wise sometimes."

Their laughs went long and deep. Both women were wiping away tears and breathing heavy when the timer went off for Faith's hair.

"Faith, let me let you go, I gotta go get an umbrella and can opener for these worms," Ebony said before devolving into a mess of giggles again with Faith joining her.

EBONY WAS STILL CHUCKLING WHEN SHE TACKED HER LISTS UP ON THE corkboard in front of her desk. She reread her goals list again, letting her next assignment solidify in her mind. [1]

<u>Goals / Wanted Outcomes:</u>

1. Identify past healthy + unhealthy patterns of partnership for future forever love. (Am I the drama?)

2. Give resources, closure questions for readers. *give, not just receive*

3. ~~2.~~ Book deal.

4. ~~3.~~ Wrap this shit up so I can get back to Saturday brunches w/mimosas.

Her eyes cut to the standing mirror next to her desk. "Ebony Elizabeth Jones, are you ready to change your life?" she whispered to her image.

---

1. "WHERE IS MY HUSBAND" - RAYE

Bright and early the next morning Ebony was back in her office professionally pushing back against Bea's suggestion that she trim on-location interviews.

"I'm asking these men to revisit a private, intimate relationship for public consumption. They need to feel comfortable," she said evenly. "You don't get that over the phone. You don't get it via video calls. And as a story it has to move beyond men vs. women. It has to become something of value beyond a quick laugh and to do that the people involved need to be seen as fully human with flaws and feelings and honesty. Meeting them where they feel comfortable, watching how they navigate their spaces...that context matters."

"Depth," Bea countered, "doesn't require a flight and a hotel stay."

"It requires access," Ebony replied.

Bea editor exhaled through their nose. "You're a strong interviewer. You can get what you need remotely."

Ebony tilted her head slightly. "Can I? Because you've sent other reporters out for less. You sent out a reporter to cover a man for six months who landed a seven-figure book deal. He'd only been a book influencer for two months and if I recall, him being blond and heavily tattooed was mentioned more often than his skill with a pen."

Bea's expression hardened, just a touch.

"I'm asking for the same resources that have been allocated to stories with half the cultural weight and none of the long-term engagement potential."

"That's subjective."

"So is deciding my story doesn't require what I'm asking."

Bea editor studied her closely, assessing. Ebony had the feeling she'd already decided, but she wanted to test her.

"You really think being in the room changes the story that much?"

"I know it does and so do you.

"People perform differently when they're comfortable," Bea said, tapping her pen against the desk. "Off the record, I hated that book influencer story."

Ebony smiled. "So did I. It was a missed opportunity to examine online book culture, Publishing and influencer bias while highlighting authors and creators in the margins who *do* have the credentials and skills, but receive significantly less support."

Bea leaned back in her seat. "That was the original angle. The rage bait hottie angle was projected to get more engagement."

Ebony nodded. "My life isn't rage bait."

Bea nodded. "Flights, lodging, per diem, your editorial stipulations, and a first look at your manuscript BUT I have no authority what happens in that part of the company AND I want to see something on this project after the second interview." She waved a finger. "If I need to kill it I'll know by then."

"Just as long as you remember my kill fee."

Bea sighed. "Anything else?"

Ebony had thought about it all night and made a decision on the spot. Her brief interactions with Malcolm made her uneasy. No... Edgy. No... She couldn't put her finger on the emotion, but the idea of him being present while she relived the tent pole moments of her love life just felt off. She didn't want to cost him the gig, but on the other hand she needed to have her wits about her and Malcolm...Anyway, the scrutiny on this project was going to be deep.

"I'd like to choose a different photographer."

Bea paused and for the first time Ebony felt more than a difference of opinion or concern for budget, there was a bit of hostility coming from the woman.

"Knight is non negotiable."

Hmmm...

Ebony had the good sense to know when a negotiation period had come to end. Bea's response was unexpectedly terse, but she chalked it up to colleagues looking out for one another and let it go. She was walking away with literally everything Malcolm said she would, plus editorial approval and upgraded kill fees.

I can do hard things.

Her mind flashed to Malcolm's hard thing sliding in, feeling every single inch of him and his phenomenal piercing.

No wait, stop it brain!

"Malcolm is going to eat it up."

"I'm sorry what?" she sputtered because that was one of her problems. *He'd already done that. Well.*

Bea squinted her eyes for a moment. "This project. He'll bring the honesty and craft you're looking for. Every single time."

"Understood. I look forward to the next steps and working with you."

They exchanged pleasantries and set a date to connect again. Closing her computer, Ebony let out a sigh of relief and rested her head on her desk. She never lost focus in these types of moments and here she was having hot sex flashes while closing the deal.

"But I did close it."

A grin spread wide across her face and pride and excitement filled her. She thought for a moment and called the first person that read the manuscript she'd be pitching when this was all over.

"Joy? Guess what…"

"The camera doesn't lie. Neither does that pussy," Malcolm said as he stood strong and erect in front of her, coaxing her legs open before sliding in. Each thrust came with the clicking of a camera.

"Wait are you taking pictures?"

"Always baby, now ride it."

Ebony looked down and realized that instead of a penis, Malcolm had a big, phallic telescopic camera attached to his body. Weird. But…

"Smile for the crowd, Baby."

Ebony was just getting into a good rhythm when she registered his words and looked up. There was a crowd of people in stands and her bedroom was a set.

Ebony woke up sweaty to the sound of chickens. Or a duck. Maybe chickens and a duck?

Nah. Must be geese from the park strolling the neighborhood again.

She rolled off the couch fanning herself and made a beeline toward her kitchen to grab a cool glass of water and wipe the memory of Malcolm from her mind. While the dream was horny and weird, she recognized the signs of anxiety. Opening her life up, stepping in front of the camera, it was giving 'filmed in front of a studio audience.'

She was prepared for a lot of the responses to the project. Comments would be first. People blaming her and her choices, to some possible threats from the unhinged. She'd seen most of it already from the little viral video. Shaking her head, she concentrated on her water, grounding herself.

It really felt great on her tongue and even better against her heated face as she pressed the glass to the side of her forehead.

"Give it a good shake," a woman's voice called in her backyard.

The shadows from the tree she shared with her neighbor Mrs. Robinson danced more than they should have on the hot, breezeless day. A loud cacophony of quacks and clucks accompanied it.

"What in the Duck Tales?!"

Doing the 'nosey grandma side angle look out the window' she saw more than a dozen chickens and ducks wandering around her backyard. She stepped back from the window, rubbed her eyes and then opened the floor to ceiling curtain all the way.

The animals were still there and when she looked up she almost dropped her glass. In her tree looking less like football god and more like, well, a home-stealing asshole up in her tree, was none other than the hobosexual that kicked off this whole series of unfortunate, becoming more fortunate events. Back in those same gray sweatpants she'd met him in.[2]

Snatching open her back door she yelled up at him, "Marcus Montgomery, I told you to stay away from me! Get down from there before I turn on my hose!"

"Ebony, honey, that's my *nephew*," Mrs. Robinson said, chastising *her*!

"Your *nephew* and I have history and it isn't good Mrs. Robinson. I would like him to leave." She unfurled part of the hose, turned on the water and stood there, prepared to open the valve and blast his ass out of her half of the tree.

---

2. Doves in the Wind (featuring Kendrick Lamar) - SZA

"But I had him bring over my brother's animals to help with your slug problem and just because it didn't work out—"

Wait a damn minute.

"You never told me your aunt lived next door," she called up. "This was a set up."

"What was a set up?" Faith asked as she came around back, "And why does it sound like a petting zoo back... here... Oh my Old McDonald..." She took in Ebony, armed with her hose, and her elderly neighbor surrounded by chickens and ducks having the slug eating time of their life. Her mouth hung open in disbelief then snapped shut as she clutched her designer purse close, startled by Marcus just hanging out in the fucking tree above them.

"My neighbor set up Marcus to meet me at the gym and now he's being *helpful* with my slug problem - without my consent."

"Oh, *absolutely* not. You will remove yourself and your fowl from Ms. Holiday-Jones's residence immediately. Repair any damage or biohazard debris left behind at your expense or we will be filing trespassing charges which is the first step to a restraining order against Mister Climb Trees Shirtless here."

Ebony loved when Faith got lawyering, but hated she had to do it for *her*, surrounded by chickens and ducks no less.

"But he's looking for a wife," Mrs. Robinson protested. "And well honey, you're not getting any younger or thinner and..."

I'll fight an old woman.

"No more viral videos E...Breathe..." Faith muttered.

"He's looking for a mommy he can have sex with," Ebony said flatly. "Look at him! Has he once interjected on his own behalf? He's happy to let Auntie do it. I'm not raising any forty year old little boys."

She and Faith turned to leave.

"I'm a grown ass man," Marcus gruffed as he dropped down out of the tree.

Faith looked him up and down and sucked her teeth. "I can't tell. You have thirty minutes."

They both went into the house. Ebony left her hose on and ready - just in case. Sitting at the kitchen table, Ebony and Faith drank lemonade and snacked on fruit and cheese as they listened to the cleanup outside through the screen door.

"How did you sleep through their arrival?"

"I was anxious last night for the meeting today. I didn't get much sleep and when I did I had weird dreams. I decided to rest my eyes for a few minutes and had more weird dreams that were interrupted by the sound of chickens and ducks. I thought it was the geese from the park!"

Faith giggled as she shook her head. "I can't believe that man had the nerve to come back."

"Where else is he gone go? He. Has. No. Home." Ebony rolled her eyes as Faith's body shook. "And she was just asking me why I wasn't married while simultaneously telling me to keep everything in my own name. She set me up while also knowing he ain't shit. These last couple of weeks have been really unbelievable."

"Whaaa? Girl, that is some unscrupulous shit! I know the housing market is tough, but dang." Faith shook her head and leaned to look out the screen door again. "But...I see why you went there. He's got the kind of chest you want to lick ice cream off of. A tree climbing, male lingerie wearing, thirst trap."

"Faith, I normally don't see you until the sun goes down during the week," Ebony said when there was a pause in their laughter. "What brings you out of the marble halls of law on a Monday?"

The pause that followed was long and heavier than their previous subject.

"I quit my job a while back."

"Oh! Oh. Ok, when did this happen? What happened?"

"Six months ago," she mumbled.

"I'm sorry whet. How many months ago? And don't you mumble it this time."

"Six. Months. Didn't make partner. Again. And I was just so over it all."

"Oh my gosh honey I am so sorry. Those assholes!" She reached out and gripped her cousin's hand tightly. "Why didn't you say something?"

Faith's eyes watered a bit. "Because. I wanted to wait until I could announce where I'd landed, but I... I haven't landed and I'm scared and embarrassed and I don't have a plan. All I know is every time I go for an interview I have a panic attack."

"Whoa. That's serious Faith. And you've been dealing with this all by yourself. Have you seen a therapist?"

"So...I don't have health insurance anymore and I thought it would pass."

"And has it?"

"Noooo," she wailed. "Look!" She snatched her arm out of her blazer and lifted it to show the sweat stains. "I had an interview at Jacobs, Winters & Foster today, I'm a shoe in, but I sat in the car hyperventilating. It felt like an elephant was sitting on my chest. I drove away and the further I got from that damn building the better I felt. Then I had to fake an ER visit as to why I didn't show. I'm a fucking mess!" She dropped her head to the table and sniffled.

"This calls for a Holiday Sisters Meeting. I'll —"

"NO! I don't want anyone to know. Not yet. They'll hover and try to make me feel better and reach out feelers and somehow mom will find out and I just don't need another,

'Holiday Women Persevere' speech and I don't even know what I'm persevering yet. I'm already trying to figure out how to ease back on my Holiday Baby Trust contributions without her knowing."

"Oh...Maybe it wasn't a good idea to have Aunt Easter take over *all* the records. And you've been paying out of your savings for six months?"

"Double my rate," she covered her face with her hands.

"FAITH! You've put in twenty percent of income you no longer have for six months?"

"I want my nieces and nephews to be taken care of; it's not like I have any uterus prospects."

"And that was great when you had steady money coming in. The Trust is ten percentage of our *income* and you don't have any."

"I have savings, investments; I'm not destitute. Not even close, but..."

"Until you know what you will do next and when... Sabbatical!" Ebony snapped her fingers. "You are on sabbatical. Reduced income sabbatical. That way you don't have to hide that you're not at work, you can scale back your contributions, it's perfect."

"Great!" She didn't look like she felt great. "I'm too old to be without a plan. This is *embarrassing*."

"You didn't think I was embarrassing, you said I'm 'a woman in transition.'"

Faith let out a listless shrug. "You haven't had to be the perfect daughter of Easter Holiday."

She slipped out of her chair and hugged her cousin hard.

"This won't leave this room until you're ready."

"Thanks E."

Ebony didn't have any words of comfort or contradiction because Faith was right. Auntie Easter could put a Navy Seal to shame with her drive and heavily regimented existence and Faith, was a product of that. It wore on her when they were younger, but Ebony thought, incorrectly, Faith had grown into or beyond her mother's expectations.

Unease formed in Ebony's belly. Faith was unflappable and right now her flaps were being put through hurricane force winds. Keeping this a secret felt *wrong*, but she'd given her word. She just hoped she didn't regret it.

the first love.

"ARE YOU NERVOUS?"

The last few days had been a whirlwind of prep work, brain work, and emails flying back and forth between him and Ebony. He had a feeling she was avoiding him, but when he picked her up, she was friendly, if not distracted. He glanced down at her fingers now absentmindedly turning over a piece of Chuckle Taffy candy.

Ebony's fingers stilled as she considered Malcolm's question. "No. Not nervous, wary maybe?"

Malcolm glanced her way again as he maneuvered through traffic. "Are you afraid of him?"

Ebony shook her head quickly. "Of Brian? No, I'm afraid of a ruined memory. He was a lot of firsts; there is a nostalgic sweetness to it. I'd hate to have the little pink clouds in my mind popped by grown-up reality."

He nodded. "I guess you have to keep in mind that whatever was special back then is in a kind of capsule of its own. You may understand it better or differently, but how you felt back then still matters, and those moments matter because they shaped you in some way."

He felt her eyes on him. "That's a good way to think about it. Thanks. Would you... never mind."

"What?"

"Would you ever go back down memory lane? Look up your first love or the 'one that got away?'"

"Absolutely not," he chuckled. "I don't do dramatics, mess, or rewinds."

"Oh." Her head turned toward the window.

Shit, he hadn't meant to sound flippant. "What you're doing is different."

"Right." Her finger went back to fiddling with the wrapper.

"No, I'm serious. Every relationship I've ever had has always ended because of the same thing. And a couple didn't end well. Any contact would probably end with my camera being thrown at my head. Again."

"Oh, I've got to know what you did for that to happen." She'd turned toward him fully, her eyes lit up with mischief.

He felt self-conscious being put on the spot, but she was engaged so he powered through with a shrug and blunt honesty. "I'm a workaholic. Relationships take a backseat to my job. I am honest about it, and my partners say they are cool with it, and they were at first. But eventually the trips go too long, communication gets hit or miss, and they feel like they are in a relationship with themselves. I've been in some dangerous situations, and the worry takes a toll too. Eventually, reality sets in, and they choose better for themselves."

"Been there, done that," Ebony nodded. "Though I wouldn't say it was better, more like it was choosing me."

"That is better," he said, as he finally found a space on campus.

As she gathered her items, he walked around the truck and opened her door.

"Malcolm, that isn't necessary," she said, taking his hand as he guided her down to the ground. "I'm your colleague, not your woman."

Not yet.

Wait. Where the hell did that come from? He blinked the thought away like one would a gnat flying too close, irritated at the audacity. And realized he still held onto her warm, soft hand. His other hand was still at the small of her back, too.

"You have your hands full." It was a lame excuse, but if she thought so, she didn't say anything. Instead, she slipped her hand out of his and unwrapped her candy - pliable from the time spent in her warm hands - and shoved the whole little two-inch rectangle into her mouth. She balled up the wrapper and went to stick it into the back pocket of her jeans when he caught her hand again.

"May I?"

She looked at him crossways, but released the wrapper in his hand.

He smoothed it out. "What's a taco's favorite dance?"

"I can't believe you read the corny jokes off the wrapper."

"I can't believe you don't. That's the best part. Come on, a taco's favorite dance?"

She frowned and crossed her arms. "The candy is the best part."

"The candy is the joke delivery system. Now, what is a taco's favorite dance?" He shimmied his shoulders.

"Joke delivery system? In what world?"

He raised his eyebrows as he waited for her answer.

"Fine," she looked to the left as she thought.

It gave him time to study her face. Deep in dad-joke ponder, it was relaxed in slight amusement. The June sun was bright on her soft cheeks, and her time in the garden with the slugs had given her the same burnished glow she had in Cabo.

He wanted to sink his hands into her fluffy curls, now free from her braids. *But that would be weird.*

"Tick tock Ebee."

"Horizontal Tango. 'Cause it's a taco."

"What?! No! This is *kids* candy, Ebony Elizabeth. I am shocked. Shocked at your innuendo." He wagged his finger at her, and she batted it away.

"That *is* a kid's answer. Middle school. Maybe high school." She grinned up at him, and the sun got just a little bit brighter. He couldn't help but drop his mock disapproval and smile back at her.

"The answer," he said, as he took her hand and led her through an Enchufla Doble move, "is salsa." She came out of the move a little wide-eyed and maybe just a tad breathless. That made him smile bigger.

"Hey, I'm sorry I thought we were setting up at noon," a young woman said, dashing up to them. "I can get the audio up in less than five, I am so sorry."

"Anika?" Ebony dropped his hand a second time and hid hers behind her. "You're right on time. This is Malcolm Knight, photojournalist."

"Oh. Okay, I thought you were the former boyfriend, and I was really late. Whew! I thought I was 'fired on the first day.' Great. Well, I am Anika Jackson, a student here at THE Ohio State University and your audio intern for the duration of your project." And she curtseyed, then visibly cringed.

She was adorable with her pink to purple ombre braids, smooth, freckled skin, and stylish, almost doll-like makeup, complete with a little sparkle. He wanted to give her a fifty-dollar bill, like he did his little cousins. Though they preferred digital money now.

Huh. It's been a minute since I sent them anything.

Malcolm made a mental note to spoil his cousins and

watched Ebony welcome Anika, smoothing right over her awkward introduction. Malcolm shook the intern's hand and refrained from sliding her money and patting her on the head.

He grabbed his gear, slipped Ebony's bag off her shoulder, and followed the women across the street to the interview location. Scanning their route, he half-listened to Ebony talk shop with Anika. Then there was a moment when both of them turned toward each other, heads tilted, that had him reaching for his camera. Anika - tall and lithe, looking every bit of the modern student - and Ebony - lusciously curved, confident, and in that phase of life where the only way to describe her beauty was to say it was timeless - framed part of a sign touting the student center. Between their bodies - one earnest, one encouraging - was the sunlit word "student."

A perfect moment captured that gave him the 'got the shot' feels.

"So the idea is to get them comfortable to open up and have an honest conversation about our relationship and hopefully through our interviews I can figure out harmful and helpful relationship patterns."

"And all this came from a random hookup," Anika said off-handedly. "You should sell t-shirts. 'No Penis Worth Your Peace.'"

Ebony chuckled. "I'm good."

They arrived at the building, and Ebony navigated the halls slowly, the epitome of moving through a memory.

"It still smells the same." She rubbed her hand along the tiled wall and smiled.

"So, please don't take this the wrong way, Ms. Ebony, I'm pan in a polycule so no judgement here," Anika started. "How much audio are we getting? Like intimate moments? Are these interview slash dates?"

His eyes snapped to the back of Ebony's head. The thought never occurred to him.

"No! Just the intimacy of conversation," Ebony said, shaking her head. "It would be unethical for me to have a relationship with a source *during* the project."

He let out a long-held breath. "Plus, it's not like you're going into this thinking you're going to get back with any of these guys, right?"

Ebony shrugged, and his jaw tightened.

"I'm not ruling anything out after we publish the piece. I mean, the whole point is to fix my love life, soo...game on."

♡

BRIAN COOLIDGE, FINANCIAL ADVISOR
CODE NAME: THE PROFESSOR
AGE 37, MARRIED, TWO DAUGHTERS AGES 3 AND 6
NO RECORD, NO PENDING LITIGATION
GOOD INVESTMENTS
GRAD SCHOOL BOYFRIEND — THREE-YEAR RELATIONSHIP
TALKER!!

MALCOLM ADDED THAT LAST LINE TO HIS NOTES AS HE SAT WAITING for any switch in the conversation that would yield other interesting shots. It was thirty minutes into the interview, and Ebony had only asked: "How have you been? What are you up to now?"

What was supposed to be a series of warm-up questions turned into the only question this Brian dude needed to talk about himself. He'd touched on his life since they last saw each other - a blow by blow, year-by-year retelling of his career, his kids, his frat, his properties, his dog, his mother, his last trip to the Dominican Republic, and his wife.

In that order. The wife barely got a passing mention.

Anika's eyes were glazed over, and if he hadn't been shooting, his would have mirrored hers.

"You know, Ebony, I always knew we'd cross paths again someday." Brian said as he took a sip of his espresso and leaned in, licking his lips.

Malcolm's curled in response.

He had to admit, Brian was an objectively handsome man who'd paid special attention to his appearance today. He looked rich casual with his quiet labels that touted two hundred euros for a basic white tee and twice that for his well broken in jeans. Malcolm could see the appeal...*if the jackass never spoke. Or if he, maybe, asked the Ebony anything about herself...*

"Really? What made you so sure?" Ebony sipped her own drink. She was relaxed and focused throughout his monologue, but now she mirrored his posture, leaning in.

"You're the one who got away. We were great together, and I knew once you matured, you'd make a fantastic wife and mother. And then you popped up on my timeline just at the right moment."

Ebony took the opening. "What do you think was so great about us? What was your favorite thing we did as a couple?"

He's going to say sex.

"Well, when we weren't in bed," Brian said, as he chuckled, "I loved when you would cook for me at your apartment. And those Saturdays when we would study and do laundry at the place near my apartment. You know it's still there? Looks the same too, except you swipe instead of chucking in quarters," he smiled and waved his hand at the change. "Anyway, not even my wife could get my laundry smelling as good as you did. And she tried every soap out there."

"Right...right...," Ebony said pleasantly. Her pen tapped twice. "Was there anything *outside* of my labor that you remember fondly?"

Brian blinked a couple of times and sat back, his face settling into a frown as he rubbed his chin nervously. "You sound like my wife. I didn't *ask* you to cook or do my laundry."

"I never said you did." Ebony kept her face passive. "I'm just trying to understand myself better through us. What's something you learned about yourself from dating me?"

"Is that the only reason you asked me here?" He looked sullen, his hand curled into a fist in his lap.

Malcolm angled his camera to shoot him from the mouth down, capturing his posture as it transformed from prideful to engaged to taken aback to sullen.

"Well, yes. I thought I was pretty clear. And you're married."

Duh asshole, remember the wife?

"Separated, actually." His voice deepened and he leaned in further.

"Legally?" Ebony leaned forward, her gaze puzzled.

That wasn't in anything she provided; Malcolm had seen nothing in his research either.

"Spiritually."

Bruh. Malcolm almost took his earpiece out and said it out loud. Instead, he snapped the self-satisfied, almost earnest look on Coolidge's face; his face was mostly in shadow, but his grin was highlighted.

"Ah. Just to pivot back, what do you think I did well as a partner?"

He adjusted in his seat, disappointed Ebony didn't look

more enthusiastic at the spiritual uncoupling Malcolm was certain this dude's wife knew nothing about.

Brian shrugged, then after a moment, "You were dependable. Like, I never had to worry about anything slipping through the cracks with you. Do you ever think about us?"

"Yes. I think about the sweetness of that first year, how happy I was. I had stars and wedding bells in my mind." Ebony gave a small, sad smile.

"Where do you think we went wrong?" Brian asked quietly, leaning in and placing his hand on top of Ebony's.

"I think the turning point was when you started telling me to 'Hurry up and cum.'"

"I didn't say it like *that*," he protested, tapping her hand playfully. "We were both young and trying to figure it out. I think if you focused more instead of those silly jokes..."

Ebony slid her hand away from his, tucking it under the table and wiping it discreetly on her jeans. Malcolm's camera saw and captured all of it.

"I see now it was partly a nervous response; I didn't respond well being rushed to climax."

"And I didn't respond well to being told it was *my* fault you couldn't get your head in the game and being laughed at."

Ebony nodded, empathy in her voice and on her face, "I'm sorry I hurt your feelings. I handled it the best way I knew at the time."

"The best way to handle it was to tell me I screamed like Professor X from that cartoon when I came? That was childish."

"No, me yelling 'Jean no!' after you came was childish. Me telling you that you sounded like my favorite cartoon from the 90s was a playful observation. I thought Professor X was hot."

Brian's mood changed on a dime. "Do you still feel that way?"

"No. I've matured, as you say." She looked down at her notes. "I just have a few more questions, Brian, if you are up for it?"

"Fine."

"How did my way of handling disagreements affect the relationship?"

"You'd bring things up a lot. Like, you wanted to talk about it over and over. I felt like once something was said, it should just be left alone."

"Is there anything you wish we had talked about before we parted ways?"

Brian shrugged again. "Probably expectations. Like there were a lot of expectations you had, you could have made it easier for me and maybe made a list of what you wanted and needed, like a chore list."

Malcolm had to give it to Ebony; she was never an inch less than professional, even after this muthafucka asked for a chore list for his emotional heavy lifting.

"Hey... did you ever learn how to, you know." Brian nodded his head toward her crotch and winked.

"Why did you steal all my underwear?" Ebony asked back.

He licked his lips and slipped from his chair, crouched low to her ear and leaned in. "I wanted to keep your scent." His face went from a grin to a grimace. "My wife made me get rid of them when we got married. Your turn. Was it a medical thing?"

Ebony closed her notepad. "Through extensive research, I learned I need a girthier penis that could provide more internal clitoral stimulation." Ebony demonstrated how the clitoris organ wraps around the vaginal canal using her fingers. "Big dick, stretch me wide, and presto! Toes pointed to the sky."

decompress and debrief

"HOW ARE YOU FEELING?"

Ebony adjusted in her seat, opened and closed her mouth a few times, then sat up straighter. "Fine. He had an interesting perspective."

They'd just dropped off Anika at her class now that she'd been initiated to Malcolm's 'come together, leave together' code and were heading back to her house. Malcolm's truck felt too bright and quiet after being inside and surrounded by students for so long.

"Do you have decompress and debrief plans?" Malcolm asked.

Ebony was torn. On one hand, she wanted to talk about what had just happened, but on the other hand, she didn't necessarily wanna talk about it with Malcolm. She found herself opening up to him anyway.

"Well, I have a bi-weekly appointment with my therapist to check in, but outside of that, no." She pulled a piece of candy out of her bag and flicked the corner of the wrapper with her thumb back and forth. "I knew I would have some emotions after the interviews, but I didn't think I'd have them all in one day. I was going to go home, go through my notes, but..."

"You need some time to decompress."

She sighed and rolled her eyes. "I hate to say you're right, but yeah, I think I do."

Malcolm changed lanes, taking them away from her house.

"Where are you going?"

"Somewhere you can decompress."

He pulled in and parked at one of her favorite metro parks, grabbed a small bag out the back of his truck, and walked toward the lake. The closer they got to the lake, the quieter it became. Gentle bird calls and lapping water replaced the roar of cars and trucks from the nearby freeway, and as she pulled a deep breath in, her body filled with the grounding scent of wet earth and sunshine. Ebony felt her body relaxing with each step until she realized where they were going.

The Columbus Kayaks sign loomed large, with a happy little cartoon kayaker beside the operating times and pricing. She slowed almost to a stop.

"What's the matter?" Malcolm slipped his sunglasses off to look at her.

Ebony was embarrassed, but she soldiered on. "I tend to avoid putting my larger body into toy boats. Yachts, cruise ships, large container barges - cool. A kazoo with oars? No thanks. In fact, this is giving me the opposite of decompress. I'm compressing."

He grinned.

Did the sun just glint off this brotha's teeth?

"I'd never put your safety at risk. I'm a bigger body, I'll be right beside you, and we'll be wearing life vests. If you'll trust me with your beautiful body one more time, I promise, I'll take care of it."

Then his charming ass winked at her. The innuendo hung heavy in the air as he reached out his hand.

"Come on, Ebee, I think you're up for the challenge."

Gosh dangit...

OPEN WATER STRETCHED OUT UNDER A BIG BLUE, LATE AFTERNOON sky, its surface twisted and rippled from the steady dip and swish of their paddles.[1]

Ebony adjusted her grip, feeling the effort to move the kayak in her shoulders. "This is work."

"Yeah, but you're taking to it like a duck to water," he said from the kayak beside hers. "You feel better, don't you?"

She gave him a look. "I do. It's peaceful out here. But do not mention ducks to me."

"Did you date a duck once?"

"Ha, ha. No, but I dated a man that filled my backyard with them this week."

As Ebony told him about her unexpected visitors, his face alternated between amused and irritated. "You've had some wild moments lately."

"Literally. Though I guess chickens are domesticated, right? And those ducks would be too, because they are kept livestock, or is that a thing? I wonder what the industry behind them is like. Ohio is huge in chicken and eggs, but ducks isn't the first thing I think of..."

Her brain clicked over and recognized she was doing her thing. Rabbit holing, as her sisters called it.

"When you think of what?" he urged.

"I'm going down a rabbit hole. Pay me no mind."

---

1.   I Want You Around by Snoh Aalegra

"More like a duck hole. Nest? Duck dive!" he said excitedly. He carefully placed a hand over top of his oar and held his other hand up for a high five. She was too far away, but laughed as she gave him an air one. "Have you ever seen how a duck dives? I got a friend who's a nature photographer, and she has this amazing series that focuses just on this family of ducks and what happens below the surface. Even when you see part of the surface, the water line acts like a membrane between realities."

Ebony had never dated anyone in her field before, and she wondered if she had missed out. *That kind of curiosity though... times two? No one would get anything done.* Shaking the thought out of her head, she made him promise to send her a link to the coffee table book.

They drifted for a moment, the current dying down enough that neither of them had to fight it. A breeze skimmed across the water, lifting the edges of her curls, cooling the heat from the low sun.

"Why did you pick this spot?"

He turned his paddle once with slow, deliberate movements. "It's my favorite. And... it felt like a good counterweight to the busy vibe of campus."

She nodded and sighed deeply, relaxing her posture. Something niggled at her just under the surface.

"You were disappointed with the interview."

She frowned slightly. "No, I wasn't. The pacing after he caught me up on all of his life was good. Anika said the audio was great. There are some good quotes and —"

"Let me clarify, you were disappointed in him," he said.

She let that sit, then pushed her paddle into the water again, setting a rhythm that he matched. *Stroke, glide. Stroke, glide.*

"He valued my labor. All these years later, he remembers

our relationship as if I were an assistant available for sex. *That's* disappointing. And he was actually a sweet guy at first. During our relationship, his ego took over. Unfortunately for his poor, 'spiritually separated' wife, it's gotten worse."

For a while, they didn't talk. They just moved and Ebony's mental checklist went quiet.

"I got over being fat," she admitted out of nowhere. "Or, at least the fat I thought I was back then. I was smaller, but still never the petite girl a boy could pick up with one arm. I got over it because he was sweet and tender, and I felt beautiful, even sexy in his arms."

She shook her head a little. "I rushed too quickly into 'playing house.' I was mimicking the marriages I saw in my real life - the care and partnership through thick and thin. But I wasn't married, and I'd forgotten something my Aunt Evie would tell us Holiday Sisters: 'Dating should be fun, especially when you're young.'"

"What was the lesson of the relationship?" He asked, slowing his rowing and letting the question linger.

"I moved too quickly, stayed too long. When I told him I thought we should see other people the first time, he said, 'We are this far into it; what was the point if we break up now?'"

Malcolm grimaced.

"Right," Ebony agreed. "I want someone who will show up for me like I do for them. And I want to have *fun* with the man I'm with. Brian couldn't laugh with me, at himself."

"That Jean Gray line was fucking hilarious. I thought Anika was going to pee herself trying to stay quiet. Did he really sound like that?"

"He did. And he really stole all my underwear."

Malcolm whistled. "I had a hookup steal my camera equipment, passport, and pants. Left me in Turkey with just my draws and shirts. I was tempted to Donald Duck it to the embassy but…"

Ebony's bark of laughter was so loud some nearby birds took off. She tried to censor herself, but giggled for a good while. The picture he created in her mind was priceless. "What did you do?"

"Made a manly skirt out of one of my shirts and inquired at the front desk about a charity lift to the embassy to replace my passport. I got some looks, but I pulled it off. I've got great legs."

Ebony laughed even harder with him joining in, almost dropping his paddle in the water, which made them double over, kayaks swaying dangerously.

As one, they decided it was probably a good time to get to shore. After they returned their boats and vests, they retrieved their shoes and socks from the gravelly shore. Ebony plopped down on a nearby bench and tried to get the motivation to move her arms, but boy, her shoulders and arms were like lead. Seeing her struggle with removing the water shoes he'd loaned her, Malcolm patted his lap, telling her she should put her feet up.

"No, you'll get sand all over your pants."

He rolled his eyes, reached down and grabbed both her legs, pulling them onto his lap. Without a word, he got to work on peeling the damp, mesh contraptions off her feet.

"How often do you bring dates out here?" She asked, breaking the intimacy of the moment. She needed something to distract her from his large hands wrapped around her ankles and feet.

"Is this your way of asking if I'm seeing someone?"

"No, I — these shoes are much smaller than yours."

"My *mom*," he raised an eyebrow and smirked at her, "liked to come out here after her in-center dialysis treatments. She said it reminded her that 'in the middle of pain, beauty still exists.'" His eyes clouded with a sadness he didn't have to vocalize.

"In the middle of pain, beauty still exists," she repeated. "That's powerful. When my Granny Holiday went on dialysis, she wasn't eligible for a transplant, and she kept her diagnosis, treatments, even how she really felt so private. It was her choice, of course."

"That's rough. Mom's eligible; it's just a waiting game. Probably a long one because of her age. I'm not a match which makes me feel like a terrible son, but at least now she has dialysis at home, she's more comfortable, and she has the beauty she curates around her. She still comes out here every once in a while. No matter how she's feeling, she likes to walk along the shore, but hates wet socks." He waved the floppy water shoes at her.

"Who doesn't?" She quipped, feeling entirely too comfortable with her legs in this man's lap.

He smiled at her, still holding her legs, his thumb stroking the skin on her ankle just below her hastily rolled-up cuff.

"I'm not."

"Not what?"

"Dating anyone."

"I didn't ask."

"And yet, now you know."

The space between them shifted—it was electric, and familiar feelings started dancing beneath the moment, not breaking the surface, but moving them along just the same.

Ebony looked away first, focusing on the water, on the way the sunlight fractured across it. She exhaled slowly, trying to settle herself and ward off the goosebumps his hands on her skin created. "We've been out here for—what—two hours?"

"Closer to three."

Her head snapped back toward him. "Three?"

"Time moves differently when you're not watching it."

"That's not—" she stopped, recalibrating. "I have notes to organize, social media posts to approve, prep work for the next interview—"

"You will get to it all," he said.

Ebony looked down at her hands, then back up at him.

"I lost track of time," she said. "And I can't afford to do that now."

He looked at her a moment longer, then gently slipped on her socks, tied her sneakers and set her feet down. Standing, he held out his hand to her. "Understood."

Her hand in his for like the sixth time that day Ebony couldn't shake a quiet, persistent thought settling in the back of her mind: the hours she'd just spent out here, the ones she couldn't account for in her notes or her outline, might be the hardest ones to examine.

trauma bonding

MALCOLM HAD NEVER HAD that much fun at the lake before his time with Ebony. When he was with his mom, he was tight, pensive and worried, watching every move and mood of hers as she worked through her physical and mental pain.

Being out there with Ebony calmed him and returned him to the peace he loved when he first found the place. Maybe it was because she wasn't grappling with life and death. Maybe it was her laugh. Either way he was grateful to her for bringing good memories to the space and for trusting him.

He glanced over at her, wide awake, staring out the window. "I thought you were asleep; you're so quiet."

"Oh no, I can't fall asleep when - that doesn't matter," she waved her hand at her interrupted thought. "Thank you again. I'm going to be broke up around the shoulder area tomorrow but... I'm in a good brain space to get into my notes now."

"Do you know what you're going to write?"

"I never start writing until I have all the information. I'll tag quotes, interesting moments, make all my observation notes etc. What about you?"

"I mark the ones that grab me first then work with the writer to see if we are on the same page. Most of the time we are."

"Are you going to email them or—"

"Do you want to grab some food and go over—"

He chuckled. "Go ahead, I'm sorry."

"If you could drop a link that would be great. I don't want an audience while I go over everything."

He turned that over in his mind, his empathy for her growing. "I'm starting to really appreciate how difficult this will be for you."

She sucked her teeth and shook her head ruefully. "So am I. Plus I'm familiar with your work. There is a depth and emotion that stays with me. It might be weird navigating it with me as the subject in front of you."

"My work stays with you?" Malcolm asked without thinking it through.

Shit.

He braced for the photo everyone brings up. And the inevitable guilt that follows. He'd been so into talking to her that somehow he forgot one of the worst moments of his life.

"Two in particular. The shooting at the West Lake concert. Everyone talks about the blood on the camera or the man's open eyes as he held the kid he saved. I always remember his hand and lip placement. The protection of his hand flat over the child's ear and his lips on the top of their head. To me, that's the power of the moment, not his agony frozen in death but the tendency of good people to comfort and be tender to strangers in the worst of times. Like your mom said, 'in the middle of pain, beauty still exists.' I was shocked as shit it ran. Then I thought about the photographer who took the photo. I couldn't imagine being there let alone having the presence of mind to capture the moment rather than run for cover. I wanted to call when I saw your photo credit, but it didn't seem like right time for a fling to reach out."

As she talked Malcolm felt his throat closing up and the thump, thump swell of a headache forming. A headache that lately was always accompanied a prickle behind his eyes.

"Are you okay? I shouldn't have brought that up, I wasn't thinking."

Forcing a tight smile, he shook his head. "It's fine. It's the job."

"No, seriously, I—."

"It's. Fine." Malcolm said more harshly than he meant to. *Fuck.* He pulled his shit together long enough to steer them safely to a parking spot in front of her house. "I'm sorry Ebony. That sounded... Fuck. I'm sorry. I asked the question."

"Do you want to talk about it?"

"I have no interest in trauma bonding with you." He gripped the wheel tightly then let it go. "Goddamn it, that is also not how it sounds."

Malcolm turned off the car and pinched the bridge of his nose. After he took a deep breath he turned to her and fuck if she didn't look like her feelings were hurt.

"Ebee, what I'm fucking up in saying is I don't want to dump this burden on you. I don't talk about it because I don't want anyone else to live with it, not even second hand. Just the fact that the photo was published, that it *sticks with you*. With the world. With his fucking wife..."

He blinked past the fucking eye prickles because here he was, oversharing with her just a few days after he said he wouldn't. "I should go."

She nodded, but sat there several beats longer. She unsnapped her seatbelt and placed her hand on his as it rested on the center console.

"It was important you showed the world—"

"His horrible death?"

"What kind of man he was. His final act was to make sure a child he didn't even know was protected and comforted. Your photo made sure he wasn't just a sterilized statistic tossed out to a numb country. Thank you for being brave."

MALCOLM WALKED AROUND HIS MOTHER'S HOUSE CHECKING THE locks and windows and noted the kitchen could use a good coat of paint.

"You seem restless kiddo," his mom said. She sat down and removed the bandage cover that kept her injection site clean and dry. "How's the assignment?"

"Good Ma, I'm fine. What did you eat today?"

"Food. What's her name?"

"It's not about a woman."

She leveled a mom gaze on him and he stood still under her scrutiny. "Then what's it about? How's your sleep? Have you talked to Lauren? You need to tell her about what really happened with the photo, does she even know you were shot too?"

Shit, he really did leave that opening for her.

"I'm fine Ma, I'm not bothering Lauren so close to the anniversary. Especially... Anyway, I was just checking on everything for you." He picked up her tablet and scrolled through reading the numbers from her last treatment. "Blood draw numbers should be back by tomorrow and I'll be back from Kentucky in time for your treatment the day after."

She waved his info away. "I can shoot myself up."

"Ma." He shook his head at her flippant attitude.

"Maybe I'll wear that gold dress of mine and pretend I'm back at Studio 54."

"Ma. You did not shoot up at Studio 54.

"Nah, I never got into the heavy stuff."

"Wait, you went to Studio 54?"

She shrugged. "It was a lifetime ago, but it was the place to be seen. It wasn't as fun as people made out to be, but it was *great* people watching."

Malcolm's brain rebooted. The life his parents lived filled him with wonder. "Where was dad during this?"

"Right beside me." She grinned. "Back to my question, what story is taking you to Kentucky? And why does she have you wandering my house flipping locks?"

His momma was like a dog with a bone.

"I'm under NDA, but it's to cover an artist."

"Is she pretty?"

"MOMMA. The only women involved is a colleague and a twenty-one-year-old intern."

"You're too old for the intern. Old men give young women worms."

"I'm not old!"

She gave him a look that said *yeah right.*

"Wow. I come all the way around the world to hang with you and you call me old."

"You too old for the intern. This colleague, however, is she age appropriate?"

"Ebee is a fully grown adult Momma, but we are, she is, it's work."

"Mmm hmm." She gave him the stink eye, then her face lit up in a grin. "I hope she doesn't leave you pantless in Kentucky."

Malcolm put on another forty-five on each side of the bar and looked around. Spotting the only other brotha working out this late, he asked for a spot and started his reps, working until his body couldn't physically throw up any more weight.

Still his mind buzzed. He couldn't get what Ebony said out of his head so he ran on the treadmill until he could barely stand.

Finally, he dragged his sleepless ass home and sat in the car flipping through his contacts. He wasn't fooling himself with the 'absentminded' scrolling. Fed up with himself he just hit the name. It rang three times before she picked up.

"Malcolm?"

"Lauren, hey I just wanted to check in on you."

"I— I'm alright. What time is it there?"

"Late."

He heard her sigh and he regretted calling.

"You're still not sleeping are you Mal?"

"I was. Then I stopped again."

"Shoot, so did I."

He jingled his keys a few times. "Besides sleep, how is everything else?"

She chuckled. "I'm getting ready to celebrate the wrong kind of anniversary and my mother-in-law dropped off a black dress and itinerary for the occasion."

"Shit."

"I really just want to crawl into bed and not come out until it's over."

"I think Justin would think that was a great idea."

"Maybe... I think he would think we both should get more sleep like him."

His laugh took him by surprise. "The man could sleep literally anywhere. We were in Kabul one time, shit is poppin' off all around us and he's like 'it's going to be a while, I might as well kick off,' and catches a few winks through the siren."

Her gentle laugh met his and something in him unlocked. "I never apologized—"

"Mal, don't. I know you just did your job, but I'm not ready to talk about it. I lost my world that day and found out the same time, same way everyone else did, looking— looking into his eyes... It changed me in ways I don't even understand and haven't figured out how to handle. Take care Malcolm. Get some sleep."

"You too."

Malcolm went into the house and his body's needs overtook his mind's restlessness. He did get sleep, but he didn't rest.

ANIKA WAS ATTEMPTING to be professional as she mic'd up a shirtless Diego Washington, looping a lanyard-like device around his neck with halting fingers. He attempted to engage her in polite conversation, and her little face flushed red underneath her tawny, freckled complexion, and she quickly mumbled her major. When she finished setting up Ebony's mic, she found the darkest corner in which to blend in, putting significant distance between herself and him.

Ebony understood her struggle. Diego was captivating and magnetic.

Still. [1]

Deep-set, dark eyes beneath sharp brows gave him a dangerous and mysterious vibe. He had highlighted locs that graced his face like a crown, especially when the sun hit as it was doing now. His long and rangy build, complete with Adonis cut, was a testament to one of two constants in Diego's life - yoga. No matter where they had been in the world or how long they'd partied into the night, he'd start his day with yoga.

---

1. Could've Been (feat. Bryson Tiller) by H.E.R.

Then sex. Intense. Creative. Exploratory. Diego had made up for every orgasm she'd ever missed with Brian.

Good times.

Where they were standing - barefoot in a barn in the middle of southern Kentucky - was a testament to his art, the only other thing Diego fully committed to. It took him, and for more than a year, her, all over the world.

Ebony thought it best to bring him back to his art after he started to fidget following set up. Part of Diego's conditions for participating in her project was that his art couldn't be photographed, alongside the standard anonymity granted each of her former lovers. Malcolm was quiet, laser focused, and efficient. Something she noticed with her interview with Brian. He became almost invisible once he started working, but Diego's nature was to notice.

As Malcolm captured some setting shots - paint cans in a corner, clay in another, Diego watched him closely.

"What are you working on that excites you today?"

The fidgeting stopped, his focus zoomed in on her, and his face lit up.

There he is.

"I was deep on this piece," he said as he placed his hand on the small of her back and led her through the barn to a series of oil paintings in various stages of creation, "those hinge together to complete one half of a larger idea on the tension between ego and insanity." He stood back and looked at it a bit longer. Then looked over at her with a wink, "I call it a self-portrait."

"You've never been insane, Diego," Ebony chided.

He shrugged. "Sometimes it feels better to say crazy instead of broken."

"You were never that either; I don't know how many times I have to tell you."

Diego had spent much of his childhood on various medicines to "calm his behavior." When she met him at a festival in Columbus' Arts District, he'd given up on trying to find something that worked with his impulse control issues that didn't leave him in what he called a zombie state.

"You've always been generous, Baby Girl. Anyway, when I took a break from my electronic fast, I discovered your message, and it gave me inspiration to finish. I stitched the last stitch just before you got here."

Ebony stopped still, excitement filling her. "Did you... did you finish Eve?!"

Diego nodded slowly, delighted that she knew exactly what he was talking about. He led her around another tall island of rolled canvas and stacks of fabric. She always loved the smell of his workspaces, no matter where they were in the world. They always smelled like the environment he was in, and his scent - a deep, rich wood, a hint of apple, and sweet almond oil. This workshop smelled of earth and hay with notes of aged wood. The pathway of throw rugs around the barn made their journey a cozy, sensory-rich one for her bare toes, and something about the space made her feel energized and itching to create.

That was the power of Diego.

There was a kind of distortion field around him that made your creativity peak as if it were plugged into the universe. It could also be overwhelming and all-consuming if you stayed in it too long.

Ebony sensed Malcolm trailing close enough to monitor her and get 'the shot' while not spooking Diego. She wondered if it was a mark of maturity or growth that she noticed him at all. Diego had a way of blotting out the presence of others, but somehow Ebony still sensed Malcolm's quiet movements.

Focus.

She'd wasted that thought because when they rounded the final shoulder-high pile of cut jean material, "*Eve*," a piece Diego had been working on since before they met, came into view and it knocked Ebony on her ass. Literally. She had to sit, she was so overcome.

At least eight feet high, *Eve* was a mixed-media wonder that took a generously plus-size woman's form and placed the natural world upon it. It was as if Earth birthed Eve and Eve had birthed Earth. There were mountains, valleys, volcanic rivers, florals, rivers and green rolling hills, stone and crystal, thin sheeting of various materials with a cloud-like substance woven within acted as a veil that reminded her of atmospheric layers. All the beauty and color set against an impossibly black sky.

"She is magnificent," Ebony said in awe, lying back on the rug to really get a good look from that angle.

"Do you recognize yourself?"

"What?" Ebony stood up and squinted. Then walked backward until she bumped into Malcolm, who had stepped in behind her to stop her before she stumbled over a low stack of paints.

She thanked him distractedly before turning her head this way and that, trying to see it. "I'm sorry, I don't see it. She still looks like your mother."

"Yes, in parts, but those are your stretch marks."

She squinted again and walked up to the piece. "Negro, you immortalized my stretch marks?! How did you even..."

She reached out to touch the material that was sewn to be the deep valleys between mountains and pulled her hand away at the last minute. She always had trouble *not* touching art. The golden embroidery string actually *look*ed like the inside lighter skin of a stretch mark in terms of color and texture. It was wild and... intimate.

"Go ahead, feel."

Mesmerized, using a single finger, she followed the string on its back-and-forth journey, carving out its form on the canvas. She used her middle finger for the second one. And so on. "You mean you made these and thought of me?"

"Nah, look." He reached over and pulled a photo from the wall on his side. It was her when they were at the naturist village of Cap d'Agde. She was naked, in water up to her thighs, peering at something out of frame. Her arms were crossed over her breasts, hugging herself. And as big as day were her stretch marks. She glanced from the photo to the art in front of her and back.

"Do you have a mirror?"

Diego grinned and held up a finger. He disappeared whistling a tune and returned with a gilded monstrosity that looked out of a Vegas casino demo. While he held it, she lifted her shirt, tucking it under her chin and yanked down the side of her loose, floor-length skirt. "Well, I'll be damned. There are a couple new ones but... huh. That IS me."

She ran her finger down her own skin, feeling the texture. "How did you get the *texture*?"

"I remembered."

"Essentially, Baby Girl, we didn't work out because I ain't shit."

Ebony barked out a laugh that was as loud as it was unexpected. She covered her mouth with her hand, her pen resting against her lips. "I'm so sorry. I didn't mean to...I wasn't expecting that."

After staring in complete awe at *Eve* and her own small, but perspective-shifting part in it, she and Diego finally sat down for their interview. And by sat she meant she sat in a tall director's chair near him while he rolled out clay beads that he would later glaze and fire.

Now she was trying to regain her professional, but open, decorum, but Diego was making it hard.

Diego chuckled watching her, his hands on autopilot. "That's what you're here for, right? To get to the truth of your human experience so far? That's the truth. When it comes to relationships, I ain't shit. I'm unsteady in all the ways that matter, selfish and self-centered. The only thing that has changed in me since you left is that I'm honest with myself and everyone else in my life now."

Diego walked over to the kitchen area and opened a small bread box. "Banana bread?"

Normally, that non sequitur would have thrown Ebony, but this was Diego, and that's how he was. "Is there anything *medicinal* in there?"

"Ebony, love, you eat a few brownies, have a bad trip and you never trust me again?"

Ebony sipped her water - that she brought. "I could hear colors, missed a deadline, and nearly broke my coochie messin' with you."

Diego grinned. "Yeah, see, that's why I ain't shit because I remember it as being a good time."

She laughed harder.

"We could've been together forever if it'd stayed like this."

She met his eyes at his words. "Maybe. It's tough to keep up with you."

"I loved our trips. The spontaneous stuff. When we weren't... stressing about 'serious' things. Like Texas, your birthday that year—that was fun. Juneteenth in Texas, the air was electric."

"I remember having to plan the trip."

"And there it is. The trip *was* the plan. You always wanted… more… structure than I did. I go-with-the-vibes. You'd get stressed about the future, and I'm like—why not just enjoy the moment?"

"If I knew we'd have a room to stay in and not some stranger's living room floor, I'd enjoy the moment."

He held his hands up in surrender and went back to rolling beads and chewing bread. She noticed he didn't say the bread *didn't* have extra "seasonings." She looked at her notes and tapped her pen twice.

"Were there ways I supported you that felt especially helpful?"

"You held things down," he said with a nod. "You were always there when I needed you. My art reached new levels with you backing me, and you didn't try to control me like some women do."

"Looking back, what patterns do you notice in how I handle relationships?"

He stopped rolling long enough to consider her. "Honestly? You're a lot."

Ouch. She made sure to carefully arrange her face so he focused on his thoughts and not her reactions.

"You go all in. Like… fast. I could match your energy when it's about creating, or fucking for hours. Seeing new shit. Seeing the world through your eyes is amazing. But you expect a lot early on too."

"Like what?"

"Sometimes you'd overreact. Everything isn't always a whole conversation. You wanted to talk everything out right then. I'm not like that. I need space. Maybe I'll come back to it, maybe I won't, but I wanted you to be cool with my decision either way. I'm not saying it's right… but like I said—"

"You ain't shit."

He shrugged. "Is this helping at all?"

"Surprisingly? Yes. If you could give me one piece of advice for my next relationship, what would it be?"

"Find someone more on your level... someone who wants the same life you do. The kids, the family barbecues, Holiday Sister Brunches, and orgasms that end in time for work on Monday. Someone dependable with the mortgage and you."

Ebony made another note on her pad and tried to put a lid on the feelings that were becoming a familiar part of this process. She wondered if Malcolm would want to debrief with her again.

"I want you to have some of these," he said, scooping up beads that had already been glazed and fired.

He placed over two dozen of them in her hands while he looked for a container. She examined them in the natural sunlight streaming in from large windows added to the front of the barn. The colors and designs were beautiful.

Diego came back with a small, translucent drawstring satchel and held it open as she tipped them inside.

"They're beautiful, thank you."

"They're made with my own semen. I dried it, mixed it in with porcelain clay, and rolled these right here in the studio. These are my favorite glaze designs."

Diego Washington Notes
Age 39 | Artist | Codename: The Artist
- He reframes my needs as issues
- Avoids most responsibility

-Accountability is chalked up to 'not being shit.'

-Centers fun and freedom over real attachment and responsibilities

Me:

-I tolerated behavior others wouldn't.

-I'm dependable... Am I a good support person or steady like your favorite milking a cow? Just labor?

-I'm a lot.

-I give too quickly.

-Diego was the exact opposite of Brian, from no fun and sexual dissatisfaction to fun without boundaries and cosmic orgasms

Two different extremes...

debrief part deux

"SO HE EATS banana bread with the same hands he's rollin' jack-off beads."

Ebony and Anika's laughter filled the cab of the rental. They had been on the road for less than five minutes, all of them pondering the same thing, but apparently he was the only one impolite enough to say it.

"Diego is...himself," Ebony said, still giggling and holding up her bag of jack-off beads to the light. "These are beautiful. And intricate."

"And filled with powdered jizz juice, sorry Anika."

"No worries, Mr. Malcolm. I'm an adult."

"Noted," he made eye contact with her in the rearview mirror and nodded that he got her. He glanced at Ebony. "Can those go through security?"

Ebony snorted and dropped the bag full of prettily decorated cum in her bag and pulled out some hand sanitizer. "It's not liquid—"

"Ha!" Anika yelped from the back.

"Spooge sniffing dogs," he muttered.

In between wheezing laughs, Ebony hit him on the arm as if she were trying to stop herself from laughing so hard.

"You seem awfully *wheeze* distracted by someone else's *wheeze* semen. He's an artist."

"So am I, but you don't see me passing out bodily fluids like trail mix."

Anika slid to the side, holding her stomach. "Help!" she crowed from the backseat.

He shook his head at the howling women in the car, steering them to the airport.

"I'M SORRY, WE ONLY HAVE ONE CALIFORNIA KING ROOM LEFT," THE clerk said with a shrug. "We're maxed out with all the flights canceled."

"We'll take it. You two take the room," he said, turning to the women. "I've got some work that'll keep me until our next flight. It's only a couple hours." Malcolm held his card out for the clerk when Ebony bumped his hand out of the way, handing the clerk her card and held up a hand to his face as soon as he opened his mouth.

"Spare me the drama; I have an expense account, remember? Your buddy Bea is picking up this tab and the tab I'm going to run up at the bar, because we need a drank."

Ebony signed the check-in form and stuck out her tongue at him. He let her carry on with a faux-defeated shrug. Taking a pay cut for his project to support hers, he'd already paid for this trip, the drinks, and the flight to transport jizz beads back to Ohio.

"I know you're down, Mal. Are you comin' Anika?"

"Nah, I've got a paper due tomorrow at 8 a.m. Which is why you two should take the room. I'm going to—"

"Yeah, no—"

"Absolutely not," Ebony agreed. "I'm sorry this storm has us stuck until tomorrow, but at some point you're going to need to sleep, girlie."

"Come on, this can't be the first time you two have shared a room; it's not that big of a deal."

He and Ebony looked at each other in shock. She shrugged wide-eyed, so he knew she hadn't told Anika about Cabo.

"Why would you say that?" Ebony asked, her voice a higher pitch than normal.

Anika frowned. "You guys work together a lot, right? This can't be the first canceled flight and booked hotel."

His grin grew as he watched Ebony fidget. She was such a cutie. One minute she's all nonchalant cum bag handler, the next she's worried about a college student in a polycule learning about their fling years ago.

"This is actually our first gig together," he said, stepping in. "We've known each other a lil while outside of this."

"Oh! Then yeah, that would be a little awkward," Anika nodded, taking a room key and Ebony's bag. "In that case, I'm ordering room service!" She made the little heart sign with her hands and headed for the elevator.

"So... I guess it's just you and me," Ebony said, biting her lip and clasping her hands together.

"Let me check in on my mom and I'll join you in a moment."

She smiled at him and moved to turn, but something came over him. He reached out to still her movements. Just a palm against her lower stomach and closed the space between them. She took a sharp inhale when he put his lips by her ear. "Order yourself a sweet treat. You deserve it. You did so well today."

Ebony's face lit up at the small recognition, and his body

responded to her delight. It was then he knew he was in fucking trouble.

They stood there, in the lobby of the Grand Marquis Hotel by the airport in the middle of Kentucky, alone in their own moment. The world fell away, and it was just her smile, the pleasure sensors pinging around his head, and the heat from her body radiating through his hand. He wanted to bend and kiss her fluttering eyelashes, and just as gravity and lack of decorum pulled his head down to hers, the desk clerk popped up next to them.

"You're in luck; someone just canceled and I have a double queen available!"

Ebony jumped back like she'd been caught doing something naughty and quickly rustled up a grateful smile towards the agent. His was definitely more flat.

"That's perfect," Ebony said. "Add that one to my card as well, and Anika and I will switch rooms. That way you can stretch out in the bigger bed." She tossed that last line over her shoulder as she walked away, following the clerk back to the desk.

Grrr...

"Hey Ma."

"There's my boy! Are you back?"

"Nah, I'm stuck in a hotel until tomorrow."

"Did the intern steal your pants?" She laughed.

He chuckled. "No, Momma, there's a storm and our flight was canceled, but we leave out at six in the morning so I will be back in time for your treatment."

"Don't worry about it, I need to stay in practice putting myself on the machine."

"You sure?"

"Yes, I have a visitor coming by later in the afternoon, and I don't want to be on the machine when she gets here. Someone from the neighborhood association."

"Dang, I'm sorry I'm messing up your plans."

"You haven't messed up anything, honey; you have a life. Work. It's why we *both* learned this."

Malcolm sighed. Guilt gnawed at the pit of his stomach.

"Son, chill. I'll see you in the morning. Go get a drink."

"Actually, I was about to have one with my colleague. See, I can relax."

"Order something stronger than ice tea."

"Not on assignment, Ma."

She chuckled. "Alright son. I love you. See you in the morning."

"Love you, Ma."

"This was a good interview to have after Brian."

Ebony sipped her lemon drop and picked up another French fry, dipping it in ketchup.

"You definitely seem lighter after this one." Malcolm took another bite of his burger and grabbed a spicy fried pickle off the share platter of appetizers Ebony ordered.

"There weren't any illusions shattered. In fact, he was more frank than I expected. With Diego, I kinda knew it was going to be a limited time. A fun time, but limited. It was what I needed in that season, but at some point it's time to leave the party and go home. Plus, how can I be sad when I'm taking home a sack full of jizzy jewelry?"

Malcolm choked a little on his iced tea, causing some of it to dribble down his chin, which made Ebony holler with laughter. Malcolm grabbed a napkin and wiped his face, shaking his head at her.

"Here," she said, chuckling as she reached out with her napkin and dabbed at a spot in his goatee. When she looked up, there was a certain shyness in her eyes. It was sweet and endearing.

She dropped her eyes quickly back down. A couple of dabs and she finished.

"There. All good." She tried to pull her hand back; he caught it. Holding her in place with his hand, her pulse racing under his fingertips.

"Thank you."

Her eyes fluttered as she gave a little shrug, and his mind flashed back to her eyes doing the same thing when he told her to bend over the railing of her private suite in Cabo.

"Would you like anything else?" The blonde, perky waitress asked, staring directly at Malcolm as if Ebony didn't exist.

Ebony pulled her hand back more firmly this time, and he reluctantly let it go.

"Nah, I'm good," he said, glancing briefly up at the woman and immediately bringing his eyes back to Ebony. "Did you get your treat?" He asked, leaning toward her.

"You sure *you* don't want dessert?" the waitress asked, tossing her ponytail over her shoulder.

Ebony raised her eyebrows. "*I'd* like the check," she said, a slight edge to her voice.

Malcolm tilted his head to the side a bit, eyeing her. "What about your reward?"

She glanced up at their waitress. "I'm good."

"I would like to watch... you enjoy yourself."

Ebony froze at his tone, her breath quickening.

"Damn, lucky girl. Cake. Get the chocolate cake," the woman above them whispered, nudging Ebony.

"I, uh, will get the chocolate cake." Ebony blew out a breath.

"Good...job." *Shit. He almost gave this high-achieving, self-sufficient woman another kind of reward.*

The waitress fanned herself as she walked away. "Goodness."

THE CHOCOLATE CAKE WAS THICK, RICH, AND LAYERED.

The same could be said about the woman sitting across from him, who insisted he share her dessert. He was obsessed with the way her mouth closed around her fork, but he was more obsessed with the way she let out a small sigh from the pleasure.

Why hadn't he fed her chocolate in bed in Cabo? Wasted opportunity.

"Was the puzzle incident the first time you picked up a camera?"

"No, my mom had been teaching me about photography for a while, but it was the first time I really focused on getting a particular shot. It immediately changed how I saw the world and my place in it. I started to see the stories in the way people lived, if that makes sense."

She leaned her face on her hand as he spoke and really listened to him. "It was your missing piece. What a blessing to figure out early what you're passionate about."

"Well, don't make me sound too studious. I abandoned it in high school for sports. Girls liked dudes that ran around with a ball, and you don't get a letterman jacket for taking pics," he grinned, shaking his head. "Photography kinda fell by the wayside until college."

Ebony smiled. "Did college girls catch up to the superior coolness of aperture and shutter speeds?"

Her teasing smile made his even bigger. "Nah, I just did both."

She laughed big, and the sound of it wrapped around his heart and squeezed.

"You carry a bit of your mom on every assignment then. How did your family receive the more dangerous aspects of the gig?"

He blew out a big breath. "My parents were wanderers. The time they spent in Columbus after I was born was the longest time they had stayed in one place since their own childhood, so they were excited for me to experience the world on my own. The reality of the work and its effect on me didn't really show until the first time I landed in a hospital. They were panicked, dirty, and exhausted after a thirteen-hour flight to find me in a small South African hospital. I was beat to shit, suffering from PTSD, and mentally exhausted. I'd never seen them like that before, and it was the same for them. It sobered all of us up real quick."

She placed her hand on top of his. "I'm so sorry you all had to experience that. What made you continue?"

"The work. It's important. It's too easy to ignore the hard things, the beauty, the horror if you don't see it. Every human deserves to have their story told. I got smarter, which meant becoming more humble, stronger -physically and mentally — and went back to doing what I could to tell those stories. My parents bought me a piece and were beside themselves when I wouldn't carry it. They thought it made me a bigger target."

Ebony nodded. "When having a gun is probably the worst thing you could do in your area of work."

"Exactly. It took a while to get through to them; explaining gun restrictions in other countries helped break through their panic. They're world travelers; so they got it, but it was a hard conversation to have. Especially since it was a written conversation, because my jaw was wired shut."

"Wow," she said, shaking her head. "If I were a parent, our code of neutrality and safety protocols would go out the window if my child was hurt."

They sat quietly together for a moment.

"When did you get the bug?"

"I was one of those kids who got 'talks too much' written on their report card every quarter," she said with a rueful smile. "And I possess an insatiable curiosity about everything and everybody. My mom said company would come by just to listen to me talk."

She pushed away the rest of the cake, offering it to him. He took another bite, savoring the intense chocolate flavor and light texture.

"I was on my way to class one day and discovered they had automotive certification classes. By the time I'd asked everything from the history of the program to the type of students they served, the instructor wanted to know if I was a cop or a journalist and offhandedly suggested I should become the latter. Once the idea was in my head, I couldn't shake it. I switched my major from English to journalism a week later."

"Well, you're incredibly talented. I've read a lot of your work. Your pen is top tier and the way you actively listen to people...you make them feel heard. Most people are interested in my work, but not necessarily in me. You make me feel interesting."

She frowned a little. "You *are* interesting."

"What I do is interesting."

"The 'why' has always been interesting to me; it's just as important as the what, where, and how."

He didn't know why that made him feel good, but it did. "You would make an excellent CIA agent."

"I thought about it. I always end up being everyone's secret keeper."

His eyebrows shot up in surprise. Unknowingly, she had confirmed what he knew to be true. "You make it easy to tell you everything. You'd have a brotha revealing all his inner thoughts."

"Like what?"

"Like, I'm glad we got stuck here for the night."

EBONY LAY there in bed thinking about Malcolm and listening to Anika type her ass off. There was more to him than she thought or had been willing to acknowledge. Before, he'd been the sexy, fantasy version of himself in Cabo, but now…

Actually, if she were being honest with herself, *she* turned him into that version in her own mind to distance herself. Most men were more than happy to talk about themselves and get fucked well with no strings attached. Malcolm, however, had several moments of real where he opened up to her.

She was, for her part, only interested in screwing his brains out and redirected any personal questions. *She* had been the one wearing a mask, determined to have a good time and leave her cares behind. And while Ebony didn't blame herself for who she was at that time, she did feel some kind of way about holding Malcolm not calling against him.

Was she seeing what Faith called the "Precious Moments" version of people or acknowledging a man's humanity? She rolled her thumbs together as she pondered. She'd actually enjoyed his company in Cabo. They both agreed it was a fling situation. Should his not calling affect them now? Back then she was in no headspace to carry on anything but luggage onto a plane. Why did it bother her that he didn't call?

She was a stickler for follow-through.

Ok...so should I bring it up?

No, I'll sound obsessed. A grudge holder.

But he brought it up...

Yeah, a while ago, if I bring it up now I look... we still have to work together.

She wanted to do more than work. Especially after the way he spoke to her tonight. She could still feel the heat from his hand on her lower belly when he told her to get a treat and praised her.

In fact, she had enjoyed everything tonight. It wasn't a date, but it was an intimate conversation, even if it was over fries, cake, and fried hot pickles.

"Ms. Ebony, am I keeping you up?" Anika asked quietly.

Ebony rolled over to look at her. "No! Not at all, I just can't sleep."

"I can hear your mind racing from over here."

Ebony laughed. "Really?"

"It's your vibe. It's pensive, restless."

"You are really perceptive.

Anika shrugged. "I'm an empath."

"I think I'll take a walk." Ebony sat up fully, slipped her feet into her sneakers, and put her bonnet on her pillow. "Do you want anything?"

"Cold caffeine. Please. I've got six more pages."

"Whew, chile, I do not miss that part of college. Caffeine coming up."

Ebony should have hit 'L' for lobby. Instead, she hit the up arrow to go to Malcolm's floor. She was just going to clear the air. Just a quick convo.

"And you will not think about how he had you bent over a balcony."

When the elevator doors opened on her floor, Malcolm stepped out.

"Oh!"

"Hey—"

"I was coming up to—"

"I was coming down to—"

Both of them laughed. "Ladies first," Malcolm said, reaching out to adjust the collar on her pajamas.

"I couldn't sleep and I wanted to clear the air about —"

A woman's scream echoed somewhere in the distance. In unison, they turned toward the sound, with Malcolm already moving up the hallway she'd just come from. A second scream and loud thump sent them running, her heart dropping.

"It sounds like Anika," she said in a hushed voice as they rounded the hallway. When they arrived at her door, they heard movement, banging, and another screech. Without hesitation, Malcolm raised his foot and with one swift kick, the door flew open, splitting off its hinges. The boom reverberated through the hallway, and he immediately rushed in. When Ebony tried to follow, he threw out his arm without looking back.

"Wait," he barked.

Guests opened their doors, and people poked their heads out or came out into the hallway with their phones aimed at the broken door. A single second or a million passed once Malcolm went in. Ebony's heart beat in her throat, and when she was about to say "fuck it" and go in, Malcolm came out with a sheet of paper covering the top of a drinking glass.

Anika sheepishly stepped out of the bathroom, face red, hands clasped tightly in front of her. "Thank you for kicking in doors for me, Mr. Malcolm."

"We're a team."

"I'm sorry for waking everyone," she said to the hallway with a shrug. "But that's a big ass spider.

Confused, everyone in the hallway, including Ebony, looked from Anika to the glass in Malcolm's hand and collectively jumped back. It looked like a freaking tarantula, and he was just casually holding it in a glass with a piece of hotel paper and a finger on top. The spider was brownish and hard to see in the dim light of the hallway, but when Malcolm moved the glass and adjusted his hand, the genuine horror came to light.

"I think it just winked," a woman from across the hallway said, and shuddered.

"That's a Carolina wolf spider," someone else chimed in.

"It's a wolf alright," Ebony said, wrinkling up her nose. "Should we be able to see each individual hair?"

As guests started shuffling back to their rooms, security came around the corner. Ebony immediately started explaining that they were on assignment and offering I.D. The woman from across the hallway blurted out, "You're the 'no penis is peace' lady!" which started another round of explaining, the video being shown, the lady asking for an autograph and Ebony taking a group photo with security and two gentlemen from Kentucky Highway Patrol.

In the end, the hotel was understanding; Malcolm walked out with security to release the spider outside, and the hubbub died down. Unfortunately, by then it was basically time to head to the airport, so Malcolm retrieved Ebony and Anika's belongings, as neither was going back into the room in case the spider had a friend. And because the entire hotel was now suspect, Malcolm first did a thorough check of his room before all three took turns getting dressed in his bathroom.

They dragged their tired souls through the airport and only perked up when Ebony, despite having all the airport security passes available, had to go through additional security screening for her bag of dried cum bead art. She mustered every skill she had to keep a straight, professional face. After a cursory glance by the agent, she got her property back, and the three of them kept it together until they arrived at their gate, where they dissolved into laughs way too loud for that early in the morning.

I'm home. Well, I'm at my mom's. I'm gonna crash here until her treatment's done. I'll send a link tomorrow of the shots so we can prep before our meeting with Bea

Sounds good. I hope your mom is doing well. Hey what were you going to say before you kicked in the door and did your Steve Irwin thang?

It was a spider not a crocodile.

It was a wolf from Carolina masquerading as a spider that flirted with that lady across the hall. Tew much.

...

I'd rather tell you in person. What were you going to say before taking paparazzi photos with six men in your pajamas?

I'm so glad I took off my bonnet before I left the room.

And same. In person

Let's meeting prep together after you review the pics. tomorrow good?

Tomorrow is full, I'm moving everything I have today over. I'm exhausted. Day after?

Perfect. I'll bring snacks, you already paid for dinner once.

I didn't, Bea did, but sure. See you then.

Sleep well Ebee

You too

Hey E, so I'm coming home for your birthday but I got something to tell you first.

Pumpkin for real?! YAY! I cannot wait to see and kiss your face! How long are you staying?! Where are you staying?! Want to stay here or at your mom's? What's up?

I can't stay at mom's not enough room.

She added a Yurt behind her tiny home last month but it's RUSTIC. I like to go there and write but I come home to pee. I can't do the composting bucket.

I'm bringing someone.

> Oooh! Sounds serious. You guys can absolutely stay here. I've got plenty of room. Tell me about this person. Male? Handsome? Is he Australian? South Korean? Does he treat you like the treasure you are?

Well…he is male. Chubby and is a US citizen, but was born in Australia. I'm his favorite person.

> Aww! I love this for you! And I love a thicc man. Pics! Or is he there? Call me quick before I fall asleep, I just got in from Kentucky and have been up for twenty four hours.

…

Pumpkin?

…

EBONY HIT THE ANSWER BUTTON THE SECOND PUMPKIN'S VIDEO CALL came in. "Anyeong!"

"Aww! Ebony, Anyeong. Your pronunciation is getting really good!" Pumpkin said, grinning and doing a small head nod.

Pumpkin was what Ebony thought of as a cultural chameleon. She adapted naturally to her environment, not appropriative, but more like culturally community aware. She owned her Black American identity, but moved seamlessly with others, picking up mannerisms and subtleties better than most. Ebony really admired her skill and talent.

"I'm trying not to be an embarrassing American when I come visit you next year."

Pumpkin laughed, her dimples flashing. When she stopped, Ebony noticed a hesitancy in her eyes.

"Ok so…what's up?"

"Don't get mad."

Ebony braced. "I'll try, just remember, I haven't slept all night."

"Oh. Maybe I should call back later; this can wait."

"Akiko Marie Holiday, if you disconnect this call, I sweartagawd I will be on a flight to South Korea tonight."

"See you already sound mad."

"Because you're stalling, girl! Is he an abuser?"

"No!"

"Ugly?"

"No, he's the most beautiful being I've ever laid eyes on." A soft peace settled on her face.

"Oh god, does he wear a red hat?"

"The hell?! NO!"

"Then everything else we can work with, Pumpkin. What. The. Fuck?"

Pumpkin bit her lip, then flipped the camera, and bedding came into view. Ebony really didn't want to see Pumpkin's man in bed, but folks in love get weird about over sharing.

When the camera focused, she saw the cutest little toddler napping in deep navy pajamas. He had short, dark, curly hair, beautiful, long, straight lashes resting against soft, chubby brown cheeks she instinctively wanted to nom nom nom. His little face twitched, and a dimple flashed. He was gorgeous. He was also...

"Bish that's a whole ass baby!" Ebony whispered. She was gobsmacked. Like her gobs were smacked. Pumpkin had a baby, and no one knew. Or at least *she* didn't know, and she wagered the rest of the cousins didn't know either.

The camera flipped around to Pumpkin's worried face. She should be; the family was going to flip their shit. Collectively and individually, creatively.

"Pumpkin, did you... *adopt* a beautiful, Black baby with a dimple like yours?"

"No." She bit her lip again.

"Pumpkin, did you create with your body a whole ass, absolutely BEAUTIFUL Black baby with a dimple like yours approximately three to four years ago and ain't said shit about it?"

"Yes, Nicholas will be three soon."

Ebony's eyes grew even bigger. "Does *anyone* know about this beautiful Black baby with a dimple like yours named Nicholas that you created with your body?"

She shook her head.

"Whoa." Ebony sat back in her bed. "Excuse me, I'mma jump in your uterus a sec. Um...in vitro, or is there a baby daddy?"

"Out of the picture." And Pumpkin steeled her spine, giving Ebony a stony look. "And I'm absolutely okay with it."

"Okay. Okay. Okay. Okay... Cool. Cool. Cool. You have a baby."

"Yes."

"And Auntie Evie doesn't know."

"Nope."

"And...you're coming to do a big reveal on my birthday."

"The day before, I don't want to take your shine."

"Girl, I have birthdays every year. I've had thirty-five already. I don't give a shit about that. YOU have a BABY!"

"I know."

The realization hit her. "And he's a boy! The first boy on this side in ever!"

Pumpkin's pensive face returned.

"And he's beeeeeeeautiful, lemme see him again."

Pumpkin's face brightened, and she flipped the camera on her phone around again. Her hand stroked his little curls and

Ebony fell deep in love with lil' Nicky. She was going to buy all the things for her lil nephew in love, but cousin in life.

"Those cheeks! I've got a lil cousin nephew."

Pumpkin flipped the camera around, and she had tears in her eyes. "He's the best thing I've ever done, and I love South Korea, but I miss my family."

"Then come home, Akiko. Wait... when's his birthday?"

Pumpkin's eyes grew wide, and she hurried out of the room and shut the door. "June 19th," she whispered.

"Holy shit," Ebony whispered back, her heart thudding in her chest. "The Holiday family legend continues. You got the magic Pumpkin!"

"It freaked me out. I was due June 10th. And I couldn't help but be a little disappointed, and I was alone and honestly pretty fucking scared to do this by myself... The Holiday legend was messing with my head. I felt like a disappointment to the whole family. But Nicky is stubborn. He wasn't budging, and then the day before your birthday, BAM, contractions started. It was as if the family was with me. It was peaceful and beautiful, and here he is."

"I would've been there, without question, Pumpkin, and no judgement."

"You're always there for everyone, E. I couldn't interrupt your life and ask you to fly halfway around the world for my drama."

"You are my sister. That is what we do for EACH OTHER. You have your reasons for keeping this part of you secret and I won't pry. But listen to me when I say I'm here because I want to be. I give what I have to give. Let me be the judge of what I can handle. And don't ever make that decision for me again."

A tear rolled down Pumpkin's face. "I'm sorry. I really wanted you here."

"I know. I love you, Akiko. Congratulations, I'm so proud of you."

"Thanks E. See you in a lil bit."

"See you in a lil bit. And Pumpin? A MUTHAFUCKIN' JUNETEENTH BABY?! I GOT A BIRTHDAY TWIN AND YOU GOT A HOLIDAY BABY! AAAAAHHHHHHHH!!!!!"

whatever you need

"E..."

Ebony sat straight up at the voice, the tone, the pause, the heaviness on the other end of the line. In the couple seconds of silence a question lingered.

"Whatever you need, Love."

"You."

"Where?" Ebony was already out of bed and at her safe. Tapping in the passcode, she pulled out everything she needed.

"I'll text it. Come in the back, please. And E? Tha—"

"No. Thank you for trusting me. I'm twenty out. Stay safe."

She disconnected, jumped into a pair of black sweatpants and wiggled her feet into sneakers; she didn't waste time on untying them. After zipping up her sports bra, she threw on a tank and strapped on her holster. Grabbing a heavy tactical flashlight, she tore down the stairs, snatched her second set of keys mid-stride and threw open her door.

"Ahh! Malcolm!"

They both jumped back from the doorway. Malcolm sloshed coffee over his hand, just missing his sneakers. With a grimace, he switched the cup to his left hand and sucked coffee off the side of his right. "Sorry." He shook his hand and grinned. "It's my turn to bring snacks."

"Shoot, I forgot what day it is. I'm sorry we need to reschedule, something's come up and I didn't get a chance to review the pics. My load has been heavy." She slid past him, pulled her door shut and dashed down the stairs. His heavy footsteps were quick behind her.

"Should we take my truck?"

Ebony almost tripped over her own feet as she turned around in surprise. "This isn't work-related."

He shrugged and crossed his arms, his eyes serious. "If you have to go strapped; you shouldn't be going alone."

"It's a *private* situation," she threw over her shoulder as she walked up her driveway to her detached garage.

"Bet."

He turned and ran - literally ran away. She heard his car door as she opened up her garage door, and she had to admit, she thought he'd put up a little more chivalrous fight. Shaking her head, Ebony refocused and opened the back of her black Suburban. She did a quick visual check of her supplies.

"Boxes, tape, moving blankets, cleaning supplies, shovel," Malcolm said from behind her. "Do I need to call backup?"

She slammed the doors shut without a word and hopped into the driver's seat. He was opening the passenger side before she got the truck in gear. As she slid smoothly down the driveway, he fastened his seatbelt.

"I thought you always needed to know what you were walking into," she tossed out.

"So tell me on the way, Stagecoach Mary."

And damn if she didn't smile just a little. [1]

---

1. Let 'Em Know - T.I.

"So you bought a Suburban in case your cousin left her husband?"

"I bought a large, nondescript vehicle for *when* my cousin *needed* to leave her husband. I told her when she was ready to make that move, I'd be there, no questions asked."

"You really love your cousin."

"She's my sister. A ten-year-long side quest into an unfortunate marriage doesn't change that."

"Are these window tints street-legal?"

"Somewhere, probably."

Malcolm let out a derisive chuckle.

"How dangerous is he?"

She glanced over at him; the tension in his jaw belied his relaxed voice.

"He's neglectful, selfish, and manipulative. He's siphoned off her glow, her soul, steadily for ten years - that's dangerous. But physically, for the most part, I think he's a punk." She shook her head and stopped at the umpteenth red light. She glanced at Malcolm again. "But you never know what goes on in someone else's marriage. The most dangerous times for a woman in a relationship is when she's pregnant and or when she tries to leave. And I'm picking her up at a fucking hospital. So..."

"So we are either moving her out or burying a body."

"Basically."

She didn't catch his expression because she focused on merging onto the freeway and praying that Central Ohio traffic, weather, and construction cooperated. Rain could add *years* to the drive because many Columbusites caught weather-related amnesia and forgot how to drive, or an entire ramp or lane that was intact the day before could be completely ripped away twenty-four hours later.

She did notice he said "We."

Eleven tense minutes later Ebony rolled to the back of the outpatient care building, scanning for the door Joy told her to use.

"Don't park in a spot. Pull as close to the door as you can."

Nodding, Ebony bumped the vehicle up over the low curb, smooth as butter, leaving a few feet between the back passenger door and the door of the facility.

"Will you stay in the car until I check everything out? What does he look like?"

"Afraid of what I might do to him?" Ebony swiped through one of Joy's social media accounts to find a pic, and her tummy flipped over. "She's already removed him from her socials."

"Your grin is a little crazed."

All Ebony could do was giggle like a serial killer as she went through her own photos. *It's going to stick.*

"Joy can be really deliberate, methodical. When she's locked in, she's fucking locked in. The world could burn around her and she'd still be locked in." She swiped through Christmas photos from the last time Eric had bothered to show. "This was five years ago; he's a little thinner now. Or at least he was last year in the hospital."

Malcolm's jaw twitched a few times as he examined the photo and joined her in scanning the parking lot and surrounding decorative vegetation. Then he got out of the car and did what Ebony could only describe as a security sweep that looked well-practiced before coming to her door and helping her out. Out of habit she locked the door and kept her thumb on the fob as she walked around the car, Malcolm her shadow to her right.

She'd been prepared to get Joy on her own, but honestly,

she felt better having him there. Not just because he was a built wall of muscle, but him specifically. He made her feel... calm?

Hmm... That was a nugget of interesting information she didn't have time to wrap her mind around today, but maybe later.

The sun-faded, heavy, gray delivery entrance door was hot to the touch when Ebony rapped her knuckles against it.

Knock, double knock, knock, knock

She used the special knock the Holiday Sisters had used since childhood. They had been deep in their secret society phase when they came up with it.

There was movement on the other side, then the door creaked open. A woman in scrubs with braids pulled into a high bun poked her head out. "You look just like your photo. Love your hair."

She opened the door wider, and a relieved Joy walked out into the sun and into Ebony's arms. Her sweet-smelling locs were soft against Ebony's nose, her body rigid with unshed emotion.

After a moment, Joy turned to the woman at the door. "Thank you for sitting with me."

The woman shrugged. "I've watched you for months, Sis; he didn't deserve you. It might be too soon, but congratulations." And with a wink, she closed the door.

Joy shook her head. "Even the nurses at Eric's doctor's office know I'm stupid."

Ebony turned Joy toward the car, unlocking the door. "That is not what she said. You just made the smartest move ever - you chose yourself."

Joy gave a small nod and squeezed Ebony's hand as they walked.

Malcolm opened the door and stood to one side, his long

arm holding it open while they both slipped in. He closed the door behind them and stood in front of it.

Ebony took inventory of her cousin. No visible bruising, she moved with no obvious injuries... but she had a haunted, sad look in her eyes.

"You don't have to talk now. Just tell me what you want to do next, or do you know?"

Joy looked at Ebony with an exhaustion that rounded her shoulders and hollowed out the area under her eyes. "I just want to sleep."

Ebony closed the door to her guest room, where Joy had fallen asleep. Leaning against it, she sent up a quick prayer of thanks to her family's traditional God - the brown Jesus with skin like copper and hair like lambswool; she thanked the saints she could remember from Catholic school, sent a note to Allah, and mentally dapped up Lakshmi on behalf of her cousin. Glancing at her watch, she was surprised it was still decently early.

She'd always thought Joy's extraction would be way more dramatic and take much longer. Instead, it was a little more than an hour to pick her up, bring her back, and get her settled in for a much-needed nap.

Ebony pushed off the door with a shrug. "Not going to complain about that. It probably saved me jail time," she mumbled.

She found Malcolm in her dining room rubbing her deep green wallpaper and laughed. "I did that before I hung it. After feeling miles and miles of the texture, I was kind of over it. Or it could've been that I picked the worst wallpaper as an amateur to hang."

"You did this yourself?"

"I did that over there," she pointed to the wall where the pattern didn't quite match up. "My Uncle Ron did the rest. He came by to check out the house and found me on the porch crying and sticky."

Malcolm let out a bark of laughter, then quieted down, his eyes on the ceiling. She waved him off. "She's sleeping as if she hadn't slept in a year. I thought you'd be elbow-deep in my bookcase by now."

"Nah, your house is beautiful. You have to slow down and take in all the details. I can tell you worked really hard on it. It feels modern without clashing with the age and style of the house."

Pride and that ooey gooey girlish feeling blossomed in her tummy — and lower. To counter, she reminded herself of the last man who complimented her on her home: he washed his dirty man panties in her machine without her permission. Ebony cleared her throat and adjusted her rarely worn holster, drawing his eyes to it.

"You're still expecting him to make trouble for her."

Ebony nodded and tipped her head toward his own. "You said you didn't carry."

"On assignment. This is Ohio."

"Ah, well...you right. Pew, pew." She made finger guns and fired them at him. Why? Who the fuck knows, but he smiled at her again, and it felt like a reward.

"Thank you for coming along. I could focus on Joy, and that really mattered."

He shrugged. "I don't know what man wouldn't come with you."

"Ha! Plenty, especially Eric. If it were one of us in trouble, he'd happily let Joy handle it, like he let her handle everything else in their lives. She did everything for him *before* he had a heart attack. After she had aged ten years caring for him." Ebony shook her head. "Anyway... I should order food. When she wakes up, she'll be hungry. I'm so glad your cousin delivers now. I can get Joy's favs."

"I'll go get them; it's faster. Have you eaten yet? There's homeless dogs in the car." He pulled out his phone, and she watched his thumbs fly over the screen.

"That's a tragedy..." His thumbs were distracting. His hands in general. They were big, yes, but the way they flexed when he used them. Ebony's mind pulled up a memory: *his hand gripping himself. He was rock hard as he moved his hand up and down, his thumb spreading his pre-cum around the head and telling her to —* "Open for me."

Her eyes snapped up from his hands, and she gulped. "What?"

His head tipped slightly, his brow furrowed. "I said I got okra for me, do you want some?"

"Oh! Yes. Mmm hmm. Love me some...okra."

"Are you okay? Do you need some rest? I'll grab the food and drop it off. I'll bring in the cinnamon rolls first."

"Yes, I'm — what cinnamon rolls?"

Malcolm paused, his brows dipping lower. "The cinnamon rolls I just said were in the car, and you said it was a tragedy."

The heat of embarrassment flushed from Ebony's armpits to the top of her scalp, making it tingle. *This assignment will never work if I can't stay focused and keep it in my pants.*

"Malcolm, I'm sorry I am..."

A horndog that wants to slut your sexy thumbs out...

"...Distracted. I'm probably not the best company right now."

Unless you want me on my knees...

He nodded, his eyes and voice gentle with concern. "That

makes sense. I'll take care of everything." He tapped rapidly into his phone as he walked toward her, stopping briefly to kiss the top of her head, and walked out.

copper smile

"WHY DID I DO THAT?"

Malcolm made his way out of Ebony's house before he did anything else inappropriate. The woman was fresh off a serious family issue, and he kissed her. On the forehead, yes, but that felt more intimate than if he'd motorboated her breasts on the way out of the room.

He let out a chuckle at his own random thoughts and started his car. Halfway to the restaurant, he realized he hadn't asked exactly what Ebony and Joy wanted besides okra.

"Fuuuuuck."

At the next red light, he called Armello. "Cuz! What do the Holiday women eat?"

"Uh, which ones?"

"All of them, but especially Joy and Ebony."

"Lemme think, Joy ain't been in for months." Armello rattled off a list of dishes, and by the time he got to January's substitutions and why they tickled him so, Malcolm cut him off. "Okay, bruh, never mind. Can you make whatever it is they like - double portions - and put it on my order?"

"Are they coming in?"

"Nah, I'm picking it up for Ebony."

Armello went quiet, then busted out laughing.

"What's so funny?"

"The way to a woman's heart is through her cousins' stomach, huh?"

"Man, shut up. I'll be there in a few."

"Alright, alright... I got you." He was still giggling when he disconnected. *Punk.*

Malcolm stopped at the grocery and grabbed some soda, tea, and a decent bottle of wine. He thought better of it and grabbed a second bottle. Next, it was a quick run down the magazine aisle to grab his mom a couple of Sudoku and word finder books to help with her disease-induced brain fog, and he paused at the flowers. There were bunches of different colored daisies that just looked cheerful. Hopeful. He grabbed a bouquet of each color and headed for check out.

Fifteen minutes later, he swore under his breath. His plan to grab the food and go was spoiled when Armello insisted on helping him carry out the massive haul. Armello spotted the daisies and started giggling again.

"Stop it, you sound like a three-year-old."

"And you're going to look like one with that rainbow bouquet."

Malcolm stopped loading the food. "Too much?"

"For Ebony? Wrong kind of flower. These say, 'Get well soon, Grandma.' Ebony seems like a rare flower kind of woman. January likes lilies."

It was Malcolm's turn to laugh. "Why don't you just ask her out?"

"Who?"

Malcolm gave him that 'come on bruh' look, and Armello squirmed for a second or two, then took a deep breath and squared his shoulders.

"Chemo does a number on everything when you're ten years old." Armello looked around at everything but him. "She wants a family. I hear her and the girls talk about it all the time, and man, to see her face when someone with a baby goes by. I can't give her that. Plus, I work hella long hours trying to keep the restaurant going. All my money goes into it and helping my sister with her kids. I literally have nothing to give her. I won't waste her time like that."

"Damn, Mello, I'm sorry." He set the food down haphazardly and hugged his cousin as hard as he could. "There are other ways to build a family."

He shook his head. "Too much to unpack, too much of a burden on someone like her." He sucked in a deep breath and put the food in the car. He gave Mal one last bruh hug, beat the shit out of his back, and walked back into the building.

All the way back to Ebony's home, Malcolm's mind was on his cousin. Mello was the picture of health now, but the acute sadness in his voice was such a contrast to his normal demeanor that it shook Malcolm.

Suddenly, all of those old feelings he had when Mello was sick came rushing back. Like the world was too big, and he was powerless in it. When the road got blurry, he pulled over before he hurt someone.

Looking around for something, anything to ground himself, his eyes landed on the happy flowers, and he felt the tightness in his chest ease some.

"In the middle of pain, beauty still exists," he whispered as he fingered the soft petals.

"That is... a lot of food!" Ebony exclaimed as Malcolm hefted the last of the food from Armello's on the counter in her kitchen. He winked at her and stepped out one more time while she unpacked everything. When he came back in, there was cash on the counter.

"That's for the food. Thank you so much. This will really be a nice treat for Joy."

"No problem, and keep your money," he said, shaking his head and hip-bumping her out of the way so he could access her deep sink. He unwrapped the bouquets and slid his eyes to her when she didn't say anything.

"Those are beautiful."

"I thought Joy would like them, give her something to look at to remind her while in the middle of her pain—"

"Beauty still exists," she finished for him.

He took an especially bright white daisy out of the colorful array, pinched the stem high on the flower, breaking it in two, and tucked the shorter end with its perfect bloom into her thick curly hair, just above her ear.

"Gorgeous."

She looked at him in surprise, then her expression softened. "Are *you* okay?"

With her face upturned, her expression so sweet it would have been easy to bend down and touch his lips to hers. They were calling him with their soft, glossy glow, and his body started moving before his brain gave permission, and she certainly hadn't. That stopped him in his tracks. Reversing course, he patted her on the arm like the colleague she was and turned back to the sink to flip on the water.

"Do you have a vase?" He looked over his shoulder and he could have been imagining it, but she looked disappointed. *That he didn't kiss her? Or because he didn't answer her question?*

He broke eye contact and looked around her kitchen. The room was beautiful, spacious, and tidy, and it only took him two guesses to find all-purpose shears. Moving back to the sink, he held the stems under water and cut them at an angle. "I'm fine," he said, glancing at her. "Talking with my cousin brought up old memories. The kind that make you remember the worst parts of being a kid - so much was out of your control."

She leaned a hip against the counter, nodding. "Shoot, I still feel that way."

He nodded, "Right. Growing up is a scam."

She grinned brightly. "Completely overrated. Though you get to stay out as long as you want."

"Which got old a while ago."

"Right!" she laughed. "Okay, all the hot chips and cereal you want."

"Ugh, spicy food gives me heartburn bad now. I still eat it, but I've gotta plan on being home so I can take something for it. No way to look cool at the club knocking back antacids."

She stepped out of her slippers and climbed up onto the counter on her knees, reaching for the cabinet above the sink.

"Whoa, girl, I can get that for you." He grabbed her waist and guided her and the heavy, leaded glass vase down off the counter. "Do you hop up and down on that every week?"

"Oh, no. I can't remember the last time I bought flowers. I keep saying I'm going to treat myself more often, but I forget or I buy up flowers for the house and leave them too long, and every room smells like rot. It feels disrespectful to my granny to leave her vases with slimy, swampy yuck festering in them. I have houseplants and don't have to worry about replacing them nearly as often. Only when I travel and Faith is taking care of them. There are always a couple that don't survive her."

He laughed with her as he arranged the flowers in the vase. When he finished, he looked at her for approval.

"They look cheerful."

"That's what I thought when I saw them." It pleased him

to no end she felt the same way. He busied himself cleaning up the cut stems and stripped foliage and put them in one of the empty grocery bags. After he cleaned the sink, he nodded toward the vase. "You gonna be okay taking that wherever you want it to be?"

She just stared at him.

"What? I could move it if you know where..."

A thousand thoughts chased themselves across her face until she landed on one, and her face tightened.

"We really are a nice family, a little overly involved in each other's lives maybe, but normally no one needs an armed escort. Well, except Pumpkin, but that's only when she cosplays."

Malcolm double blinked. Ebony grinned nervously and twisted her fingers around each other before answering what must have been a confused look on his face.

"My cousin Pumpkin's got this Janet Jackson-in-Poetic-Justice-Before-She-Met-Tupac vibe that transforms into dark anime catnip when she puts on a tail or fangs. She needs security at events because someone might try to carry her away again."

Again?

"I say all that to say, we are an almost normal family and I appreciate your help today, but don't expect to ride out any more during this project... I feel like I'm rambling."

Malcolm chuckled, leaned his hip against the counter, and ran his hand over her twisting ones. "You are, but it's cute. For the record, I'd never judge you or your family. It's good that you are there for each other, and I'd gladly ride out the next time you need it."

She scrutinized him for a moment, and he let her until he realized, belatedly, he'd been holding her hands for too long.

Releasing her, he took a step back and shoved his hands into his pockets. "I'm going to let you relax."

She definitely looked disappointed for a split second before she schooled her face into a friendly blank canvas. "Who's going to eat all this food?"

"I thought this would be a meeting of the cousins, kind of thing."

Ebony shook her head and blew out a breath. "Joy doesn't want anyone to know just yet. She just wants to sleep and give herself some time. I'm going to respect that."

Her eye twitched a little.

He barely held in his laughter. "You're ready to rain hellfire down on him now."

"Just one little throat punch," she pinched her thumb and index finger together and held them up to her eye, "and the protection of tangible and financial assets, that's all."

He couldn't keep the laugh in this time. Her face cracked slowly, and when she let her full laugh out, it took his breath away. Her cousin may be *named* Joy, but Ebony, when she smiled, radiated it. An errant set of curls dropped onto her face, and his hand was already sweeping them away before his brain could do the decent thing, which was leave her alone. [1]

Her laugh died in her throat at his touch, and she leaned ever so slightly into his palm, and damn... He felt that shit deep. "You shine like copper when you smile. Your skin tone, the way you light up, just rich and radiant."

She smiled bigger. "Copper is now my favorite element."

"Same," he whispered, leaning in and closing the space between them.

"SON OF A BITCHASS MUTHAFUCKER CUNT PUNK BITCH!"

---

1. I Found My Smile Again (Radio Edit) by D'Angelo

They jerked back from each other at the interruption and waited as footsteps rapidly approached. The steps paused at the door of the kitchen before Joy appeared, appearing calm but seething.

"Hey cuz, hello Mr. Security man. Have you been hired the whole day?"

"He's not—"

"Yes, ma'am," he interrupted. He ignored Ebony staring a hole in the side of his face. "How can I help?"

"I need to go get my items OFF THE MUTHER FUCKING LAWN BECAUSE I MARRIED A CHILDISH, HYSTERICAL, NO, *TESTERRICAL* SONOFABITCH!"

She took a deep breath, apologized, turned on her heel, and marched back through the door.

"You don't have to—"

"Ride out, Copper."

IF THE DRIVE OVER TO JOY'S CONDO WAS ANY INDICATION, HE WOULD have to run zone defense until his crew arrived. To protect Joy's husband. The tension was *thick*.

"I can't believe he changed your gate code," Ebony said as she cracked her knuckles.

"I can," Joy sighed. "I was going to leave Friday, but today at the doctor's office... the way he talked to me...I just...I was too fucking rash. E, it's Mom's stuff and none of the neighbors are answering." Joy slammed the phone against her thigh.

Ebony whipped her head around to look at Joy for a moment.

"I see."

And the next thing he knew, Ebony was out the car and preparing to scale the fencing around the condo community.

The hell?

He threw her SUV into park and stepped out to convince her not to do it or to do it in her stead. "Ebony let me... do absolutely nothing... Damn."

She had scaled up one side of the fence and down the other before he got his door open good. After activating the gate on the other side, exposing a serious security flaw, she waved them in with a degree of impatience. But in his defense...

"That was smooth as hell."

She climbed onto the seat and shot him another copper smile, "Don't let the fluffy fool you."

"No ma'am."

Any levity among those in the vehicle leaked out like a sad party balloon when they rounded the block and Joy's condo came into view. It was easily identifiable with the front yard strewn with clothing, paper, cardboard boxes, and a man pacing back and forth, yelling into his phone.

"My god, how pedestrian," Joy murmured under her breath. "His stupid ass insisted we move 'out the hood' only to throw a ghetto tantrum for the whole block... He wants to show his ass? Fine." [2]

"Oh shit," Ebony whispered.

"I BET YOU'RE FUCKING *HIM*."

Joy had already cussed the man up one side and down the other and apparently he still hadn't had enough. He just had to have the last word.

At her husband's accusation, Joy stopped collecting her

---

2. Plan B - Megan Thee Stallion

things and looked Malcolm up and down, assessing. His ears heated when she nodded her approval.

"I wish. I'd let him and the neighbor run a high-speed train on my ass if I wasn't too bone-fucking tired from putting up with your lying, cheating, selfish ass. It'd be nice to cum after three dry years."

"You are one cold bitch."

"So is yo' bald-headed, chap-lipped, loose-coochie mamma."

"At least she's alive."

Three things happened at once.

The neighbor invited on Joy's sex train stepped in front of her, Malcolm stepped between the neighbor and Joy's husband stretching his arms wide to keep the men apart, and Ebony slipped under Malcolm's outstretched arm and popped up like a meerkat with a solid, closed fist punch that dropped Joy's husband instantly.

"Throat punch!" Ebony sang as she skipped, literally skipped away from the man writhing on the ground.

Malcolm didn't bother to hide his snort when his little maniac jumped and clicked the heels of her sneakers together before she pulled a flattened box out of the SUV.

"Stay down, man," he instructed Joy's husband while Joy and the brotha from next door walked past to load up a couple of boxes.

'Thank you for this Ty," Joy whispered.

"I would have stopped him if I'd known what was going on," Ty said almost tenderly.

Malcolm stole a quick glance at Ebony, who raised her eyebrow and twisted her lips into the universal Black woman sign of *"Yes, I clocked it and ain't mad at it."*

Something told him that when she was ready, Joy already had an eager volunteer to end her orgasm drought. Malcolm's attention swept to a white utility van that slowed and parked behind their SUV. He smiled when Armello and their cousins Dank and Smoke got out.

"Ayye, sorry it took a minute man, Smoke had to hop the fence to get the gate open. Them knees ain't what they used to be."

Joy made her way over, her eyes wide. Malcolm introduced Smoke and Dank. "They are discreet," he assured her.

"I'm going to call the police on all of you," Eric rasped from the ground.

"Been there, done that," Dank said, shrugging.

"And we don't mind goin' back," Smoke offered Joy a wink. "What happened to him?"

Eric was still wheezing and rubbing his throat in between unimpressive threats.

"She did." Malcolm tipped his head in Ebony's direction, who waved happily before she wrapped a damaged Christmas angel in paper and placed it in a box.

"Nice."

Soon they had everything Joy wanted from the home and arranged for his cousins to follow them to Joy's job where she'd been quietly moving and storing her things. Eric watched from the front steps, a sour expression on his face. A rumpled gray cat trotted up to the bottom of the steps, meowing loudly until Eric kicked it away.

"Ruckus!" Joy yelled, taking off in a sprint toward the animal. Eric instantly backed further up the stairs.

"You can't... touch me," he rasped.

"No, but they can," she tipped her head toward Smoke and Dank walking up. She got down on her hands and knees and tried coaxing the kitty out from under a nearby bush.

"Aye, bruh, lemme holla at you for a min," Dank said as he advanced on Eric.

"No, please, I just want to go," Joy said as she clutched the bedraggled cat to her chest. She sounded exhausted, like all the fight had gone out of her in her husband's last act of casual cruelty.

Smoke and Dank were definitely reluctant to go without feline justice, but in the end they escorted Joy to the white van where they cut holes in a small box and gently placed the kitten inside with Smoke using his own work shirt to tuck around it. They offered to take the cat to their vet to get checked out and then bring it back to Ebony's.

"We'll be seeing you, dog," Smoke called out to Eric. Eric looked terrified by the prospect.

Good.

I SHOULD WAKE HER UP.

In the many hours since they left Joy's condo they'd gotten the stray cat Joy had been feeding for months checked out with Dank's vet, shopped for cat food and toys to make the stray's transition to its new indoor life easier, met up at Joy's job and transferred all of her worldly goods from the warehouse to a storage unit. Ebony slept all the way from the storage unit to home. She didn't stir when his cousins unloaded Joy's other items in the house, and now, two hours later, she was still knocked out.

She must have really needed this nap. Almost like knowing her cousin was safe, she could relax.

His stomach rumbled loudly, and he thought about the Armello's he left in his car. He dismissed the thought quickly, not just because it was courting food poisoning, but it would mean leaving Ebony in the car by herself. He didn't want to risk her waking up disoriented and alone. Instead, Malcolm checked her glove compartment for crackers or gum and discovered a cache of Chuckle Taffy candy.

That'll work.

He grabbed some, ripped open two at once, and popped the chewy cherry goodness into his mouth.

"Are you stealing my candy?"

Her voice was soft, and her face the sweetest thing he'd had the pleasure of seeing in a long time. Turning fully in the seat, he nodded.

"Yes."

"And you're not even going to offer me one?"

"That would defeat the point of stealing it, Sleepyhead."

That copper smile came out again, softer, shyer, lit by the soft glow of those decorative black streetlights some neighborhoods had.

"I'm sorry I fell asleep I—" Her face froze as she looked past him out the window. "I fell asleep."

"Yes, but it's cool. My cousins took care of everything; Joy probably went back to bed immediately. She looked beyond exhausted."

She looked at him as if she'd never seen him before.

"What's the matter?" He picked up another piece of candy, peeled the wrapper and handed it to her, but before he withdrew his hand, he tucked away another one of her voluminous section of curls. "Want to talk about it?"

Shaking her head slowly, she nibbled off a piece of candy, deep in thought. "How long was I out for?"

"A couple of hours. You seemed like you really needed it."

"And you sat with me the whole time?"

"Of course," he scoffed. "I wouldn't leave you alone in the car asleep. Anything could happen."

She took another nibble and held the piece between her teeth. Leaning, he tipped her face to him and closed his mouth around the rest and pressed his lips against hers, savoring the feel of their pillowy softness against his. He'd missed them, missed her this close, and couldn't believe he didn't realize that simple, powerful fact until right in that moment.

"They taste better when I steal them like this."

She quirked up another quiet smile. Her eyes swept his face, settling on his lips. When she lifted them again, they were heated, and his body responded in kind. She had him hard with just one look. Just like Cabo, but more...just more.

"I have more candy in the house."

you told me to sit on your face!

IT WAS ALL WARM, searching touches and desperate, knowing kisses. Memories of stolen Cabo nights and breezy ocean mornings heightened the anticipation of this moment. They weren't new lovers eager to unwrap and see each other's offerings; they'd had a taste, a sip, a generous gulp, and were ready for more.

That long weekend in Cabo taught Ebony a lot about Malcolm: he had a birthmark in the shape of Italy along the right side of his ribcage, that his eyes rolled back when she ran her nails up his side while circling his nipple with her tongue, and that in bed, he was very vocal.

Vocal in his pleasure, vocal in his praise, and commanding in his handling of her body. She kicked the bedroom door shut just as he picked her up and wrapped her legs around his waist. Her brain vaguely registered that she was no longer alone in her house. Horny hormones pinged throughout her system, clouding her judgement, but she didn't want to subject her soon-to-be-divorced cousin to an auditory play-by-play of what they were about to do.

Malcolm nipped at her lip, whispering against it. "Shower first, then sit on my face."

Oooh goodie.

One of the first things she invested in after she bought her home was her ensuite bathroom. It was the stuff of dreams, from decor to amenities, including a tankless water heater. Was it more environmentally friendly? Sure. But right now she was happy it meant she could take the longest, hottest shower she'd ever taken in her house.

A shower that started the best way possible - with Malcolm gathering her curls high on her head and wrapping a satin scrunchie around them, then licking his way down the back of her neck to that sensitive spot between her shoulder blades. When she moaned, she felt his mouth smile against her skin.

It sent shivers down her spine.

Over the next hour or so, he dedicated himself to ensuring she was very clean and tasted every inch of her to be sure. His touch was gentle as he slid the soapy cloth down her neck and across her décollctage. He paid special attention to her taut peaks, drawing another moan from her. A swirl of the cloth, followed by his thumb repeating the motion - a smooth glide made slick with soap. A swirl of cloth, then his thumb, swirl... thumb... until her eyes closed, her head dropped forward, and she swayed - almost losing purchase on her balance. He placed a firm hand on her hip, steadying her.

"I think I should move on, but first, offer them to me." His voice had deepened with need, and she felt the vibration of it zing from her ears straight to her clit.

A grin crinkled his eyes, and her smile mirrored his.

She did as she was told, cradling and lifting both of her breasts, made heavier with desire. She pinched her own nipples. He moved the detachable hose slowly over and under her breasts, rinsing her, before dipping his head low and taking her right breast into his mouth. Too soon he switched to her left breast, licking a droplet from the tip before sucking it.

The water was hot; his touch - scorching, but still the flush under her skin felt hotter. It flowed molten and punishing, threatening to steal her breath before Malcolm mercifully, or regretfully, moved on with his deliberate cleansing.

Added to the things she knew about Malcolm: she now knew how it felt to be caged in by his large body as he stroked her to her first of several expected orgasms of the evening. His stomach, his chest, his hardness pressed against her back, his mouth licking, sucking and nipping at her neck, one brawny forearm wrapped around her chest keeping her clenched to him while his other hand pressed and rotated against her freshly cleansed clit.

And when she said, "Right there, baby, please don't stop..."

HE STAYED RIGHT THERE. Same rhythm, same stroke, same pressure.

It really is the simple things.

And she lit up and came apart in his arms. The fire beneath her skin reached an almost unbearable peak before setting off prickles across her scalp and down her chest and arms in a cascade of goosebumps.

He moved his hand from between her legs to around her waist, careful to keep her fully immersed in the shower spray and anchored to him.

Eventually the high subsided, and he lowered her onto the corner bamboo bench and washed her legs in long, slow strokes that somehow always went high enough to brush teasingly across her lower lips.

Finally, after washing, rinsing, and sucking her toes, he backed away, turned off the shower heads that had the potential to spray her, and used his long arms to snag a couple of her fluffy towels.

"Stay here, rest up."

She wanted to protest, to have her own fun with soap and droplets, but *damn*, she was so cozy wrapped in towels watching him soap himself.

It was a great show.

Especially when Malcolm took himself in hand, his Apadravya piercing winking in the light. After a few strokes, Ebony got the distinct feeling he wasn't just being thorough.

Rock-hard and beautiful, watching him pleasure himself did things to her. Ebony lifted a foot and placed it on the bench, opening herself to him and showing him exactly what. His smile in response was devastating.

He gripped himself harder and moved his hand faster, then he suddenly stopped.

"Damn Ebee," he gasped, closing his eyes for a moment as he struggled to get himself under control. "The way you look at me. Be good or I'm going to end up coming all over you and your shower."

Ebony shrugged, like, "*And?*"

A deep chuckle rolled up from his chest, and he shook his head. Adding more body wash to his washcloth, he finished cleaning himself, never taking his eyes off her.

ANOTHER THING EBONY NOW KNEW: HOW DELICIOUS WATER DROPLETS tasted on Malcolm's skin and how gorgeous his skin looked against her plum sheets. His eyes were heated as he crooked his finger at her.

She'd just finished applying moisturizer while he did the same.

"You don't mind smelling like orange blossoms?" she'd asked.

"I'm about to smell like all of you in a minute," he replied with a wink.

In one smooth move he stretched out his full six feet, three inches, fluffed up her pillow and patted his chest... "Come moisturize my beard, Ebee baby."

Ebony grasped her sturdy, mounted headboard and graced his face with her essence. And from the first swirl of his tongue, she was gone. In the zone, his groans of appreciation, her own moans of pleasure, his grip on her thighs pulling her down further, her hips acting on their own as she greedily, wantonly chased another explosion.

That familiar flush returned, and her hips pistoned, and Malcolm, caught up in the moment, was trying to talk her through it, or at least that's what her horny mind thought. Just like she thought the double tap on her thigh was the encouraging equivalent of an ass smack.

But by the time he gripped her tightly and pulled her back enough to let loose a wheezy gasp for breath, her thoughts had switched.

"Oh my god, I'm suffocating you!"

Ebony, horrified and deeply concerned for the man who was lying in her bed, dick on brick and still gasping she did the only thing she could think of - she screamed for her cousin.

"AND HOW LONG AGO DID YOU ADMINISTER THE EPIPEN?" a paramedic asked Ebony.

"I didn't. Joy did while I called you all."

"Sir, is this lotion on your face? Are you allergic to aloe?" asked a second paramedic.

"What were you doing at the moment of contact with his allergen?" the original paramedic asked her.

"It's me," Ebony whispered as she wrapped and unwrapped the tie of her robe around her finger.

"I'm sorry, ma'am, what's you?"

"He's wearing me," she yelled, and the room came to a halt. "I was riding his face, and he started to suffocate, okay? In Cabo he...*enjoyed* when I got..." She gestured wildly with her hands, "you know... comfortable. I did the same tonight and almost killed him."

The paramedics all looked at each other for a second.

"Sir, I need you to put the mask back on!"

Ebony looked up to see Malcolm shaking his head and hand back and forth.

"Sir!"

"Maybe we should go into the other room," the first paramedic suggested, opening his arms and gently steering Ebony and Joy into Ebony's sitting room.

"At 12:07 a.m. I heard Ebony scream. I came in and recognized the signs of anaphylaxis. Malcolm pantomimed that he had an EpiPen. I ran to my room to grab my own and administered at about 12:10 a.m. Because of his facial swelling and labored breathing, I propped him up and gave him his dignity with a blanket; then I took his blood pressure. It was initially 221 over 128 and dropped with each check every three minutes until your arrival when it was within normal range."

Ebony stared over at Joy in awe. She was so calm and rattled off blood pressure numbers and intervals like she was an ER doctor instead of a historical preservationist.

"Are you a nurse?"

"No, my shithead husband, ex-husband, umm... soon-to-be-ex husband had a heart attack last year. Since then I've been waiting on him hand and foot and recording everything from his medicines to BPs to his goddamn shit color until that lying, cheating asshole got too lazy to cover his tracks. Or maybe he thought I was stupid. Do I look stupid to you?!"

The paramedic blinked. Joy cleared her throat, smoothed back a loc, and with the motion, regained her composure. Ebony had whiplash from Joy's outburst and switch up and she would've laughed had she not been worried about her body count, including an actual dead body. How was she going to explain this to Malcolm's mother?

"Ebony! Ebony!"

"Where's my baby?!"

At the sound of her mother and father's voice Ebony simultaneously wanted to hide and run into their arms. They pushed their way into her sitting room and rushed to her side.

"Little Bit, are you okay? Joy, are you alright? The neighbor called us," Ebony's mother said, pulling them both to her, pulling back to give them the once-over and then snatching them back close to her again. "Ran, baby, what did the man say?"

"Mom, I —"

"He said Ebony had some *boy* up here that is allergic to our daughter's lady parts."

"Oh god, Dad just—"

"Uncle Randy, maybe—"

"Allergic to what? What's a lady dart?"

"Noel, put your ears in, baby," her dad said, motioning to his own ears.

"Oh, I was in such a rush, let me get my aids on," Noel muttered as she searched her purse.

"Or maybe not," Ebony said in dismay, wishing the floor would open up and swallow her whole.

"Uncle Randy, we should probably—"

"Ms. Jones, just a few more questions. Mr. Knight will be

fine, but it would help us if we could isolate what triggered his allergic reaction. Did you use any new lotions or food, latex or silicon tonight when…"

"No," Ebony closed her eyes and tried to focus on the paramedic while Joy took her mom and dad to the side, whispering quickly. "We hadn't made it to latex and silicon yet, but it was our first time. Well, not the first time, but first time in a couple years. I don't remember what lotion I used back then. We showered, moisturized, and I broke the man with my… Jesus."

"Oh my god!" Noel whisper-yelled from the corner. "Is his *member* swollen?" She held her hands entirely too wide. Ebony would have checked into the Upper Room if it had swollen that damn big.

Right then. Right then was the moment they wheeled Malcolm out, and even though he was wearing an oxygen mask, anyone could easily make out the hives spreading across his face, and his eyes were almost swollen shut.

"Oh!" her mother gasped as she took in Malcolm's appearance with surprise and concern in her eyes. Then. The realization. "Oh. Ohhhhh…"

This is a new low.

Ebony's heart banged painfully in her chest from the sight of him, the extent of his reaction, and the level of mortified adrenaline coursing through her veins.

"We found hair on the pillows; he's allergic to the cat," another paramedic announced to the room.

Malcolm took his mask off to say something, but before he could, her daddy fussed from the corner.

"What kind of man is allergic to coochie? A lil bush ain't never hurt nobody."

"Ran, is that the unhoused man she met a few weeks ago?" Her mother whispered loudly.

"No, Auntie, that's..." Joy started to explain before the buzzing in Ebony's brain took over and drowned out most of the noise in the room.

I have to move. I have to make sure Malcolm is okay, then move... to a new planet.

Overstimulated, embarrassed, worried, she pushed the mask back onto his face, but snatched back her hand when he tried to touch her. She didn't want to set off another reaction. Things were very much out of control and Ebony kinda forgot herself.

"But, you told me to sit on your face! Why would you tell me to do that if you're allergic?"

It wasn't her finest moment.

Ordinarily, she wouldn't yell at a man experiencing a medical emergency.

Ordinarily, she wouldn't have yelled about a recent sex position in front of Columbus Fire Department Ladder Number 4. Ordinarily.

But in her defense, good sense was thin on the ground hours ago when she rode out to claim Joy, later her stuff, and hauled off and knocked the shit out of Eric. It would've been patchy after a couple of good orgasms on a regular day. Once the man almost died under her, and her dad started yelling about coochies, good sense left on a first-class flight for parts unknown. A bitch's system was dysregulated.

"Oh my gosh, E! Ruckus! I shooed him out of here earlier," Joy snapped her fingers as she put it together. "I didn't realize he'd gotten on your bed. I'm so sorry."

Ebony's mouth formed an 'o' while her father said it.

An actual cat. Not *the* cat. She'd forgotten about Joy's new buddy.

Ebony reached back out and gripped Malcolm's hand. "I'm so sorry. I'm going to be right behind the ambulance. And I'll call your mom."

Malcolm shook his head no and pulled down his mask briefly. "I never call her until I'm alright."

"Okay," she whispered and slipped the mask onto his face.

He pulled it back down. "It wasn't you. You are incredible."

She wasn't sure if the man could even see her through his puffed-over slits for eyes, but she smiled anyway and once again slid the mask into place.

Joy was at her side, slipping a pair of leggings, a cami, and an oversized sweater into her hand while her father followed the EMTs out of the sitting room door and down the stairs.

"I'll stay and change your sheets and get the second guest room ready for your gentleman caller," her mom said. "I don't like that you let him back into your bed after he tried to manipulate you into letting him move in, but he's a human being. We can't put him out on the street after a medical event. Just make sure he doesn't start receiving mail here, or he'll have squatters' rights."

my teddy-weddy

"YOUR FIANCÉ IS HERE, MR. KNIGHT."

He schooled his face to neutral at the announcement of a fiancé he definitely didn't have until Ebony, clad in leggings, a sweater, and hair still up in the puff he put it in earlier, walked through the door of his room in the ER. Then he relaxed. It was automatic. And disconcerting.

"Hey Honey, how are you?" she whispered, coming in, sitting on the bed and taking his hand. She brushed her soft fingers lightly over his brow.

He did not hate that at all.

"My Teddy-Weddy has an ouchie wowchie," she crooned, kissing his hand in hers and crossing her eyes at him, her back to the nurse.

He leaned in to kiss her cheek and whispered, "You're such a little weirdo."

"Err... I'll leave you two alone," the nurse said, stepping out and closing the door behind her.

Her beautiful face broke into a big smile. "The swelling has gone down some."

"How bad is it?" He patted his face, noting that the

tightness was easing some and that he could see better out of his eyes.

"Like you went two rounds with black towel, no socks, 1990s Mike Tyson." She leaned in and looked closer, and kissed him gently above his eyebrow.

"Damn. I'm sorry I ruined our evening. I had so many plans and positions for you."

Ebony chuckled quietly. "You didn't ruin anything; you can't help your allergies. Plus, it's probably for the best."

He felt himself frown. It felt weird, like his skin was a mask, but he was more distracted by what she said. "Why do you say that?"

She shrugged. "We were about to get complicated."

"We don't have to be."

She gave him a long look and nodded with a yawn she tried to stifle. He watched her for a moment and decided it could wait. This wasn't a conversation for one in the morning. But they *would* have this conversation. Instead of pressing her, he scooted over in the bed, turned on his side and patted the empty space. "Come, lie down."

"No, I'll just pull up a chair—"

Malcolm sat up, wrapped his arms around her, bear hug-style and pulled her down with him. She let out a muffled yelp on the way.

Grabbing her leg, he yanked it on top of his legs and tucked her head into his chest. "I'm stuck here for another couple of hours for observation. You are too nice to leave me, and I'm not going to let you sit in a hard chair all night."

"But—"

"Ebee. You're tired, I'm tired. Go to sleep."

She blew out a frustrated breath, then snuggled into him a bit. "Fine."

Malcolm traced slow circles on her lower back, and soon her

breathing slowed and grew deeper. He let himself luxuriate in her softness, in her closeness, and inhaled deep, taking the scent of her deep into him. The last thing he remembered before the nurse woke them hours later with his discharge papers was kissing the top of her head and the soft sigh she let out in her sleep.

♪♫ *Don't you remember you told me you love me, baby...* ♪♫

"Shit."

His mom was blasting Luther Vandross. It must be Saturday morning, and she was about to kick in his door with a list of cleaning to-dos.

Wait. I grew up.

Malcolm cracked open an eye, still half expecting his mom to burst in. Instead, he was in a very well-appointed, deep navy bedroom with bronze accents. The summer sun peeked through floral, but not fussy curtains, and it took him a moment to remember where he was... Ebony's.

The night came flooding back and he scrubbed his hand down his face. Ebony's father had driven him and Ebony back from the hospital in what was probably the most awkward ride ever. The man had thought he was allergic to his daughter's "coochie" and took exception.

Which... Fair.

Then, instead of letting him leave, her mother insisted he sleep in the "absolutely cat-free guest room" so they could keep an eye on him

The whole time Ebony, looking like a teen with her scrunchied poof and oversized sweater, mouthed, "I'm so sorry." He chuckled despite himself.

Life with her ain't dull.

He sat up and really got a good look around. Ebony had a wonderful eye; the room was cozy and cool. No wonder that dude she ranted about tried to move in.

Are these sheets bamboo?

He wanted to snuggle in and sleep the day away. Instead, he reached out and turned off the small bronze humidifier next to him and got out of bed. After making the bed, he stretched and headed to the bathroom.

Laid out on the counter on a beautiful bronze tray were a new toothbrush and travel-size toiletries. *Damn, a dude could get used to this.*

And as soon as he had the thought, he remembered that he wanted to talk to Ebee. He quickly freshened up, put on the hospital sweats again, and went looking for the lady of the house. Following the music, he found her in what he assumed was her office. She was staring off into the distance, her hand on an old-fashioned, non electric carpet sweeper, wearing snug biker shorts, fuzzy, mismatched socks, and a cut-up sweatshirt that hung off one soft and sexy shoulder. Her hair was still up in a giant puff on the top of her head, though it looked neater than what he'd done. She was a beautiful sight for no longer puffy eyes, but...

"You look worried."

She jumped out of her skin and turned off the music.

"You look better. Much better. How do you feel?"

"I'm fine. What's up with you? I could hear you thinking from the doorway."

She smirked. "Are you an empath too?"

He shrugged and waited for her to talk. She sighed and leaned her butt on the edge of her desk.

"Three of my favorite people in the world are dealing with serious issues, turning points in their lives, and not only can I not do much to help them, I have to keep everything a secret from everyone else."

"The downside of being the one everyone tells their deepest, darkest to."

"Right. And it's all happening simultaneously, and each one is worried about what everyone else is going to think or do, and no one — never mind."

"No one is thinking about the impact on you."

"Gawd that sounds so selfish," she whispered, peeking out the office door. "My life is a doggone slapstick comedy compared to what everyone else is going through, and none of them know that I'm holding something for someone else, and I can't talk to any of them about it. My normal sounding board is them. And then I have to juggle the questions from the aunts and my parents or play stupid. BUT," she whispered yelled, "if they say they didn't want to bother me, I feel bad. Offended even. I insist harder I *can* handle it because I *want* to help and in the moment and most of the moments I have the capacity, but lately when I step back and look at all the plates spinning... I'm overwhelmed and I don't want to mess anything up, because one plate could be the domino that sets off the whole house of cards to come down. Shit, I'm mixing the hell out of these metaphors."

She sighed and scratched her head in frustration. He had an overwhelming urge to sooth her.

"Hmm, do you want advice, an ear, or someone to kick ass?"

Ebony's eyes lit up. "You sound like my dad."

"No, if I sounded like your dad I would say, '*What kind of man is allergic to coochie? A lil bush ain't never hurt nobody.*'"

She covered her cheeks, looking equal parts horrified and amused. "Mal, please don't remind me. I am thisclose to leaving the planet for parts unknown. A year-long study on the space station or something… I can't believe you heard that."

"Oh, I heard it. Your neighbors a mile away heard it. Your cousin's seen my dick… It's been a banger week."

She covered her entire face with her hands after that. "I have never been more terrified or embarrassed for myself and you," she said with a muffled voice from behind her hands.

Laughing at her antics, he peeled away her hands. "It was a moment I'll never forget. The before and the after. Especially the before."

Especially the after. The after where she crawled into bed with him and let him hold her so close…

Her eyes heated and he needed to focus. "You need to put on your own mask first before helping anyone else, Ebee. You seem to have trouble saving enough of you for you. Do you have a therapist? Or someone who's better able to helping you figure out strategies for balancing everything?"

"Yeah, but I feel like I should be able to do this on my own. Faith was right, though; I'm opening up a can of worms in the rain and need an umbrella." She paused, her head cocked slightly. "Shoot, that actually makes sense the more I think about it."

"You're in a storm, undertaking something difficult, and need protection so you can focus on the task at hand."

"Holy shit, you speak Holiday."

He felt a sense of pride warming him. At a loss with what to do with himself, he looked around the room. Large sunny windows dominated one wall, shedding light on an absolute fuck ton of papers and debris.

There were piles of papers and boxes arranged in stacks surrounding the sides of the room. Her desk was neat and organized, as was the center of the room, but the rest was a disaster. Surprising, considering how beautiful the rest of her home was.

"So, is this where you hide the bodies?"

"I'll drop yours over there if you don't hush talking about my office." She pointed to an especially wicked pile that had several full wicker baskets stacked. "This is organized chaos, genius in motion. This is—"

"A mad professor's laboratory?"

She smiled big. "Exactly. I know where everything is."[1]

Before Malcolm could stop himself, he bent and pressed his lips to hers. First her body froze in surprised, and then she melted against him and kissed him back. He wrapped his arms around her, pulling her tighter into him and deepening the kiss. Her full lips and searching tongue wrested a moan from the pit of him.

"Thank you for taking care of me last night," he took her hands and kissed them with one peck, two pecks, and then a third. "Thank you for staying with me."

She shrugged and looked up at him through her lashes. "It's the least I could do after almost killing you."

"You didn't almost do anything, but if I had died with you on top of me, it would have been a great way to go."

"You know I'm scarred for life now." She twisted her mouth up in a teasing smirk.

He chuckled. "I guess we're going to have to do another kind of therapy to cure you. Multiple aversion sessions where we get you comfortable. Start with you in my queening chair and move on from there."

When she looked puzzled, he pulled out his phone and did a quick search, and the way her eyes lit up got him hard. He grabbed her luscious ass and pressed her front to his so she

____

1. Thinkin Bout You by Frank Ocean

could feel how he reacted to her. She gifted him with another kiss that had him slipping a hand under her shirt to tweak her nipple. Movement and a loud laugh somewhere in the house reminded them they weren't alone. Reluctantly, Malcolm ended the kiss.

"I could kiss you all day and never get tired. These lips..." He dipped back in for another taste. "And I hate to kiss and leave; but I have to go check on my mom."

"Ooh, about that," Ebony said, biting her lower lip and giving her head a quick scratch. "So last night, my mom insisted on calling your mom. Joy held her off until this morning, and now your mom is on her way to check on you."

Malcolm was in shock for a moment.

"Remember when I said that we were pretty much a normal family? This is the part that's not included in the pretty much. We're actually really overly involved in each other's lives, and sometimes that bleeds out into the rest of the world."

She searched his eyes for his reaction, and Malcolm tried to tamp down the anxiety and slight anger he felt at his mom being contacted. Her health was fragile, and he'd seen the toll of that kind of call before.

"You're upset."

"I am, honestly. I know your parents didn't mean any harm, but I don't tell my mother about any hospitalizations until I'm fine and she can lay eyes on me. I never want her to have to go through what she went through that first time, especially with her condition now."

He patted his pockets, looking for his wallet and keys.

"I'm sorry, I really am. If there's a way to make it up to you both—"

"No, I just — I really need to get to my mom," he bent down and gave her a quick forehead kiss, then pulled out his phone and moved toward the hallway. Malcolm didn't get as far as the doorway before he was already connecting via video call. When he finally saw her face, she was smiling. The sight pulled most of the tension out of his body.

"There's my boy! I am right outside the door on my way in. You look worried."

"I'm worried about you."

"Oh, I'm fine. Mrs. Holiday-Jones told me everything."

Malcolm moved down the hallway with Ebony close behind, then rounded the stairs in long strides, arriving at the bottom of the steps at the same time Ebony's mother was opening the door.

"I thought that was you, Noelle Holiday," his mother fussed, working her neck in indignation. "I'm finally gonna get a chance to kick your behind, you man-stealing heffa!"

Ebony and Malcolm's eyes were as big as saucers as they looked to each other for confirmation that they were truly hearing what they thought they were hearing.

"Mabeline Carter?" Mrs. Jones asked, pointing a finger in his mother's face. "Listen, sistah, don't start nothing you can't finish. "

The two women glared at each other, hands on their hips, squaring off.

"Mom?" Ebony squeaked.

The two women suddenly threw their arms open and fell into each other, hugging hard and rocking back and forth. "Ooh it's good to see you!" his mother crooned.

"It's been decades and you still look nineteen!" Ebony's mother said, rubbing his mom's back before squeezing her again.

"How do you guys know each other? Malcolm asked.

"Miss Mabeline is your mom?" Ebony asked.

"You know Mabeline already?" Noelle asked Ebony.

"Yeah, from Armello's Saturday Brunch!"

"That's right. We miss you and your sisters. You need to come back on Saturday. We'll make sure no one bothers you." Mabeline put her hands back on her hips. "Well, isn't this a small world? I used to date, well, Noelle stole my boyfriend, Randolph. The captain of the football team with the broadest shoulders and the prettiest brown eyes."

"And you stole Jet from me! His real name was Jetson and it fit. He was the fastest man on that track. Could jump hurdles with his eyes closed; he was that good. And the boy could fill out a pair of shorts."

"I only stole him to get back at you!"

Ebony and Malcolm looked at each other again, their eyes wider still.

"*Oh shit,*" Ebony mouthed.

Malcolm shrugged in response. He was simply floored.

"When I heard your name, Noelle Holiday-Jones, I had to come see if it was you so I could lay eyes on you and tell you after all this time: girl, thank you for taking that man off my hands!" Mabeline fell out laughing.

So did Noelle.

"Girl, I was going to say the same thing. If I had known then what I know now, I would have given you that man."

"Where's Mr. Big Shot Randolph Jones?"

"He's at home now, cutting the grass, taking a nap, and probably farting up my den."

Mabeline cackled.

"Did you marry Jet?"

"And did. And then he had the nerve to die on me, almost two years ago. Just irresponsible."

The two of them cackled again. Then hugged each other hard, as hard as long-lost friends could.

"I'm so sorry to hear about Jet, Shuga."

"He was the love of my life; we had a good time together." They rocked some more.

"I understand. I fuss about Ran. He's retired and getting on my nerves, but I love that man."

Noelle wiped a tear off Mabeline's cheek. And Mabeline clasped her hands over Noelle's. "How have you been?"

"Oh, girl, I'm just fine. Getting ready to get a new hip."

"What?! Mama, you didn't tell me you needed hip replacement," Ebony said, her face scrunched in worry and shock.

"Oh, chile, I'm sure I did."

"No. No, you didn't."

"Well, anyway, how are you?" Noelle asked, dismissing her daughter, who stood there with her mouth hanging open.

"My kidneys are shot," Mabeline said, shaking her head. "I'm on dialysis three times a week. My baby boy has basically become a dialysis tech; he knows as much as the doctors do. He's been helping me with my treatments."

"Well, you don't look like what you've been through. We over here getting ready for Ebony's birthday party. You know, my mama was on dialysis. Come on into the kitchen. I got some tea cakes and hibiscus tea. That tea is good for your blood."

"Let me guess, she was born on Juneteenth!"

When Ebony's mom nodded yes, Malcolm's mother cackled. "I see the Holiday women still making Holiday babies!"

And the two women linked arm in arm, heads bent toward each other, talking a mile a minute, moseyed off to the kitchen, completely forgetting why Mabeline was there in the first place. Ebony and Malcolm, two fully grown adults, stood there in the foyer of *her* home like two kids while the adults went on about their visit.

"What in the world just happened?" She wondered out loud.

"So your *mom* used to date my *dad*?"

"And *your* mom used to date *my* dad. You could have been Malcolm Jones, and I could have been Ebony Knight."

Something about her saying her first name with his stopped him in his tracks. His heart started beating hard. His head felt funny, and his ears tingled. It felt like premonition, promise, and possibilities, a possibility he hadn't considered before now.

"Malcolm, you all right? You look a little funny."

"Uh, yeah, let's go see what our moms are up to."

uncomplicated

EBONY TURNED to see her back in the mirror. Her birthday dress was fire: a brick-red halter top that cinched in at the waist with a flared skirt made her feel like a pinup. The cotton fabric was light and airy, perfect for what was turning out to be another hot weekend. Her nude sandals made her legs look long, and they were comfy enough for running around the yard all day.

"Gorgeous as always, Sis. That booty lookin' right!"

She looked past her reflection to Pumpkin standing in the doorway of her bathroom with a sleeping toddler taking up half her body, and her heart cartwheeled at the sight.

"OH MY GAWD!" Ebony excitedly whispered so as not to wake the baby. Jumping up and down, she ran to her cousin and enveloped both of them in a hug that was as gentle as it was fierce. She motioned Pumpkin into her bedroom and arranged pillows on the bed to form a little barrier to keep Baby Nicky from rolling off. Then she ran to the Blue Room and back, waving her recent purchase.

"Why do you have a baby monitor?" Pumpkin whispered, tucking her waist-length brown braids behind her ear. She was wearing a whimsical black and white dress that reminded Ebony of Wednesday Addams, but in a summer dress with puffed sleeves.

"Because you had a baby. Duh," Ebony whispered back. "The crib is still boxed up in the Blue room. I thought the weather delayed your flight!"

Pumpkin grabbed Ebony into a long, rocking hug that had more than a few sniffles. They closed the bedroom door and sat holding hands on the settee in the sitting room.

"There was a break, and I took the first thing smokin'. I'm not staying long; I just wanted to wish you happy birthday and give you your present. Then I'm going to a hotel room and lie low until everyone leaves."

"What? Why?"

"Because I will not take away from you and your day. We slipped in while everyone was in the back and I'll slip out when you go out."

"Pumpkin, I really think you should reconsider. This is low key, not everyone is going to make it today. It could be a soft launch, and I can't think of a better reason not to be the center of attention."

She looked unsure.

"Just think about it."

She nodded. "Wait here."

Pumpkin stepped out into the hallway, and Ebony heard her collide with another cousin with a secret, and there was a muffled scuffle. The next thing Ebony knew, Pumpkin had yanked Joy inside the sitting room with a hand clamped over Joy's mouth. Joy was holding a large, wrapped package.

"I'm going to let you go, but don't scream. I'm not staying."

"What do you mean you're not staying?" Joy hissed as she hugged Pumpkin and kissed her and hugged her again.

Pumpkin held Joy at arm's length, looking at her closely.

Joy had pulled it together, mostly. Her locs were twisted up high at her crown, emphasizing her striking cheekbones, and she wore her favorite "Preservationists do it for historical record" tee, shorts, and strappy sandals. She needed a second coat of concealer, but Ebony wasn't going to tell her that.

"Why were you coming out of the guest bedroom, and why do you look like you've been crying all day?"

"Uh... just studying here so I could help with setup. And these allergies have been terrible this year."

Pumpkin narrowed her eyes at Joy. "I got some Korean Red Ginseng that might help."

"Yum!"

Pumpkin looked at Ebony, and Ebony found the hem of her dress fascinating. Pumpkin sucked her teeth and dug in her purse, producing a small container and handing it to Joy.

Joy handed Ebony her present from Pumpkin, her eyes wide to reiterate '*keep yo mouth shut.*'

As if she needed that extra eyeballin'.

A knock at the door made Ebony tense and wonder which one of her family members was coming to jeopardize their secret next. Instead, six feet three inches of thick Black man goodness stepped through the doorway, looking expensive in navy shorts and a cream shirt - a departure from his work uniform of pants with hella pockets, dark tees, and heavy boots. He scanned the room until his eyes quickly settled on her.

"Ebee, happy birthday. Wow, you look beautiful. Your mom sent me up here to tell you to come down because people are hungry. However, I know for a fact that your Uncle Ron just started the coals, and it is not you they are waiting on, so take that with a grain of salt. She's put everyone to work, and you're next. Even Anika is making hibiscus tea."

And then Malcolm smiled and Ebony's panties went poof

because he'd put in a grill for the occasion. Nothing ostentatious. Just a little gold on his eye teeth. It was unexpected and hella hot. Sensing eyeballs on her, she stood and introduced her cousins before they went in on her. It was the most Holiday family introduction ever, and she hoped he picked up what she was putting down.

"Malcolm, these are my cousins - Akiko, also known among family as Pumpkin, who you actually don't see unless she changes her mind and comes downstairs, and Joy, who was studying in my guest room to escape my mom's wrath." She winked at him, her back to her cousins. "Holiday Sisters, this is my colleague Malcolm Knight."

Malcolm acted as if he hadn't heard a word she said.

"Ebony... Really, you. Are. Stunning."

Buoyed by the current of his palpable awe, his words floated around her and settled lightly on her shoulders - a cloak of the finest gossamer that stirred gentle, soft feelings.

"Thank you, Malcolm. I like your," and she pointed to her teeth, "they suit you."

"Thank you."

The sound of a baby stirring interrupted their long stares. Ebony's eyes went round, and Pumpkin moved to Ebony's bedroom without a thought and with Joy on her heels. Ebony just held a finger to her lips and shrugged at Malcolm as a whispered argument broke out in the other room.

"Nicky!"

A toddler wearing just a pull up on the bottom came streaking out the door, past Ebony before she could react, and was on his way out of her sitting room. Malcolm responded quickly and blocked the door. Swooping Nicky up in one arm and closing the door with his other hand, he looked back at Ebony with a grin. "He's fast, he almost snuck me."

Nicky, for his part, was all in Malcolm's mouth, trying to

reach for his gold adornments. "What's that?" he asked, his adorable voice hinting at an Australian accent.

"Nicky, baby," Akiko fussed, coming out of the bedroom with his little shorts in her hand. She thanked Malcolm, retrieved the cherubic toddler and marched back into the bedroom where there was more whispered conversation.

"That's a whole ass tiny human!" Joy said loudly before more whispers.

Ebony turned to Malcolm. "I said the same thing."

"Is this a recent development?" He asked, genuinely confused.

She nodded.

"Wow."

"I said that too."

He smiled at her again, and she returned it. "I think we need to let them work it out; those two have several points of beef," she said, and headed for the door with Malcolm following close behind her. When they got down the hallway, she found herself pressed against the wall and caged in by Malcolm. [1]

"You really look amazing in this dress," he kissed her cheek near her mouth. "I don't want to mess up your lipstick yet."

He kissed her jaw, down her neck, and gently sucked on her shoulder. "I wonder what you have on underneath this," he said as his hands slowly slipped under her dress and up her thighs, lifting her dress as he went. He felt his way up, squeezing and kneading until he reached her thong. "Hold up your dress, baby, I don't want to wrinkle it."

"Anyone can walk up or out here, Mal," she said, even as she did what she was told.

---

1. That's Why I Love You (feat. Sabrina Claudio) by SiR Chasing Summer R&B/Soul 1 70

"Then I guess you're going to have to be quiet and I'm going to have to be quick."

And quick he was, he slid her panties to the side and circled her clit with his long finger before she could even mount a bullshit protest. Instead, she bit back a moan. He moved closer, his big body shielding her.

"Spread wider. Let me wish you a happy birthday," he whispered in her ear.

"You already did," she said breathlessly with a low, guttural groan as she complied. Her head fell forward against his shoulder as he slid a finger into her while working her clit. The world faded to nothing but the feel of his hands on her, his soft kisses against her throat, and the warmth of his body - close but not pressing against her so as not to wrinkle her dress.

"And now I'm going to do it all day."

"Oh, fuck." Her nails bit into his neck as she came in an embarrassingly short time with deep, intense waves.

Malcolm slid his fingers out of her and sucked them, smiling down at her. "Mmmm," he nodded. "Let's clean you up."

She nodded and started to lower dress when he shook his head no.

"Hold it higher."

Confused, she held the skirt of her dress higher, and he dropped to his knees, threw her leg over his shoulder, and with a flat and focused tongue, he...

Licked.

Her.

Clean.

Her hips chased his tongue, but he stilled her movements with his big hands spanning her hips. Malcolm finished the job like he was being graded, then carefully slid her red thong back in place. Looking quite pleased with himself, he gently lowered her leg, rose to his full height, straightened her dress, and smiled.

"Happy Birthday, Ebee."

She was speechless, and stayed that way after he tagged her hand and led her to the hallway washroom where he positioned her next to him while he washed his hands, ran a hot soapy washcloth over his mouth and goatee. When he finished, he used the lotion available to moisturize his hands, ran a palm over his goatee, and glanced over at her. "Cat got your tongue? 'Cause she got mine."

Ebony's head was spinning and wrestling with what was happening between them.

Was this a part of the uncomplicated? Uncomplicated meant just sex, right? Having a good time, but probably not a long time.

She'd invited him and Anika because it was the polite thing to do, especially once they learned their parents had been friends. But now, this didn't feel uncomplicated. This felt... fun and exciting. She felt safe enough to fall asleep in the car with the man and... it was a lot of feelings. Her racing brain paused long enough to look up at his expectant face.

"I—that was corny."

He shrugged. "At least I don't have hives."

Despite her distracted thoughts, she laughed. "I already warned my parents not to say a word."

"Good to know. I'd hate to have to explain to your family just how unallergic I am to you." He flipped up her dress and gave her mound a playful pat, drawing a surprised squeak out of her.

He took her hand again and led her down the stairs. As the voices of her family grew louder, panic set in. Hand holding in front of the fam? They'd have them engaged, and the Holiday Baby Betting Pool would activate. Quickly she slipped her hand out of his and met his eyes. "This is 'uncomplicated.' Which means I don't need my entire extended family in my business."

She left him with a question on his face and moved into the kitchen, pasting a smile on her face.

"AYE NEPHEW! I HEARD YOU WERE JET KNIGHT'S BOY." [2]

Ebony's ears perked up. Like they'd done all damn day whenever anyone mentioned or spoke to Malcolm. It was irritating. Well, it was irrational. And that made it irritating. She was a grown woman; it was her birthday; it was Juneteenth, and a lot more of the family from both sides made it after all. She should focus on catching up with the cousins from the Jones side of the family. Instead, she was now half-listening to her cousin Bianca from Houston share her brush with Beyonce's play cousin at the nail shop and half-listening for Malcolm's response.

His deep voice rumbled underneath her Cook Out playlist, while his smile and grill caught the sunlight. She watched his throat move as he drank hibiscus tea, savoring it. He looked around, and after catching Anika's eye, he lifted the glass and gave her a nod. She gave him a thumbs up and accepted additional praise from Ebony's Auntie Eve.

Ebony was glad she'd had the mind to invite her, and that she wouldn't be alone on the holiday. Anika was from a small town in Texas, near where Ebony's dad's family hailed. Getting home during the summer was tough and expensive. She looked back at Malcolm in time to catch him watching her.

"That man is fine as hell," her cousin Bianca said. "How are we related?"

---

2. Tell Me by Groove Theory

"He's a colleague." Ebony said as she got a little more thirsty for Malcolm herself when stretched his long legs out. The muscle in his thigh flexed for the whole world to see in his hoochie daddy shorts.

"Damn. I'd watch the news more often if he were reading it."

Ebony laughed off-handedly, not bothering to correct her about either of their jobs. She waved her fan harder and crossed her legs. His eyes dropped to them.

Jesus.

"Ebony, your dad can't find Momma's Anniversary Champagne in the basement for the toast."

Her mother's voice was enough to break the connection and give her an excuse to move out from under his gaze. She was grateful for her mother's incessant aversion to relaxing for once. Hopping up, Ebony excused herself and headed for the basement to grab a few bottles of Granny Holiday's special occasion champagne. She'd made it to the bottom of the stairs when footsteps materialized behind her. She turned expecting to see her dad, but there Malcolm stood.

"Happy Birthday, Ebee."

The husky need in his voice sent chills through her.

"Mal, it's dirty down here. I haven't remodeled and..." She trailed off when he made a little circle with his finger, indicating that she should turn around. And she wished she could say she hesitated, but nope. Around she spun.

"Thank you."

Stepping in close, he wrapped his arms around her, cupping her breasts through her dress. He pinched her nipples, sucked on the back of her neck, then growled in her ear, "Grab that ankle chain."

Shit! She was drenched already, but somewhere in the back of her lust-filled mind a practical thought formed.

"I've been outside all day, Mal."

"I don't give a fuck."

When she still paused, he almost brought her to her knees with:

"Come on, Ebee. Let me please you."

He pressed her forward with a large, flat hand in the middle of her shoulder blades.

As soon as she had achieved the position he requested, he flipped the back of her dress up, slid her drenched panties to the side, and with a deep squat got face to puss. Malcolm leaned in, took a deep sniff, made a noise of approval in the back of his throat, then disrespectfully ate her as if her pussy dripped hibiscus tea and he was *parched*.

"Ebony, did you find it?" Her mother called from somewhere near the door, but gratefully nowhere near where she could see them.

"Almost!" she cried out, her legs shaking.

Malcolm latched onto her clit and she found it alright. He anchored her against him as he sucked her through the deep waves of her orgasm.

"Happy Birthday, Ebee," he moaned against the back of her thigh.

HE WAS CLEANING HER UP GENTLY WITH WATER FROM THE UTILITY SINK when her mother yelled down again.

"Do you think it's in the garage?"

"Maybe! We'll move a couple of these boxes to be sure," she yelled back.

"You should've had it ready," she grumbled, walking away from the door and summoning her dad.

"She acts like I asked for this party. I never do, and every year she works herself and everyone else like a dog during it," she lamented, shaking her head as Malcolm washed his face. "Day-to-day Mom? Awesome. Party day Mom? Low budget Mommy Dearest."

She pulled her underwear off, dropped them in the sink and added some detergent and hot water. Malcolm turned her around, brushing her hair out of her face. "What do you mean?"

She gave him a rueful smile. "Every year this is a chance for family to get together, which I love. It's billed as a combo birthday Juneteenth situation, but honestly, she never really asks what I want to do for my birthday; it's just dates, times, and relentless prepping and serving."

"Ebony—"

"I found them, I'm coming, Ma!" Rolling her eyes, she pulled out two bottles from a crate clearly marked "Champagne, Vivian Holiday," in large, curling cursive. "Can you grab two more? Auntie Evie will do at least two more toasts tonight once she gets a little champagne in her."

"What would you rather do on your birthday?" Malcolm asked as he took her bottles and followed her up the stairs, a hand held out to keep her steady. She focused on walking and his question and not the mind-blowing experience she just had, and she certainly didn't wonder what other isolated areas she could wander to in her house .

"Game and talent night," she said without hesitation. "With food that someone else prepared. And carrot cake."

Her voice dropped to a whisper. "I never get carrot cake because chocolate and vanilla are easier with a crowd, but it's my favorite."

"Ah, 'bout time!" Her mom thanked Malcolm and pulled the first two bottles out of his arms. "I'm going to set these to chill. After the toast, we'll cut the cake, and then it's music until the fireworks."

She wasn't really talking to them, just running through to-do lists with them as witnesses, but at "fireworks" Malcolm tensed behind her.

He pressed his hand into her back, and they left her mom, her list, and Ms. Mabeline alone in the kitchen before the moms found something else for them to do. When they got through the house and to the front porch, Ebony closed the door behind them. With most of the family in her house and backyard, the porch was quiet.

"Hey is everything alright? I felt you tense back there."

"My passcode is 3326." He chuckled at her confused face. "I always feel compelled to tell you every secret."

"I'm sorry, I didn't mean to pry."

He waved her off and sat down on her porch swing. When she didn't join him, he reached out his hand to her. Her mind flashed forward to a future that held a thousand reach outs just like that.

It was the orgasms' fault.

But she sat down anyway and tucked her legs to the side while he rocked them.

"Why don't you tell your mom about your birthday wishes?"

"I don't want to be ungrateful. She works hard and looks forward to this every year. Everyone does. Plus, all of us put up with birthdays that don't just belong to us; it's the Holiday way."

Shit.

"DOES the Holiday Way have anything to do with why my mom thinks all of your family members have magical holiday birthdays?"

Ebony cringed. "You caught on to that, huh?"

Malcolm pulled back and looked at Ebony in disbelief. "I'd be a shitty journalist if I hadn't. Wait, it's true? I thought it was Mom's brain fog getting the better of her."

Ebony took a deep breath and speared him with a look, surveying him before her eyes flashed. "I don't tell secrets. And my sisters and I don't let just anyone into our circle, so if I share something with you and you let it leave this porch, you are untrustworthy, and that is the worst thing you can be in my world. Do you understand?"

She was fierce in her delivery, steady in her gaze, and Malcolm nodded. "You have my oath to you. Nothing leaves this porch."

Ebony took a deep breath. "Two generations ago, my grandmother Vivian Gaines-Holiday was in labor with my mom, Noel, and it wasn't looking good. They told my grandfather, Tibbett, to prepare. Family history says he went to the hospital chapel, laid facedown on the floor of the church and prayed for God to save them the entire time they were in the delivery room. Granny always said, 'God was so touched by his dedication and faithfulness He blessed the family especially.'"

She paused and checked him out, eyes narrowed. Malcolm didn't know what reaction she was expecting from him, but he wasn't having it, so she continued.

"My mom was born Christmas morning, and Granny obviously made it through because she had Evangeline - Aunt Evie on Halloween, Aunt Easter on Easter, and my Aunt Glory, who passed away when the twins were eight, was born on Fourth of July."

Malcolm had questions and mentally calculated possibilities.

"I know what you're thinking, but what is the luck of castor oil or any other intervention back then, besides surgery, working on the exact day you want it to? And we are all girls for two generations."

"You were born on Juneteenth…"

"And my dad is from Texas; it has *been* celebrated there since the 1800s. Joy and January were born on New Year's Eve and New Year's Day. Faith was born on Easter like her mom, but they don't share a birthday since Easter moves around the calendar like a drunken floozy."

"Was Akiko, uh, Pumpkin born on Thanksgiving?"

She nodded, watching him absorb it all like a Sith Lord. The light bulb went off. "But she had a boy."

"I *KNOW!* Shocked the shit out of me," Ebony said, throwing her hands up in the air. "I guess the blessing doesn't really care about gender. But it does care that he was born…"

He was leaning in so hard his leg was on her thigh, and he

knew he looked like a gossiping fool, but he was intrigued beyond measure.

"Today."

"No!"

"Yes! In Australia, no less."

"So it is only American holidays?"

She shrugged. "I guess? He's the first baby born from our generation, so not a lot of data to test."

"This is an incredible story, Bea would love to have it—"

"NO. Once people find out, they accuse us of doing it on purpose, and men become obsessed with having a 'Holiday Baby' to prove something to themselves or whatever. It's been dangerous for us, so we agreed to stop telling people until we were really sure about them. My aunts too. You'd be surprised how competitive people, men, get. Then there's the Holiday Trust we all pay into that supports each other when one of us starts a family. My grandparents started it, and we all contribute a percentage of our income. You get a payout when you have a child. Eric was obsessed with it to the point Joy changed her birth control because she was worried he'd tamper with her pills."

She slapped her hand over her mouth. "I wasn't supposed to say that. That is ninety-nine percent speculation on my part just off of things she'd said from time to time. Don't say anything."

He laughed and shrugged, "Who am I going to tell? It sucks she didn't feel safe in her own home."

"Seriously. Casually throwing out 'Imma get you pregnant' is a threat, especially in this country and as a Black woman."

"Is it a lot of pressure having this kind of family history? How do you hide it? Is that how you got your house?"

Ebony started to speak, then stopped and blinked up at him. "You believe me."

"It's extraordinary, but why lie? To me of all people, who can run all that through our info systems?"

"Eric didn't believe Joy until she told him about the trust."

"Eric is a punk-ass bitch."

He was gifted with more copper and a laugh that lit up the street. Her laugh. It was musical, holding notes to a refrain that was both familiar and new. He wanted to write a symphony with the sounds of her joy. The thought was as jarring as it was comforting.

Ebony looked past him, and a line appeared between her brows. He turned to see a brotha with long locs carrying a small duck wearing a bowtie stride confidently up Ebony's walk.

Well, that's not something you see every day.

The closer he got, the more tense Ebony became.

"You have got to be fucking kidding me," she said under her breath.

That's when it clicked. *PlayStation/Laundry/Duck Dude.* He rubbed Ebony's arm.

"Sit up a little, Ebee."

Malcolm slid forward in the swing, resting his arms open-handed on his legs. He scanned the street for anyone who didn't fit the scene or who lingered, and after determining Duck Dude to be alone, did a brief scan of him. His extra smedium, hot ass dress shirt and slacks left little room for a piece. He looked him directly in the face and let his eyes do the communicating.

Duck Dude slowed.

Smart.

Then he glanced at Ebony and kept coming.

Stupid.

"Aye, bruh, nah."

Ebony jumped a bit at the bass in his voice.

Duck Dude stopped on the walk. "What?"

"Get on with that, she already told you."

Duck Dude sucked his teeth, and with a bravery that didn't quite reach his eyes, took another step. Now Malcolm was irritated.

So he stood. Slowly. Allowing his size to unfurl in the most dramatic fashion because fools like this always fell for the dramatics.

Falling back a step, Duck Dude flicked his nose. "Oh, so you the new man? Ol' Michael B. Jordan Creed lookin' ass."

At Malcolm's silence, he shifted.

"I came to apologize, and I brought you a gift, Ebony."

He tried to look around Malcolm at her. Instead, Malcolm matched his movement, blocking his access to her.

She doesn't need to be dealing with this bullshit.

"No thank you!" Ebony said from behind him.

Malcolm raised an eyebrow.

Another teeth suck, then the save face look up and down and dude spun on his heel in his dress shoes and walked off. He gave the little duck a kiss on the top of its head as he put it in the front seat of the car.

"That was sweet; he actually cares for the duck."

"Maybe he needs to date ducks instead."

Ebony chuckled, then sighed dramatically. "Tell me you have a duck-toting one-night stand somewhere in your archives, or I'm going to feel very weird."

Malcolm thought for a minute. "No, but I had a night with a woman who claimed to be the reincarnated soul of Cleopatra."

"Well, that's just exotic and mysterious. I can see a long night in a canopy bed in Cairo…"

"Ebee, it was in a third-floor walk up in Brooklyn and her mattress was on the floor. The sistah came, said goodnight, then grabbed an ankh and staff off her nightstand like one grabs a teddy bear."

Ebony looked at him for a long minute, and when she saw he was serious, she fell out laughing, giving him more copper than he could hold and enough notes for a song.

Ebony stood with her hands on her hips as she looked for the extra camp chairs for even more Holiday-Jones relatives. She turned around when he closed the door behind him.

"Malcolm, no. No more illicit licks. I cannot leave a snail trail as I walk through the family cookout."

He took a step toward her. And she took a step back. He noticed her breathing kicked up a notch.[1]

"I just want to sing Happy Birthday to you before everyone else."

"Yeah, right."

He took another step toward her. And she took a step back. Her fingers played with her dress hem, absentmindedly lifting it.

"That fucking dress is going to make me lose my mind. Just let me sing Happy Birthday and give you your gift, Sweet Ebee."

He pulled a small box wrapped in red and white polka-dotted paper from his pocket and handed it to her.

The smile she gave him was so big and bright it lit his entire soul. How a man could look at that smile and not do everything in his power to *keep* her smiling was lost on him.

She accepted the gift and played with the bow. "Thank you, you didn't have to get me anything."

---

1. All I by Jill Scott

"I was raised better than that. You've met my mother."

She laughed again and looked up at him through her lashes. "Okay, Mal, you can sing me one round of Happy Birthday—"

"While I bounce you on my dick."

She burst out laughing, then covered her mouth, looking behind him at the garage door. He stepped forward again, and she kept taking steps back until he could barely make out her features in the dark corner of the garage.

"One round. Happy Birthday. And you better make me come."

"Challenge accepted."

AT SOME POINT EBONY MUST HAVE PUT ON FRESH UNDERWEAR, WHICH was a disappointment because he liked the idea of her bare under her fantastic dress granting him easy access, but one quick yank and her barrier was removed. She reached for the zip of his shorts, pulling him out and gently caressing him, flicking his piercing causing him to hiss in pleasure.

Ebony took the condom out of his hand and rolled it down his length, all the while never taking her eyes off of him, a playful glint in her barely visible eyes. "One. Round."

He nodded, grinned, and bent, reaching his arms between her legs and hooking them behind her knees. "Hold on to my shoulders, Sweet Love."

She moved with some hesitation, and his alarm bells went off. He stopped immediately to check in.

"Are you okay? Are you still good with this? There is no pressure, Sweetheart, you understand me?"

"Yeah, but I'm heavy, Mal."

Ah.

He worked out to keep himself strong and safe, yes. But he also worked out so he could deliver pleasure in a variety of ways.

"I promise Ebee, nothing about you is too heavy for me."

He lifted her in one move, her legs over his upper arms, and balanced her opening at the tip of his dick. Slowly he slid her down, inch by inch, then raised her slightly before sliding her down a little more, working himself into her. He carefully monitored her reactions, sensitive to when she held her breath, when she sucked breath in at a sensation, when she released a breath as pressure eased.

When he had her fully seated, she let out a low, heavy groan. He bit his lip against the sensation of her wrapped around him, her softness yielding to his opposite.

"One round of having me folded like an ornamental crane," she panted with a smile.

"You feel so good, Ebee baby." She clenched her inner muscles, and he swore deep. Sweat broke out across his skin, and she blew a cool breath against the droplets. The act caused goosebumps to break out down his neck, shoulders, back, and arms.

"A single breath from you is almost sending me over. One good round of Happy Birthday before you reduce me to a fucking puddle at your feet," he growled out.

Now, while he had agreed on one round only, he hadn't agreed on which version of Happy Birthday he'd sing so when he started bouncing her on him to the opening lines of the Stevie Wonder version that clocks in at over five minutes, he caught her off guard.

Her eyes lit up, and that copper smile, barely visible in the dark, took on a distinct lusty filter, and he wished he could see it in full light. That kind of smile, that kind of heat deserved every good thing, and he was committed to giving it to her.

Malcolm and Ebony locked in on each other, in words and deed. She allowed him to pleasure her, encouraging him softly. She gently laughed with him when it became harder to concentrate and he mixed up and improvised lyrics. And she was free and trusting in his arms, and he did not take a single fucking thing for granted.

She was sharing her body, her time, her family, her humor, her trust...

"Let go when you're ready, baby, I've got you," he gritted out, holding back his own release.

"With. Me." She groaned out as she let go, lighting up. Her body squeezed tight, a deep sacred moan releasing as she convulsed in his arms. Whatever she asked for, he felt it an honor in his soul to do it, and so he let go, exchanging energy and breath with her as he stretched her inner walls with all of him.

♪♪ "Happy birthday to me... happy birthday to me... happy biiiiirthday..." ♪♪

At Ebony's quiet voice, Malcolm looked up from her cousin telling him about her run-in with Beyonce's cousin's nail tech or something. She was setting out plastic forks and small dessert plates with a little smile on her lips as she sang Stevie Wonder's version of Happy Birthday under her breath. Ebony was near enough and the ambient music low enough that he caught her.

She paused as if she felt his eyes on her. Glancing up, she looked around and, spotting him, gave him an eyebrow raise before going back to what she was doing.

"What I want to know is why you lied?!"

Ebony's head popped up at the loud voice, and he followed

her eyes. Faith and an older woman who looked just like her were in a heated conversation.

"Oh boy, Auntie Easter is on one." Ebony's cousin shared.

Damn, what was this woman's name again? He never forgot a name, but was distracted when she introduced herself because Ebony had been dancing, and that's really all it took.

She leaned in and whispered conspiratorially, "Auntie Easter is on the Holiday side of the family. That side is *very* dramatic. It's all the women and their legend — well, never mind that. I hope they calm it down before Auntie Evie steps in."

He nodded noncommittally because he would not wade into those waters. He was a guest and would not get into family gossip. His momma raised him better than that, too, *and* she was in the kitchen.

"I'll put your name on my gift," Auntie Easter grumbled.

"I don't need you to; I can handle a gift to my cousin."

"Well, it needs to be a good one and you can't afford it," she leaned in and whispered in the loudest whisper ever, "unemployed."

Malcolm wondered if she was hard of hearing. She seemed to be concerned with appearances, yet she was loudly sharing her and her daughter's business.

"Wow, Mom."

"Hey Auntie, hey Faith girl! That is a gorgeous dress," Ebony slid up smiling. "Momma made tea cookies, Auntie Easter, do you want to—"

"I want to know if *you* knew about this." Easter seemed beside herself, and he'd never met her before.

Ebony's neck twisted and her eyebrow arched just slightly at her aunt's tone.

"Oh shoot," the Beyoncé cousin said under her breath. For their part, the rest of the guests and relatives did a decent job of pretending they weren't listening. His gaze locked on Anika's, and she gave him the "aight, Imma head out" look.

"Of course you knew, the secret keeper of the group. And you didn't think her *mother* needed to know that she was practically destitute?!"

"I don't tell business that's not mine."

"Oh, your business was everywhere already, Ebony. Don't be salty I archived it."

"Momma, I am not destitute. Please stop being so dramatic. And you know it was wrong to upload that video."

"Hey, hey," Joy said, coming through the backyard gate.

"Joy! Yay! Glad you could make it." Ebony made another attempt at a pivot from the drama.

Joy looked from Faith to Ebony. "What's up?"

"Ebony's been keeping secrets," Aunt Easter spat, "and that stops today."

"Why do you need to know everybody's business, East?" Ebony's Auntie Evie asked. "They aren't little girls anymore. Be happy they have each other and leave them alone until they need us."

"You would say that; your daughter's on the other side of the world. Doing Lord knows what in a raccoon tail."

"Yours is right next to you and is further away."

Damn. Points to Auntie Evie.

"Auntie Easter, this isn't the time—"

"Oh, what would you know about appropriate Ebony Elizabeth?"

Without a thought, Malcolm stood and made a beeline for the women. Ebony's father, who'd thankfully largely ignored him the entire day, stepped into his path.

"Let 'em be. This happens every once in a while; this is normal for the Holiday Sisters."

"No disrespect, Mr. Jones, but that doesn't make it right."

He stepped around him and was at Ebony's side immediately. "Ms. Easter, do you love your nieces?"

The question jarred the rude woman.

"Yes, of course!"

"Then why are you talking to them as if you don't?"

Easter glitched.

"No Ebony slander will be had today," Joy said. She pulled herself up to her full height and adjusted her locs. "I left Eric weeks ago. Ebony came and got me, throat punched Eric, let me stay here, didn't judge me. I told her because I *trusted* her."

"You left him?!" January asked, grinning, as she walked in with an armful of paper plates, napkins, and takeaway boxes from Armellos. "Sorry I'm late, E." She leaned in and kissed Ebony on the cheek, and Malcolm clocked a hickey on her neck before Ebony did a small double take and smoothly adjusted January's collar.

"Joy, really? You're home?" January asked.

The sisters shared a look while Faith took January's packages, seizing the opportunity to leave her mother's orbit. The various other relatives, including "the uncles" around the yard, nodded and grumbled their approval.

"And I'm not on the other side of the world, I'm right here because it's Ebony's birthday, and she doesn't judge me either and she made sure I had a beautiful place to stay with everything I need for my son," Pumpkin said from the back door. "Nicholas."

The entire backyard fell silent.

Pumpkin held her head higher and reached behind her, picking Nicky up. He looked around, yawned, and waved.

In shock, the family waved back at the giggly little one.

"I've got a grand baby?" Auntie Evie asked, stunned.

Collectively, the whole yard took a breath and started talking over each other excitedly.

HE PULLED OUT THE SMALL CARROT CAKE CUPCAKE WITH A CANDLE from behind his back.

"Oh, my gosh, how did you get that?! I literally just told you it was my favorite like five minutes ago."

"Armello's delivers, remember? Make a wish."

Ebony looked around at the family gathered, including Auntie Easter, and smiled.

"*I love you and I'm sorry again,*" she mouthed. Ebony nodded and winked.

"I know you're not supposed to say it out loud, but... I wish to see *everyone* right here next year. Ready to blow out the candles with me, Nicky? Ok go!"

"WHAT'S 48 AND SWEET?" EBONY READ ALOUD. SURROUNDED BY gifts and cards, her mother sat close, carefully recording the giver and the gift for Thank You cards. When she opened his gift, she smirked and read the sticky note attached to the single piece of Chuckle Taffy candy in the box.

"Well, it can't be me. I'm nowhere near forty-eight." He placed two identical red and white, polka dotted boxes in front of her. She let Nicky have a ball tearing all the paper away. When she read the box, she howled with laughter.

"FORTY-EIGHT POUNDS OF CHUCKLE TAFFY??!!"

HE UNWRAPPED ANOTHER CHUCKLE TAFFY.

"I can't believe you're stealing more candy. That was a gift."

"I think you can spare one."

She pointed to the candy wrappers all over their blanket. "You're going to crash."

"Look, this is hour thirty of the Holiday-Jones Juneteenth celebration. I need the sugar. Uncle Ron said he was leaving, and it took that man a half hour to get to the car."

She laughed, chewing on one herself. "Well, don't eat them all before the fireworks. Eating chewy candy, gum, or crunchy snacks can help regulate your sensory input..."

"How did you know to do all this?" Her hair, now fully fro'd out from the day's busyness and... activities, filtered and disbursed the soft glow from the park's lights. She looked as magical as her family lineage suggested.

"I texted a friend who is on your side of things. He said fireworks can trigger a lot of photojournalists, especially if they've been in conflict zones. I looked up ways to reduce its impact since you insisted on staying," she hit him with an exasperated look, "and found these sensory tools. Candy, noise-canceling headphones, visually dampening the brightness."

She shrugged like it were easy. It was a moment he had dreamed about without remembering it.

He saw others. It was his job, his calling, his passion. He stood in the shadows, on the periphery, blending in with his surroundings, a witness to and for the world. Being unseen was required and comfortable.

Malcolm didn't know *he* needed to be seen until she did. He didn't know he needed to be cared for in this way, or that it was possible until she did, and it unlocked something in him.

"I haven't seen fireworks in two years now."

She turned to him, giving him her full attention. Families

milled about, all moving closer to the best spots, but Ebony had set up a blanket underneath a set of trees that filtered much, but not all of the night sky.

He didn't know how he was going to react, but he wanted to try for her. When she mentioned it was her favorite part of her birthday, and knowing how much his mom loved fireworks, he decided he would stay. He looked across the small pond in Ebony's neighborhood park to where the lingering members of the Holiday-Jones clan gathered. He could just make his mother out, comfy in a pop-up camp chair, snuggled in a furry throw Ebony brought over for her.

Malcolm was just going to raw dog the PTSD, but Ebony saw him, researched and gathered materials when she could have been doing line dances with her cousins and loving on her nephew.

Her efforts moved him to his very core. He couldn't believe his luck or blessings that someone so good showed up twice in the most unexpected places. He took her hand in his, swallowed, and started again.

"I haven't seen fireworks in two years. The last time I was on the ground, my lung collapsed, watching one of my closest friends bleed out. He glanced down at her, then back at the crowd ahead.

"The blood on the camera is mine. Most people don't know that. Most people also don't know, and I hope they never learn, what it's like to not be able to tell the difference between fireworks and gunshots. Not just that night, but every night since. I laid there, begging Justin to blink his eyes for me. And telling him to hold on because help was coming.

The shots, the fireworks, went on forever. I watched him cradle that child and kiss his head. There are nights I dream I'm still asking him to blink his eyes for me. And he does a couple of times, and then he just stops."

He reached over with his free hand and brushed a tear just as it escaped.

"And the crazy part is I got awards and accolades for a shot I don't even remember taking, losing my friend in a way I can't forget. It's so automatic to me. All I remember is wanting people to know how he took care of that kid, because I didn't think I was going to live long enough to tell them. Somewhere along the way, someone got my camera to the office. And they ran with it. They didn't give Justin's wife a heads up, his family. They were on the other side of the world seeing him on the news, social media, like everyone else."

"He came here to hang out with me because we'd just lost Dad. We were out doing 'real American things.' Nothin' more American than a mass shooting." Malcolm looked down and shook his head. "His wife, Lauren, still hasn't forgiven me. I haven't either."

Ebony didn't say a word. She didn't try to comfort or smooth away his pain, his confessions. She simply handed him noise-canceling headphones, passed him a Chuckle Taffy, and lay back on the blanket, pulling him with her.

Malcolm lay there with her watching twinkles of color through the canopy of trees. And while his heart rate did increase, and he had a few phantom pains in long-healed holes in his body, he didn't have the feeling of overwhelming dread wash over him.

Rationally, he knew it was the techniques he had learned in therapy that helped him keep his breathing even. He also knew that time itself had worked to dampen his reactions.

But he had to acknowledge that because of Ebony, the muffled booms of the fireworks felt less intense. It wasn't a cure. No, he would not lay that responsibility on her. It was simply that the experience was better with her. She probably couldn't hear him over the noise, but he said it anyway.

"Happy birthday, Ebee."

"YOU KNOW what I'm stuck on?" January said quietly, leaning back in her chair with a mimosa hovering near her lips, the morning sun making her glossy dark hair shine even more. "The fact that Ebony really tried to casually have that man come through yesterday like we don't have eyes."

Faith let out a loud laugh.

Across the yard, Malcolm helped her dad carry folding chairs back to the garage, his sleeves pushed up just enough to show off his tattoos and make the Holiday women suddenly interested in post-party cleanup. Ebony was enjoying her cousins and the view following one of the most eventful Juneteenth they'd had to date. Her mom was at home nursing a sore body, which meant everyone could move at a more leisurely pace.

Next year, we're hiring help.

Joy followed their line of sight and whistled low. "That is some peak nineties fine."

"Exactly!" January slapped Joy's arm. "Like Ms. Mabeline had him marinating in cocoa butter and R&B videos as a child."

"Dark skin. Tall. Observant and quiet, but can carry on a conversation. Built like a truck with skin that says he drinks water on purpose," Pumpkin said as she blew another set of bubbles for Nicky, sending the toddler into giggles as he chased them and Aunt Evie ran with him. She was head over heels in love with her grandson.

"And those arms?" Joy fanned herself dramatically. "Ebony Elizabeth Jones, I beg."

Ebony rolled her eyes. "Y'all are so irritating."

"No," Faith corrected. "You are irritating. Because the last time I saw him, you were basically telling him to go fuck himself."

"Well, now, she's doing it for him," Joy added, giggling and ducking a playful swat from Ebony. "She's helpful like that."

"It's uncomplicated. We are work colleagues who enjoy each other physically."

All four cousins looked at her in synchronized disbelief.

"Girl."

"Be serious."

January nodded toward him softly. "That man looked ready to fight Auntie Easter on your behalf after 'working' with you approximately seventeen business days."

"It's been longer than that, and he did not look ready to fight her," Ebony argued.

"He absolutely did," Faith said. "Calmly. Respectfully. With diction."

Joy snorted. "The 'Ms. Easter, do you love your nieces?' almost took me out."

January pressed a hand to her chest dramatically. "'Then why are you talking to them like you don't?' BABY."

Faith shook her head. "See that right there? That's not casual sex behavior."

Ebony folded her arms tighter. "He was just trying to de-escalate."

"No," Joy said immediately. "He was protecting you, and it was nice to see a man do that."

Joy had barely come out of the bedroom for weeks, but today she had time to roast Ebony's situation. Ebony didn't know whether to be offended or ecstatic.

"He embarrassed Auntie Easter so bad she rebooted like a frozen laptop," January added.

Faith nearly choked laughing. "She really did glitch. Momma was remorseful all night. About y'all. Perfect Faith didn't get jack but a reminder to keep trying to find work. I don't know what's gotten into her lately; she's more on than usual."

"Damn, Faith," Pumpkin said. "I should have popped out of the back door sooner."

Even Ebony laughed at that one. "That was dramatic as hell. I love your flair."

Pumpkin grinned.

"Hey Ebee, do you want this in the garage or the basement?" Malcolm called.

"Basement, please."

Malcolm smiled and gave her the thumbs up then tucked a heavy table under each arm.

January pointed immediately. "See? You smiling too hard."

"I am not."

"You like him."

"I like having sex with him, and we work well together," Ebony corrected.

Faith stared at her for a long moment. "Ebony, that man had tea cookies and hibiscus tea, Grandma's champagne and generational dysfunction in the same afternoon."

"And he handled it well," January added.

Ebony laughed despite herself, shaking her head. She would *not* tell them she revealed the Holiday family lore.

Faith looked back toward Malcolm, who was now swinging Nicky around while listening politely to Ebony's father tell him some long story with excessive hand gestures.

"He fits," she said quietly.

Joy nodded. "Like… naturally."

Ebony's heart kicked over, and she promptly halted it with a scoff.

"Y'all created an entire relationship in your heads because the man has sexy tattoos and a savior complex."

"The tats opened the door," January replied. "His character walked through it."

Faith lifted her glass toward Ebony.

"And baby," she said, "that man looks at you like he's already made up his mind. When are *you* going to?"

Ebony cast her desktop screen to the large flat television in her office, interrupting the constant news stream. She was finally flipping through the trove of photos Malcolm sent over, and she'd made up her mind alright. She hated the shots he picked for her. Maybe not hated, but they were underwhelming.

She sat on the floor with a sigh that was loud enough to alert Pumpkin on her third trip past her door as she paced with a fussy, super sleepy Nicky.

"What's up?" she asked as she poked her head in the doorway.

"Take a look at these photos for the article."

Pumpkin came in, doing that momma swing-bounce.

Ebony slowly moved through the pics, and every so often Pumpkin would make a small reactive noise.

"Those are really good. He captured so much emotion and atmosphere. The men look... human. Complex, and you don't even see most of their faces. Malcolm has an incredible eye."

Ebony slipped over to the next batch. Mainly of her.

"You look pretty. Very professional. Your skin looks amazing, too. Where are the rest?"

"Rest of what?"

"You. Those all look like really nice photos for a new website."

"EXACT—" Ebony grimaced. "Sorry," she whispered as Nicky sleepily lifted his head for a second before he passed back out. "That's what I'm talking about."

"Are you sure that's all of them?"

"ARE YOU SURE THAT'S ALL OF THEM?" JOY ECHOED PUMPKIN A HALF hour later.

Ebony had already checked with Malcolm, and he confirmed he'd sent over his selections. So she shrugged with a more than disappointed nod.

"Oh."

"He doesn't respect me, my work... I may not be solving world hunger, but I'm discussing *real* things. I thought he understood, or at least supported it."

Ebony was so... disappointed. Embarrassed. Of course he didn't take her work seriously when she was offering her ass to him all willy nilly; when she was so open. Her hopes for the project crashed. It would still be good, because she was a beast with a pen and his male subject shots made up for the shiny veneer offerings of her.

"I'm so stupid."[1]

"Have you talked to him?" Joy asked.

She shook her head.

"That's what I asked. It can be worked out. He can still switch out photos before y'all submit to the editor, right?"

She shrugged. She felt like a balloon someone had slowly let all the air out of. Not popped, that was a sudden explosion with remnants. No, she was the saggy, misshapen vessel after being overfilled with hot air.

"Don't look like that, E. I'm sure there's a reasonable explanation," Pumpkin urged. "Right, Joy?"

Joy looked at Ebony, a small, sad, knowing smile on her face. "When someone shows you who they are and what they think of you the first time, believe them."

EBONY CLIMBED OUT OF HER GREEN VW BUG, AND THE DAMP SUMMER heat smacked her in the face. Sweat formed at her temples and started a race down the side of her face. Snatching a scrunchie off her arm, she pulled her hair up in a puff before grabbing her bag and trudging up Malcolm's steps. He'd wanted to meet at his house to prep for the meeting with Bea, and she'd come prepared.

Of course she had her notes, transcripts, etc.; she also wore a plain pair of cut-off jean shorts, an oversized tee, and no make-up. And underneath, for extra insurance in case hormones and stupidity took over, she wore her giant period panties that had elastic hanging from the waistband and her raggediest bra - she'd repaired the underwire. She didn't know

---

1.   Fool's Gold by Jill Scott

how to sew too well, so it had random red thread and awkward, clumsy stitches along the breastbone.

As she waited for him to come to the door, she steeled her spine, guarded her heart, and wiped the sweat off the back of her knees.

Jeez, it's almost as hot as corn sweat season.

She waited another moment before ringing the bell again. Malcolm's truck was in the driveway and his windows were open, so she sent a quick "I'm here" text. Finally, when she was ready to give up and run to the air-conditioned protection of her car, she heard movement and voices coming closer.

"Seriously, Malcolm, the budget is negotiable, and if you come to Europe, we still have a free press, your mother has free healthcare, and you have a position worthy of your talent. You don't have to be in the field to do meaningful work, but you're above this clickbait content for young hoes."

"I'll think about it, John, and listen about the piece—"

Ebony didn't want to hear anymore. She turned on her heel and took her granny pantied, clickbait ass back to her car.

"Ebony, wait," Malcolm urged as he ran out onto the sidewalk in bare feet. "Ouch, shit, this sidewalk is hot. Ooh. Sorry about that, I was on a call and making lunch. Please come in, it's hot as hell out here."

You have a job to do, and you can buy a couple of new bras if this project continues.

Putting a smile on her face, she nodded. Even though her sadness and disappointment weighed down her steps. ~~She had worked through heartbreak before.~~

Scratch that. She had worked with disappointing co-workers before. Her heart had nothing to do with this.

EBONY'S VIBE was off from the moment he opened the door. She was guarded and had given him polite, pleasant smiles all afternoon. Not the copper he'd come to ~~love~~, like very much.

He wondered if she was angry because she had to wait for him to open the door. It *was* hot as hell outside. Or maybe she was just tired. Seeing Ebony, even on a low-energy day, brought a smile to his face, and he tried everything to make her smile as she sat across from him, going through her notes.

She was on point with her suggestions on which photos would work with different pieces of copy. And her analysis of the project so far was thorough, and Bea was going to love it. As he watched her search for a notation, he realized what was probably bothering her.

Her birthday party had been one of the wildest, funniest, sexiest, most wholesome, and fulfilling days he'd had in a long time. And it was probably affecting her as much as it was affecting him. And if it was, then she wanted to have the same conversation he did about an exclusive relationship with each other.

He offered her a piece of Chuckle Taffy candy, and when she reached for it, he held it and her eyes longer than he'd gotten her entire visit.

"Ebee, do you think you could see us as more than the label we've assigned?"

Ebony released the candy, leaving him holding it. "I appreciate your interest, but I don't think it would work." [1]

She was polite even as she dropped a mallet on his face.

It wasn't as if the rug had been pulled out from under him. It was as if the *world* had been. His heart stuttered to a stop, and when it started beating again, it was in his gut.

He replayed every moment from her birthday like he had done every moment in the couple of days since. He left that night with a gentle kiss on her forehead. Her copper smile was the last thing he saw as he pulled off to drive his mother home.

What had happened between then and now? Among the millions of thoughts racing through his mind, one was clear: he wanted to make sure he didn't say something out of emotion that could damage things between them further. So, he schooled his face into the same pleasant, benign smile she had been giving him all afternoon.

"Why wouldn't we work? Our chemistry is undeniable. I've never had the kind of fun I have with you, and... I miss you when we aren't together. I think we should explore what we could be."

A flash of something — disappointment? Flittered across her face before it returned to all polite business.

"You don't really want to know, and I don't want to mess up the great working relationship we have. Things went too far on my birthday because 'uncomplicated' is really starting to

---

1.   Pick Up Your Feelings by Jazmine Sullivan

look complex." Ebony packed up her notes, careful of her annotation tabs, and sent her backups to the cloud.

Another ACME cartoon-size mallet blow. "Seriously? Ebony, I want to know."

"You don't do rewinds, remember?" She leaned against the doorframe, holding her notes close to her like a shield.

Malcolm leaned in, eyes serious. "That's different. We were never in a relationship. Not like the men you're interviewing."

Her face was resolute, even angry. "Hookups are one thing; I was down for that...while it served its purpose."

He leaned further in, placing his arm above her head on the door frame and using his hand to tilt her chin up to him. "What's changed, Ebony? I also said I don't do dramatics or mess, and I had the most exciting holiday of my life. The best time. With you. Why won't you give us a chance?"

"My family is not entertainment, and I'm not interested in exploring a genuine relationship between us because you don't respect me."

Malcolm was floored. Straightening, he took a step back, then another. He fast-forwarded through their weeks together for anything remotely disrespectful. Aside from some early scoffing and ribbing, which she returned, things between them had been great, he thought.

"Ebony, I don't know what I did, but I —"

"Every photo you've taken of me, I am gorgeous. Poised. Damn near flawless."

"I thought you liked the photos I've shown you so far."

"I did and do. They're flattering."

"So, what's the problem?"

"Flattering and flat. I don't need an ego boost. I expected the same thing you gave to the male subjects. Something...real. Photos that capture the truth of who I am in those moments, something with more depth, unless, as I suspect, your bias tells you there's nothing there. Which means you don't respect me and you for damn sure don't respect my work. Which, honestly, for me, is worse."

Malcolm instantly got pissed. He'd captured her and her 'great loves' exactly as they were. That was his job, and he was damn good at it.

She slipped out from under him and moved toward the door. "When this is all said and done, you'll publish more serious, Prater Prize winning work, the men in my life will have truth, whether or not they like it, and I'll have some great fucking headshots. Just another pretty girl in her vapid search for love. Or how was it put? Oh, yeah, 'clickbait content for young hoes.'"

MALCOLM STRUGGLED FOR SEVERAL REASONS.

One was with his ego. He was Malcolm Kingsley Knight, and he knew his work was good. The shots were crisp. Rarely, if ever, did he receive negative feedback like what Ebony provided.

He went back and forth on whether to change what they had discussed submitting, but that didn't feel right either.

Second, the idea that Ebony was putting forth work that she didn't one hundred percent believe in killed him. Compound the fact that it was his work? He had no words.

And finally, and the biggest reason he was struggling, the thought that kept him spinning in his bed all night was: she didn't think they had a future together.

It was the first time in a long time, maybe since his mother was diagnosed with end-stage renal disease, that the work came second to a personal relationship. There was an ache that spread out from the center of him when her eyes revealed the depth of her hurt.

"Fuck."

He called Mello over, and after explaining everything, Mello gave him solid advice.

"Listen, man, in the end, your integrity is on the line. If the work you selected was the best for the assignment, then you have to stand by that, regardless of pressure from your personal life. But if there is another reason, you need to hold yourself accountable."

They worked on Malcolm's puzzle some more. Dozens of black cats with glowing yellow eyes judged him the more correct pieces they added.

"As far as Ebony goes," Mello started. "I love the woman, but that whole family is a bunch of damn sirens with their sweet smiles and soft voices calling men to smash themselves against rocks in tribute."

Despite his own troubles, he recognized Mello's lament for what it was: yearning. He thought about that hickey January had alongside the takeout from Mello's at Ebony's party. "Any recent developments with January?"

"None that I want to share."

I bet she got more than her order the other day. Wait 'til I tell Ebony...

Oh. Right.

Damn.

Later, after Mello left, Malcolm stayed up late flipping back and forth through the raw photos he had of Ebony. It just didn't feel right to use them. That was his professional and personal judgement.

So, with hesitation, he forwarded what they worked and agreed on, closed his laptop, and went to bed. As he settled in for the night, he thought about Ebony and the way she felt in his arms, the beauty of her coming apart by his hands, the spiritual connection that he was sure she felt in those quiet moments together...

He slept like shit. Tossing and turning, every time awakening not to his own pleas for Justin to blink, but Ebony's eyes, Ebony's smile, Ebony's hips when she danced, the way she looked at him when she realized he believed her, the cute little way she always pretended to be exasperated when she passed a Chuckle Taffy wrapper to him.

She haunted his dreams, and he vowed that tomorrow he'd fix things.

MALCOLM WATCHED EBONY ON SCREEN FOR ANY OVERT SIGN THAT SHE was as torn up as he was. It was in vain. Ebony was a pro, and she was just as composed, just as prepared as on any other workday. He studied her and her office throughout their video conference with Bea instead of paying attention to what the editor was saying.

The area in frame of her camera was neat and stylish. Only he knew it was barely controlled chaos just outside the frame. Her hair, each curl defined and carefully arranged. Only he knew what it looked like after a day of summer heat, fun, and sex. That it reached skyward in a curly halo crown that framed her face. She schooled her face into polite, engaged professionalism, but he knew what she looked like when a moment or a joke caught her off guard and she lit up, shining so brightly she could replace sunlight.

"Malcolm?"

"Yes?"

Bea looked at him, and he could feel her suspicion through the screen.

"I asked what you thought of the intern, Anika?"

"Oh, right. She's excellent, fits right in, very professional, she makes great suggestions and is willing to take direction, asks how she can improve…"

"Yes, that's what Ebony said already. Anything substantive you can add?"

Shit. He glanced at Ebony's little box on his screen where she sat quietly, looking like she was writing something down.

"Uh, she's afraid of spiders."

Ebony's professional facade broke for a split second before she got it firmly back into place.

"Yes, well, I don't think she will have to worry about that at the London office. They don't cover many spider stories."

Bea cleared her throat and exhaled slowly. "Okay," she said. "The interviews work."

Ebony blinked. "That's it? Just work?"

"They're sharp, uncomfortable, honest in places I didn't expect." Bea nodded as she wrote something down. "Your interview with Brian was stilted, but you loosened up considerably with Diego. What an interesting, charismatic, toxic man. I hope you have more exes like him."

Ebony double blinked while Bea moved right on. "I like when you are more conversational. It really draws the readers and listeners in; you feel like you're viewing two real people in a genuine relationship versus an interrogation. Keep that angle for the next three. Now visuals. First, Malcolm, I love the title *"The Five Loves of Ebony Jones."* It's fun.

"There are some really captivating images here…" she shared her screen.

Brian from behind as he whispered in her ear. Ebony leaning away to where most of her face is out of frame.

Diego's hands covered in clay and his mid-torso highlighted by the sun as he tipped beads into Ebony's hands.

"These are strong shots. Complicated shots. Human shots. We don't have enough strong shots of Ebony."

Bea flipped quickly through shots of Ebony in the files. "She's not in the same emotional language as everyone else in the project."

Malcolm resisted the urge to scrub his hands down his face. Keeping it passive and professional, he nodded. "Understood."

"You overshoot, so I know there is something in the outtakes we can use. Find them and have them to me by tomorrow EOD. Social teasers start immediately after, before Ebony's video gets stale."

She wrote something else down on her tablet. "All right, that's everything. Ebony, I look forward to your next interview. We have...safe love, the love that almost broke you, and your almost forever." Bea looked at her. "Keep being honest."

"Can I come over? I need to apologize."

The low hum of Ebony's refrigerator and the soft, rhythmic tapping of rain against her windows filled the silence as they stood across from each other, the kitchen island a physical representation of the emotional barrier between them. The island smelled of bleach and other cleaning products.

"I'm sorry for interrupting your cleaning."

Ebony was barefoot, arms folded, watching him as if she were still deciding whether he'd earned the right to be there. She didn't appear angry anymore—something deeper than that. Disappointed. It hurt to see it, stand across it and know it was his fault.

"I did that for you. The cat slips in here sometimes."

She did that for me when she already had a full day. He felt worse, and he didn't think it was possible.

Malcolm struggled with how to start. Not because he didn't know how to apologize, but because he was afraid of making it worse.

"I need you to look at something," he said, voice even, careful not to push.

She lifted her brow slightly. "Okay."

He pulled a small stack of prints from his bag. There was something weightier about having the photos in hand, and something shifted in the room. Ebony hesitated before taking them, like she were bracing for more disappointment.

The first image: Her, alone. Waiting. Her face is pensive as she chews on her lip, a hand on her lower belly like she's steadying herself.

The second — After the interview, after Brian left. Anika's hands in frame reaching for the mic and Ebony's shoulders slumped, eyes closed. Processing.

The third — Her reflection in a mirror, Diego's hands visible holding up the mirror. Ebony's earth-toned, long skirt pushed down at the waist, her creamy top held high and tucked under her chin as she examined her stretch marks, comparing them to a photo in her hand. Her belly, rounded with an overhang, exposed, and her face was full of wonder and pride.

Ebony paused on that one a little longer than the others, but she didn't say anything.

Each photo peeled something back. Not unflattering, but unprotected. Honest. The version of her that exists in the moments, without filter. There's frustration, there's a wistfulness, there's a range of emotion that hadn't been in any of the photos before.

Ebony exhaled slowly, eyes still on the photos. "Why?"

Because I'm falling in love with you.

"Because they're different," he said. "And once they're out there, you don't get to control how people engage with them."

And I can't protect you.

She looked up at him then, really looked. Like she heard what his heart spoke.

"I've seen what happens," he continued. "People don't just look at images like these. They dissect them. Project onto them. Decide what they mean about you—your mood, your attitude, your worth."

Her expression tightened, and she crossed her arms again, tighter this time. "So instead you decided for me what I could handle."

Malcolm exhaled, nodding. "Yeah. I did."

"I thought I was protecting you," he added. "But I hear you now. That wasn't my call to make. And I wish you'd heard the rest of the call where I told him his misogynoir was showing. I took the call as a favor to a friend; I have no desire to work with someone like that."

Silence stretched between them, but it's not the same silence as before. It's less heavy, making him feel more hopeful.

Ebony looked back down at the photos, flipping through them again—slower this time.

"You really saw all of this?" she asked quietly.

"From the beginning."

She studies two images in particular—the stretch mark one and the one where she's putting a protective distance between herself and Brian. "You didn't think I could handle being seen like this?" she asked.

"I thought the world couldn't handle you being seen like that without trying to tear it apart."

"That's not the same thing."

"I know that now."

Ebony arranged the stack on the counter, aligning the edges with precise movements. When she looked up again, her eyes are steady on him. "I was so... disappointed. And... hurt. And angry. I couldn't believe that's all you saw after seeing so much of me, of my life, of my family. I felt reduced and marginalized in my own story. All of me is worthy of being documented; you don't get to decide what I can handle."

Malcolm nodded. "I understand. I apologize. It will never happen again. I wanted to... protect you."

Ebony shook her head and let out a sigh that sounded thirty-six years in the making.

"I am a brown-skinned, Black, fat woman. I am successful enough for people to enjoy humbling me. I have the nerve to have a platform, the nerve to have men who have loved me, the nerve to want and believe I deserve that good Sunday morning garden, forever love. I knew that all of those things could and will probably be vilified coming into this. I've lived in this body, in this world for thirty-six years," she threw out her arms in frustration.

"And while yes, knowing and experiencing the reactions will be different, I made the choice to do it and do it my way. When you stopped treating me as a human and just as a woman you liked to have sex with, you took that away from me. Don't you think I deserve to have my truth documented? What about other women like me? Women with less? With more? Fatter? Darker? Trans? This is my story, yes, but god, I hope it's bigger than me. That's what I'm aiming for and you said you were with me on it. That I could trust you."

She swiped at an errant tear in frustration, and he wanted to kick his own ass for hurting her. Her words landed violently, not because she was strident or forceful. She had every right to be. Her words exposed the reality of what he'd done, and it was so opposite of his intention. It shook him to his core. He maintained eye contact with her, unwilling to turn away from the pain of the moment.

"What can I do to make this right?"

"Don't edit me down to something easier for *them*," she flung her hand toward the window, "to digest."

"I won't."

Ebony held his gaze a second longer, weighing him. Taking a deep breath and slowly letting it out, she picked the stack up again and laid each photo on the counter side by side.

"These..." she said quietly, "these are the ones that matter."

Finally, they were both looking at the same version of her.

dead chickens

The wife somewhere watching this interview:
👁️⟷👁️ "SPIRITUALLY WHAT???"

This interview was basically:

Ebony: Let's discuss emotional growth.

First Love: Remember when you folded my boxers?

👀

"First Love" listing his dog before his wife told me EVERYTHING I needed to know.

MALCOLM FOUND Ebony sitting cross-legged in a flowy beige jumpsuit in the middle of her office, surrounded by even more chaos than before.

After their talk, things weren't immediately back to where they used to be, but Ebony engaged with him beyond polite work exchanges, and that was good enough for Malcolm, at least right now. His myopic decision damaged something fragile between them, something that even in its infancy was beautiful. It would take time to repair, and Malcolm was willing to do the work.

Her laptop balanced precariously near the edge of a stack of boxes she was using as a desk, and her phone buzzed every few seconds against the rug. Sticky notes, transcripts, empty tea packets, and Chuckle Taffy wrappers were littered across things like confetti.

Ebony herself looked somewhere between horrified and delighted.

"Well," Malcolm said from the doorway, "that expression usually means either critical acclaim or felony charges. Akiko let me in."

Without looking up, she pointed at him dramatically. "The internet thinks Brian is a serial killer."

Malcolm walked further into the room. "That feels excessive."

She slowly lowered the phone and stared at him. "He admitted to stealing my underwear to preserve my scent."

Malcolm paused, considering. "...You know what? That's fair."

Ebony barked out a laugh before immediately groaning and switching positions on the floor, tucking a pillow underneath her butt.

"Oh my God."

"What?"

She held her purple phone up to him. "Read that."

Malcolm took it from her and started reading aloud. *"Spiritually separated means his wife still files their taxes jointly."*

He snorted immediately. "Okay, that's funny."

Ebony rolled onto her stomach, burying half her face in a pillow. "I thought people would focus on the emotional labor discussion."

"They are."

"They're also making Professor X memes."

Malcolm sat on the floor beside her. "I mean, you did yell, 'Jean, no!' after that man came. That's the internet," Malcolm said. "You give them sociology, they make reaction GIFs."

Her phone buzzed again.

And again.

And again.

Malcolm glanced down. "How many notifications is that?"

"I stopped counting."

She finally sat back up, her 'fro disheveled and flat from the pillow. "The clips are everywhere. Somebody's already made a song out of the parts of the interview. *'Big dick, stretch me wide, and presto! Toes Pointed to the Sky'* is a trending sound."

Malcolm laughed immediately.

"It's not funny."

"It's a little funny."

"It already has ten thousand views."

"That's *hilarious*."

Ebony flicked a pen at him. It hit him in the chest and bounced off without phasing him.

"You know what the best part is?" she asked.

"What?"

She smiled at him with pride, and he was startled to see a bit of copper shining. "People are thirsting after your camera work."

He blinked once. "My camera work?"

"Yes. They thought the shot of me wiping my hand after Brian touched me was hilarious, but they keep talking about how you capture our body language and reactions without ever showing his face. "There are already a couple of think pieces on how you capture the tension that humanizes us both in 'top-tier visual storytelling.'"

Malcolm was deeply pleased that *she* was proud. "I'm glad you called me on my shit. I had no right to censor those moments of you."

"I've been thinking on it and appreciate where your heart was."

He felt a bit of relief.

"Even if your head was in your ass."

His head snapped up to look at her, but she was already back into her feed. She was a funny little thing.

She changed position again, exhaling. "I didn't expect this response."

"What did you expect?" He stretched out flat on his back, pulling his knees to his chest in a stretch.

"I don't know." She glanced down at her phone again. "Maybe people calling me bitter. Or messy."

"Some probably are."

"Yeah, but..." she hesitated. "Mostly women seem relieved."

Malcolm watched her carefully as she scrolled. "Read me one," he said quietly.

Ebony swallowed once before reading aloud. "'The labor line made me cry because I realized none of my exes remembered me outside of what I did for them.'"

She was quiet for a moment. Then she stood and pulled something off her corkboard and handed it to him, a pensive look on her face. "One and two are kinda happening," she whispered.

<u>Goals / Wanted Outcomes:</u>

1. Identify past healthy + unhealthy patterns of partnership for future forever love. (Am I the drama?)

2. Give resources, closure questions for readers. *give, not just receive*

3. ~~2.~~ Book deal.

4. ~~3.~~ Wrap this shit up so I can get back to Saturday brunches w/mimosas.

Malcolm leaned back slightly, nodding. "It is. That's a good thing, right?"

She nodded slowly. "I think so, but…"

He waited patiently for her to finish. The moment felt heavier than the conversation before, and Malcolm knew instinctively how he showed up in it would impact their relationship from that moment on.

"It's scary being on the verge of good things. Big things. Can I even maintain it? But I'm also scared of…" She looked around the room. "So many, many things. Everyone thinks I'm brave, but…Right now I feel like a big ol' chicken. And yet… it's exciting. I haven't felt this engaged with my work in a long time. Faith was right. I *was bored*."

"Brave chickens are the ones who were scared and crossed the road anyway," Malcolm said solemnly. "Though a lot of them are dead chickens now…"

Ebony paused for a second, and the moment he smirked, she started laughing again despite herself, the kind that stole her breath for a second.

Malcolm watched her quietly through it. God, he liked her

like this. Checking his feelings, he scrolled through his phone. "There are diagrams now explaining why a girthier penis helps."

"Shut. Up."

"One woman called you 'a professor of dick discourse.'"

Ebony screamed into a pillow.

Nicky came running into the office, and with a flying leap, tackled Ebony. "Auntie Neeeee!"

Ebony instantly wrapped him up in kisses and tickles. They played for a good ten minutes before Pumpkin came to take him to the park.

"You love having them here."

"Yeah, I do. I've always wanted a family; I'm trying to come to terms with it possibly looking different from what I thought."

After another hour of trawling through the discourse—something warm settled in his chest. Underneath all the viral clips and jokes and chaos, people had really understood her.

And judging from the relaxed look on Ebony's face, she realized it too.

THEY STROLLED FAR ENOUGH AWAY from the jazz concert where they could still hear the music, but it didn't interfere with their conversation or make Anika's job harder. Happy for a milder summer day, being outdoors with jazz music was exactly the place Isaiah felt most comfortable.

Sitting on the wide park bench, there was enough room for Ebony to turn and study Isaiah. He looked good. Broad and strong, Isaiah still kept his hair cut close, and was one of the few brothas that could pull off the no facial hair look. It was the cheekbones and the sharp jawline that did it. His tawny skin had the summer glow he always missed when winter in Ohio turned him into what he jokingly called a sugar cookie. And most importantly, there was a boyishness to him that just warmed her heart.

Still.

"How have you been?"

Isaiah chuckled a bit, glancing at her and rubbing his hands together in thought. "I've been better. I just went through a breakup. Mom transitioned and my baby girl is gaining a stepfather."

"Wow, Isaiah, that's a lot to handle at one time. Are you sure you want to do this?"

He shrugged. "It gives me something to do with my mind. And most of this...most of this is going to be okay. Mom didn't suffer. She went in her sleep, which is the best way you can go. Cassie's fiancé is a great guy. A teacher, loves Tiana like she were his..."

"But?" she prompted.

"She started calling him Dad-O."

"Did she start calling you Isaiah?"

"NO." He laughed, breaking some of the tension he was holding. "I'm still Daddy, but I never thought I'd be sharing the title. The first time I heard her call him that, it stopped me in my tracks and my heart dropped to my ankles. And between you and me, Dad-O sounds cooler."

"Yes, but you're the original; there is no replacing that. And she's four, her giving him a nickname like that shows she feels safe. And it's different, so she recognizes the two of you are different instead of a replacement."

He looked like he wasn't too sure. "You didn't ask to meet with me to talk about that stuff. How's all of this going for you?"

Ebony smiled slightly. "I care Isaiah. You're a good man, and you deserve all the good things."

He nodded some, then looked at her expectantly.

She raised a shoulder. "To answer your question. It's been an interesting season of my life."

"I bet. In your work life, you've always preferred to write about what's happening, not be the happening. I'm ready to do anything you need."

"What moments in our relationship do you remember as the happiest or most meaningful?"

Isaiah stretched his long legs out, his khakis neat and crisp, and thought for a moment. He smiled to himself. "I liked the small things. Cooking together, movie nights, just... being around each other without it needing to be anything big. And honestly, the few times you got me out of my comfort zone—those stuck with me too."

"Are you okay with sharing an example?"

"You really want specifics?" he asked with a small laugh, leaning back further and rubbing the back of his neck, thinking. "Okay... the salsa class."

She blinked, then immediately started laughing. "You hated that salsa class."

"I hated the first fifteen minutes of the salsa class."

"You were physically distressed."

"Because you signed us up without warning me, and then a woman named Pilar started yelling counts at me in Spanish while you spun around like you were born in Cuba."

She laughed harder at that, dropping her pen on the grass in front of them for a second. They both bent to grab it and almost bumped heads.

"Now you know I don't like you lifting a finger for labor, Ebony." He took a bandana out of his pocket, wiped off her pen and handed it back to her.

"Anyway, I was terrible," he continued, smiling despite himself. "Like, aggressively terrible."

"You kept apologizing to everyone you bumped into."

"I *did* bump into a lot of people."

"But you stayed."

He shrugged lightly. "You were having fun."

His answer came easy. Honest. Which is why Isaiah was so endearing.

"Remember afterward we ended up walking around for like two hours just talking. We had that really good beer at that hole in the wall."

"OH MY GOD with the bad cover band!"

"Yep."

Her smile softened at the memory. He looked down briefly before continuing.

"That was kind of your thing," he said. "You'd push me into something I never would've chosen myself... and half the time I ended up really glad you did."

They sat in companionable silence, slow jazz notes from the festival drifting lazily over them on gentle summer breezes.

"I think I felt more interesting around you," he admitted quietly. "Do you think I could've done anything differently that would've changed things between us?"

It was a question Ebony hadn't expected, but she should have. When she ended things with Isaiah, he was really hopeful for a reconciliation.

"Back then? I honestly don't know. I never wanted to change you, Isaiah. And what I was looking for at the time was different."

He nodded, his eyes thoughtful. She waited a moment before asking another question. The now melancholy jazz was an apt backdrop.

"What do you think I did well as a partner?"

"You were thoughtful. You paid attention. You remembered things that mattered to me. And you brought good energy—I didn't always match it, but I appreciated it."

"How did I make you feel loved or appreciated?"

He smiled at a memory, and when he made eye contact with her, there was deep emotion in his eyes that made her brace for the impact of what he was about to say.

"You saw me. The things I liked, or mentioned in passing,

you'd file away. They would show up again as a card, or a little gift, or even a meme. You always found ways to let me know you were thinking of me, and I never had to guess where I stood with you. Thank you for that."

Every so often Ebony wondered what her life would have been like with Isaiah. At the time she was almost one hundred percent certain she knew the predictability of the days, months, and years ahead. Now? She wasn't so sure.

"Thank you for saying that Isaiah, I appreciated you more than I said." She put her hand on his. "You helped me learn what being safe in a relationship felt like. And how important it is."

Isaiah looked at her with a half smile. "Safe or boring."

"Safe. And that's a really important thing for a woman." She made sure he understood her, that he understood the value he brought to her life. And she held onto his hand until he nodded that he understood.

They got up and walked around some more for the rest of the interview, mainly just reminiscing. Their relationship wasn't about conflict; it was about wanting different things. Understanding that early Ebony didn't want to belabor it. As she sensed Malcolm's presence move, she asked one more question.

"If you could give me one piece of advice for my next relationship, what would it be?"

Isaiah took both of her hands in his. "Don't ignore what you need. But also... don't dismiss something steady if it's good, just because it's not intense and all-consuming. Quiet love can be good love too."

Isaiah Langston Notes:

40 | Engineer | Codename: Black Bob (The Builder)

He values consistency, but acknowledges my influence. He understands me more than I expected. He sees me clearly, without diminishing me. He didn't blame, deflect, or minimize

What is different now vs then? Would his kindness, consistency, and quiet, settled love be enough? Is passion problematic? Isaiah is the opposite of Diego. Consistent. Calm. Another pendulum swing.

EBONY, Anika, and Malcolm sat on the video call while Bea's team read social media posts about their project. Ebony didn't know how she was supposed to look. Chill, excited, deeply serious.

> Malcolm: I can hear you thinking over here. Relax.
>
> Anika: Miss Ebony, you look constipated. It's okay to smile if you feel like it.

The two DMs made Ebony laugh out loud, which, thank goodness it was during the reading of a funny post. She took a breath and sat in the moment.

"Crazy Love is the type of man where you leave spiritually awakened, sexually exhausted, emotionally confused, and somehow carrying homemade banana bread."

. . .

"Crazy Love MADE ART OUT OF HER STRETCH MARKS?????

And somehow it was the most romantic, unhinged, heartbreaking thing I've ever read."

'"Sometimes it feels better to say crazy instead of broken.'"

Yeah this interview just drove directly through my chest."

"The interview captured something difficult to explain — how some people can love you deeply and still be completely incapable of building a life with you."

Crazy Love calling Ebony "a lot" right after describing her as passionate, devoted, creative, emotionally present, and all-in...

Men really will describe a deeply loving woman like she's a natural disaster.

"I don't know what to say; the responses have been amazing. It was a team effort."

"You sound like a professional athlete," Bea said with a slight smile. "Keep doing what you're doing and have that manuscript proposal ready. I have a feeling you can write a dictionary on butt play and get it published right now."

And that produced Ebony's very real reaction of shooting coffee across her desk and laughing until tears fell.

> *"I like Ebony, but hearing multiple exes describe her as "all in" early makes me wonder how often she mistakes intensity for compatibility."*

"SHIT... THAT IS WHAT I DO."

Ebony looked up from her phone and back down again. The comment had forty-three thousand likes.

She sat back against the couch cushions in her parents' living room, the sweet scent of pound cake wafting around her while the television played low in the background. Dinner at her parents' house usually reset her nervous system. Usually.

But today, some random woman with a butterfly avatar had slipped a few puzzle pieces of her life into place in one random comment.

"What's that look on your face?" Her dad asked from the kitchen doorway.

"What look?" Ebony muttered.

"You look like you either discovered a tax problem or a personality flaw."

Noel barked out a laugh from her seat on the couch next to Ebony.

"Daddy."

"What? I know my child."

Ebony stared back down at the comment. Then turned the phone toward them.

Her father squinted. "Why do y'all read comments? That's your first mistake."

Noel took the phone anyway and read the comment, then scrolled for a moment. "Hm."

Ebony frowned. "Not hm. Defend me."

"I can't defend you from something accurate."

"Mom!"

Randolph reached for the phone next, reading slower. His eyebrows lifted halfway through.

"Daaaang."

Ebony threw herself deeper into the couch. "This family is terrible."

"No, baby," Noel said, slowly adjusting next to her. "This family is honest."

Randolph pointed toward Ebony with the phone. "You do go from zero to 'this could be the father of my children' pretty quick."

Ebony tried not to laugh and failed. "I'm too old for this shit. Sorry Momma. I mean to keep making the same stupid mistake."

Noel waved off the swearing. "You're a very loving person. But you attach meaning to chemistry too quickly."

Ebony's smile faded. She thought about how fast she learned people's favorite songs. Their childhood stories. Their ambitions. How quickly she started weaving them into her life. Like Malcolm.

"This is the second time in a month I've realized I've been foolish."

"Oh, baby," Noel patted her leg gently, "it doesn't mean you're foolish."

"It feels foolish."

"No," Randolph said. "It means you're optimistic."

"I think..." she swallowed, "I think I fall in love with potential versions of people really fast. Like if the chemistry is there, I fill in blanks that maybe haven't been earned yet."

Neither parent interrupted.

"And then when reality shows up, I'm already emotionally invested enough that I try to force it until I wake up."

Randolph nodded slowly. "Now that? That was therapy language."

Noel patted Ebony's puff, shaping it the same way she had when Ebony was little.

"You know what I think?" her mother said. "I think you've spent your whole life being very emotionally brave."

Ebony looked at her.

"You love fully. You show up fully. You don't ration affection. That's beautiful." Noel shrugged lightly. "But sometimes people who love deeply mistake feeling something for feeling safe."

Ebony blinked. "Oh," she whispered.

"Give yourself some grace. The goal isn't becoming less loving," her dad said, bringing food from the kitchen to the dining table. "It's learning to let time reveal people before you hand them access to all of you."

Ebony sat quietly with that. Her thoughts turned to Malcolm and their intensity. They had potential, sure. They had chemistry. She had let him in and he'd disappointed her.

They were still coming back from that. But she cared for him deeply. She flicked her screen and pulled up her therapist's website. Taking a deep breath, she tapped the appointment button.

"No more skipping."

Ebony worried something was wrong when Anika called instead of texting. She looked over at Malcolm, speed puzzling. At least that's what she thought it was called. The man put together puzzles to a timer to "relax" and "work out things." It's apparently a sport.

He showed her videos. While critiquing strategy and giving background on the major players. Like it was the Cleveland Browns. He was adorkable.

"Hello?"

Anika made a strangled sound. "Oh my God. Open social media right now. Any socials."

Ebony pulled her phone from beside her thigh, already suspicious. Her notifications were chaos. Mentions flooding in faster than the screen could refresh.

"What the hell..."

She opened the first app that appeared.

A teaser clip from the interview series was posted twenty minutes ago. Nothing unusual there—except for the last slide.

PHOTOGRAPHY BY MALCOLM KNIGHT.

And beneath it?

Pandemonium.

Her eyebrows lifted slightly as comment after comment flew past.

MALCOLM KNIGHT??????
OH THIS ISN'T AN ARTICLE THIS IS AN EVENT

The man who shot the West Lake shooting?? The man who shot the G20 Summit protests? THAT Malcolm Knight??

No wonder the interview photos feel emotionally invasive 🫠

Ebony looked up slowly.

Malcolm was still putting a puzzle together, like the internet wasn't currently losing its collective mind over him.

Someone had already made a side-by-side thread comparing his photos from the project to his occasional celebrity portrait work, highlighting the way he captured emotional shifts mid-expression.

Ebony Jones interviewing her exes while MALCOLM KNIGHT shoots the emotional fallout?? Whoever approved this concept deserves a raise immediately.

Ebony slowly lowered the phone.

"People are fanboying harder over your photos; Bea added your name to the social media promos."

"Ok."

She blinked at him. He really couldn't care less. She flipped through the comments. "Someone has found a picture of you looking quite dashing surrounded by sand. Apparently, you have thirst-trap forearms."

He snorted.

He really does. Ebony watched him twist open the top of his water bottle and almost moaned. Fuck, she missed him.

Another call came through and she put her on speakerphone. "What now?"

"Behind-the-scenes footage."

"Okay..."

"People are obsessed with the dynamic between you two."

Ebony nearly choked. "What dynamic?"

Bea laughed outright. "Oh sweetheart. The internet thinks he should be your sixth love."

Ebony's eyes snapped toward Malcolm. Of course he'd heard that part, 'cause speakerphone.

His expression stayed on her unblinking. Daring her to look away, to deny it.

It's too quick. I can't mess up again. My heart...not with Malcolm.

"That's... The internet is wild," Ebony said too quickly and turned away, flipping through her notes and not seeing a darn thing. His eyes were heat scopes on her back.

"Mm-hmm," Bea replied. "Anyway, engagement is through the roof. Do not disappear tonight. We're dropping more photos at eight. And Malcolm?"

Ebony turned, shaking her head for him not to respond.

He ripped open a Chuckle Taffy like a savage, his eyes still boring into her. "Yeah?"

"Your photo essay is a go. If you include a "Behind the Lens" segment and talk about the purpose behind the project and that includes West Lake. I'm sorry, Mal, I tried to keep you out of that."

Bea genuinely sounded remorseful. Ebony watched him wrestle with it for what felt like forever before the storm behind his eyes cleared. "People need to see."

Bea sighed and cleared her throat. "Okay Mal. Give Lauren a heads-up and, hey, you can use Jasmin Johnson for the interview."

Ebony gave him a sympathetic, encouraging smile. Jasmin Johnson was the lead journalist on a national, highly rated morning show. She was a pro who asked interesting questions and was good with sensitive topics. Even so, this was going to be hard for him.

"I already have an interviewer. I'm looking right at her gorgeous brown eyes widening in disbelief."

"Holy shit, kid. You're going all in, aren't you?"

"Yeah."

"Ok well, at least you don't have to worry about cutting your fee to pay for Ebony's location shoots. The folks upstairs are practically giddy with the metrics. Ebony, send me your contract demands for the *Journalist: A Requiem* piece. We'll go from there. Good luck, you two."

The call ended before Ebony could protest or ask for clarification, or anything.

Silence settled over the room as Ebony stared at Malcolm, and Malcolm stared very hard back. Her phone buzzed again with a fresh notification preview:

The way Malcolm Knight photographs Ebony Jones needs to be studied.[1]

She set her phone face down on the table. "I think you failed to mention you have a terrifyingly observant fanbase."

---

1. i love me by Joy Rhodes

"They're usually discussing aperture."

"And that you were funding my project."

"Only partially."

"Why?"

"Because you deserved to have every resource. I didn't want to see you get shortchanged."

Her heart fell over itself and splashed out, bleeding on the floor. She wanted to run into his arms and say, to hell with lists and the cautious approach. But the part that held her back? Was hopeful, and that hope kept her steady.

"You had a project on the line?"

He nodded.

"I see."

"Do you?"

The intensity in his eyes, the caged energy in his body turned her bones to liquid. He was moments from throwing her on the table, making her see. She would enjoy it, swallow it up. Gulp it whole. And after...she would wonder.

Taking a deep breath and steeling herself, she pushed forward. "I know I over-analyze and am like a dog with a bone, wanting to examine things, and so I don't want to do too much, be too much here. But I need to know... Is that the only reason you took the assignment?"

He held her eyes, and she held her breath.

"At first, yeah, but that changed about two minutes after I saw you."

"Oh," she said, looking down at her hands.

"Why didn't you say any of this before?"

"Because if I had brought up the photo essay, I would have had to explain why it was so important to me. You look at me and I can't hold anything back. I told you my actual PIN code."

A small smile slipped out, and she mirrored it.

Malcolm shook his head, blowing out of breath. "I just wasn't ready to share that yet. It was still too raw."

His pain was still palpable.

"And now you're going to discuss it for the world?"

"With you by my side? Yeah, it's that important to me. People need to see the lives that journalists put on hold to tell the story. They need to see the life that Justin left behind."

"I asked for a new photographer in that first meeting with Bea."

His head snapped up. His frown caused a deep line between his eyebrows. "You tried to get me off the assignment, why?"

"Because deep down I was afraid of this. Because I didn't want you to see me in all my mess."

"And what is this? What are we doing? Because all I know is, we had one disagreement. An important one, and you've had your guard up ever since."

"I don't know because I've gotta work on me. I love too fast, give too much." She looked away for a moment, and when she focused back on him, he reacted to the tears in her eyes. "I don't want to see potential and fill in the blanks for the future with us. Only to find none of it's real. I'm not sure I can go through that again. So," she blew out a breath. "I'm working on this."

Ebony pulled out the activities her therapist had given her to do at the end of her first session and held them out for Malcolm. Taking it in hand, he scanned the first sheet of paper.

<u>Questions to Ask Yourself</u>

- What specifically has your potential partner

done consistently over time that makes you feel emotionally safe, not just emotionally activated?
• If physical chemistry disappeared tomorrow, what would still exist between you two?
• Are you learning your potential partner, or are you interpreting him?
• How much of your attachment is based on who he has proven himself to be, and how much is based on who you hope he'll become?
•What pace would feel emotionally responsible instead of emotionally satisfying?"
• What does quiet compatibility feel like in your body? Can you tolerate it, or do you mistake calm for lack of connection?
•What are you withholding from him right now that previous versions of you would have rushed to give?
•Have you allowed him to disappoint you yet? Healthy attachment requires reality, not idealization.
•What would it look like to enjoy being loved without immediately trying to secure permanence?

To Do's:

•Keep a two-column journal titled Facts vs. Fantasy. In one column, write only observable actions your partner has taken. In the other, write the meaning or future projection automatically attached to those actions.

• Go one full week without escalating intimacy. No defining the relationship, no future fantasizing, no emotionally loaded late-night conversations. Observe how your potential partner shows up in ordinary moments.

• Write timelines of past relationships, marking the exact point where emotional intensity overtook actual knowledge of the person. Identify recurring patterns.

• Practice "information gathering" dates where the goal is not emotional closeness but curiosity.

She stood in front of him, exposed and raw. Wishing he'd throw her on the dining room table and just fuck his promises into her, but hoping he didn't because she wanted this to be more than her imagination.

"Malcolm, I'm loving myself enough to slow down, hopeful enough that it'll matter, and wishing that you'd wait for me."

He reached out and touched her face, following the curve of her cheek, reveling in the softness of it. She leaned into it, feeling the ache that one feels when they miss home. He leaned down and instead of kissing her, put his forehead to hers.

"I miss you," he said fiercely. "I respect what you need to do to be okay. Thank you for sharing this with me and not shutting me out. And I'll be here when you're ready."

"I hope so," she whispered.

real villain

The real villain of this interview is Pilar because why was she terrorizing that man on the dance floor 💀

Isaiah describing himself as "aggressively terrible" at salsa while Ebony laughed at him the entire time is somehow the healthiest relationship content I've seen all year.

Also "I never had to guess where I stood with you" being his definition of love??? Yeah I need a minute.

Isaiah apologizing to everyone he bumped into during salsa while Ebony was apparently living her dance show fantasy is the most "golden retriever boyfriend meets extrovert girlfriend" thing I've ever read.

That's the kind of breakup that stays with you for YEARS because nobody betrayed anybody. You just realize love and compatibility aren't always the same thing.

These interviews stopped feeling like entertainment for me somewhere around episode three. Watching Ebony hear how different men experienced being loved by her has been devastating because so many women are recognizing themselves in it. The overgiving. The rushing intimacy. The mistaking emotional intensity for safety. The way we pour love into people hoping consistency will grow later.

the love that almost broke me

HE DIDN'T WANT to wake her, but they had arrived at the interview location a considerable distance away from the original location. The interview subject, Jordan Green, at the last minute had "thoughts" about the location choice.

Anika had exams, and now, because of the popularity of the series, they were on a strict deadline. Malcolm was pretty confident he would make Anika proud with the audio and after listening to her detailed process he kind of felt like he had a lot to live up to her expectations even though he had been doing his own shooting and solo videoing for almost as long as she'd been alive.

He appreciated her attention to detail.

Wanting to give Ebony time to wake up and get oriented before the interview, Malcolm ran a light touch down her arm, calling her name. She slowly blinked awake and looked at him. For a moment he saw everything good and bright and sacred in her smile.

Slowly as she moved to fully awake, he saw her guard come back up. And while painful, he understood why she needed to do it. The only thing he had in his corner was his commitment to being there for her consistently until she fully realized she had his heart, she had his trust, and she had his commitment.

"Boy, I can't believe I fall asleep in the car with you so often now," she said as he helped her out of his truck and she stretched. She'd pulled her hair back for this interview, and the coily curls at her temples and nape fluttered in the breeze.

"You mentioned not being able to fall asleep before, why?"

"Well, if you ask my cousins, I'm knocked out before I get to the outer belt." She smiled ruefully. "They make me drive so I'll stay awake on road trips."

They entered the restaurant, and she turned to him. "One night I needed a ride from the airport and Joy offered to pick me up. She ended up not being able to make it, an emergency meeting with a big money client. So she sent Eric, which I guess caused some kind of issue because there was a video game tournament or stream that he was supposed to be on. I could've taken a ride share."

"Whatever it was, he had a problem with doing the task and he had a problem with me, which was fine because I hated him." She smiled and shook her head. "It had been a long trip, I was exhausted, and I fell asleep on the way back. So instead of taking me back to my house, he left me asleep parked on the street at their condo, in the middle of the winter for hours."

Malcolm hackles were raised already, now he wished he'd let Smoke and Dank make the visit they had planned. He might have to make a trip by Eric's himself.

"He claimed he told Joy I was out there and she just didn't hear him, but the end result was I had mild frostbite and could have died."

"Since then, unless you're family? I'm awake. Except with you...And I need you to hold on to that and unpuff your chest a bit because Jordan is already here."

"What? Where?"

How the fuck did I miss that?

He scanned the dining room and didn't see anyone that looked like the man in the dossier.

"My guess? Private dining room. Now he can say I've kept him waiting, even though he's early and not where we discussed. Welcome to life with a narcissist. Don't feed or pet it."

Ebony turned on her heel, squared her shoulders and marched right to the private room entrance.

Malcolm had a heightened level of aggression that he worked the entire drive to overcome. Leading Ebony to a man she classifies as the one that almost broke her was against everything he as a professional, a man, and as a lover of all things Ebony Jones was supposed to do.

But as a lover of all things Ebony Jones, he understood that this was her journey and his job, in all roles, was to support it. Now he wanted to kill Eric, find the duck dude wipe him out, and put the narcissist through the closest window and he hadn't even met him yet.

This muthafucka has one time to get out of pocket and I'm violating the 'neutral observer' tenet without a second thought.

"AH, EBONY, I SEE YOU ARE RUNNING A BIT BEHIND. YOU LOOK incredible. You carry your weight *really* well."

Fuck. I'm going to end up killin' this asshole and needing Dank and Smoke to do the body.

Jordan stood, adjusted his suit and leaned in for a hug which Ebony deftly redirected to a hearty handshake. *Good girl.*

"Jordan, you look well. We're forty-five minutes early actually. Good thing I decided to check in here instead of where we said we were meeting," she said as she sat.[1]

"Well you know what I always say: you're on time if you're early and late if you're on time. And this is?"

"Malcolm Knight, the photojournalist assigned to the project. Malcolm this is Jordan Green."

JORDAN GREEN | THE NARCISSIST THAT ALMOST BROKE EBEE
CODE NAME: THE GREEN EYE BANDIT
37. LAWYER, SINGLE, POSSIBLY GUILTY OF INSIDER TRADING
MASSIVE DICKHEAD,
PUNCHABLE FACE.

"Oh, you're the one capturing Ebony's genius on camera. I've gotta say, it's a tall order keeping up with her."

I cannot wipe that shitty grin off his face. Ebony needs this for the series.

"No, not really. She's a pro."

"That's an interesting angle... but I've seen Ebony work with lighting that really makes her pop. You'll catch on eventually."

The asshole tracked him during his set up shots and as he made adjustments.

"I'd maybe avoid that angle—Ebony likes to be presented a certain way. I've noticed she prefers this style."

"Thanks for the heads-up."

Seeing he wasn't getting the rise out of him that he wanted, Jordan refocused his efforts on Ebony.

---

1. Oscar Winning Tears by RAYE

Jordan adjusted his microphone and gave Ebony a half smile. "You always did like closure."

"Yes, I do love clarity."

He chuckled. "Same thing, depending on who you ask."

Ebony could have easily left Jordan off of her list, but it wouldn't have been honest and she really wanted to be authentic to herself and the experience. But she had to admit her skin crawled sitting across from this man.

"Let's start simple. How would you describe our relationship?"

Jordan leaned back and smiled. "Intense. Passionate. We challenged each other. Not everybody can handle that kind of... depth."

She didn't hate him per se. She loathed him and in a small way pitied him because despite having everything that signaled success, he was empty inside.

"'Handle' is an interesting word. Could you explain what you mean?"

"You know what I mean."

"I really want to make sure I do."

Jordan sighed like the question was silly. "You're the journalist Ebony."

When she didn't give in he smirked and said, "You had trouble being challenged to be bigger, confront your flaws."

"Thank you for clearing that up."

Ebony spent so much of the relationship on her heels questioning herself, being defensive, trying to tie herself into knots for his understanding that she never really got to the root of what made Jordan a narcissist. But she did get the results.

"Were there ways I supported you that felt especially helpful?"

He frowned at her for a moment, then seemed to recover himself. "You believed in me before a lot of people did. Especially when work was getting stressful. You made home feel calm for me. That mattered."

That was... nice. Now comes...

He glanced up at her before adding cream to his coffee. "I don't think you realize how much emotional space you took up sometimes, so when things *were* peaceful, I appreciated it."

And there it is.

Her relationship with Jordan changed her brain chemistry. How she saw the world, how she saw people in it. The openness she'd had all her life was compromised by her relationship with Jordan. And it took her a long time to get back to where she trusted herself and she could trust her reality.

"Do you think you were a good partner?"

Jordan adjusted in his seat and looked off to her left. "I think I showed up in ways most men don't. I provided stability. Access. Experiences. I pushed you to think bigger."

"Did you love me?"

He tilted his head. "That's a loaded question. I cared about you deeply. Probably more than you realized at the time. You could have been the love of my life. Then you started changing."

Here we go. "How?"

"More defensive. More independent. More... suspicious of me. It started feeling like you were listening to everybody else's opinion of our relationship instead of experiencing it for yourself."

"I see."

"What do you see?" He smirked again.

She hated that stupid smirk. He was one of those men that deployed it so regularly it was their resting douche face. You always wondered what the joke was, were they joking, were you the joke... Again, back on your heels and easy prey before you even got started. She wasn't giving him what he wanted and he would escalate soon.

"Is that why you cheated?"

Jordan's jaw tightened, then relaxed. He adjusted his tie and tapped his fork against the table linens. "It wasn't a relationship. Let's not exaggerate."

"It was significant to me. Can you understand that?"

"I respect that you felt hurt."

"That's not the same as taking responsibility for causing the hurt."

"Isn't it though?"

She signaled to Malcolm she was wrapping up. Any longer and Ebony would projectile vomit in this man's face.

"Let's pivot, Jordan as our time is getting short. Why agree to this interview?"

"You asked...And I've always wanted to you to succeed in your little writing endeavors. And because... despite everything, we were good together." He looked at her and gave her a strange puppy dog face.

Was that supposed to be endearing. Jesus, he doesn't even know how to be human at all does he?

"I also don't like seeing it rewritten by those who would want to...manipulate your kind heart."

"Would you prefer to do the manipulating?"

"I would prefer to control the narrative."

"Same thing Jordan."

He shook his head like she was a child. "I read one of your articles the other day."

"Oh?"

She started closing her notebook and capping her pen.

"It was... good."

But...

"I mean, it's solid. You've always been able to tell a story."

"Thank you that's my job."

"Right. I'm just saying—it felt a little... safe."

"You don't say?"

"Yeah. Like you're not really digging anymore. You used to go deeper when you were with me."

"Ok, well, thank you for the interview Jordan. I really appreciate you taking the time."

Malcolm appeared immediately and unclipped his mic.

Her abrupt ending took him aback. He hadn't had the chance to rile her up or get her to defend herself which meant that Jordan would be unsatisfied and one thing Jordan didn't abide by was being dissatisfied by someone he once told "was lucky to have him."

"Are you sure you have everything? You know how people are... I just don't want anyone underestimating you because you let your emotions get in the way. You do have a decent thing going —"

"I'm sure, I got everything I needed, thanks." She hitched her bag onto her shoulder. "I wish you the very best in therapy."

"Wait, Ebony, who do you think you are talking to me like that?"

Jordan moved to stop her from leaving and she paused, laser focused on him. Jordan looked to his left where Malcolm stood, displeased and ready and rethought.

"Maybe I'll tell my own side of the story," Jordan sneered.

"You could, but then I and the Metropolitan Times can sue you for breaching your NDA. As a lawyer you really should read before you sign."

She started to move when she thought better of it. "Your beard lace is lifting, just right here," she pointed at his temple where that damn lace had been bothering her all interview.

And the man who thought he was better than her in every way was devastated. Over a face wig.

Chuckling, Ebony let Malcolm escort her out of the private dining room.

Faith always said that Ebony saw the "Precious Moments" version of people. The vulnerabilities, their childhood, their innocence, the things that sit underneath what they project out into the world.

And as she walked away, head held high, unbothered, and really unmoved by his manipulation tactics she realized sadly there was none of that within him, none that she could see, none that she was willing to dig for. To be a human in this world where there is so much good and beauty and life, and not have those real pieces of yourself? It was a sad way to live.

"How do cell phones get around?"

"Not now Ebony." Malcolm's jaw clenched and his grip on the steering wheel was punishing.

"That poor steering wheel," she said quietly.

He glanced at her and eased back on his death grip, flexing his fingers as he adjusted.

"I get it you're mad—"

"Oh I'm more than mad. It's taking everything in me not to turn this car around, lock you inside, and go whoop his ass."

The base in his voice made her a little wet.

Focus Ebony. Growth, change.

"Did he ever put hands on you?"

"No," she said looking out the window. "I got out before it started to feel like it could be a possibility."

"I hate this," he said after a while. "I hate this for you. I wish... I wish you'd stop, but I have no right to ask that. And I respect that you want to see this through, but hearing time and time again how these dudes didn't appreciate you or treat you well... That asshole Brian was pathetic, but that motherfucker over there," Malcolm pointed forcefully at the windshield vaguely in the direction of the restaurant. "That motherfucker is evil."

"I thought about leaving him off the list..."

"But you wanted to be true to the process," he finished for her.

Her head snapped around to him in surprise. "Yes, I did."

He nodded, never taking his eyes off the road. She watched him for a moment taking in just how beautiful he was. Not his precious moments - not him as a child doing puzzles, not him as a father swinging their potential children around like he did Nicky. Just him right now, Malcolm Knight. The one always seeing her when she wasn't quite sure she could see herself.

"So, how do cell phones get around?"

Malcolm sighed, shook his head, and eased up off the gas. All the while mumbling under his breath. Finally, he glanced over at her with a smirk like she needed to come harder if she was gonna get him.

"They're mobile."

"Did you read these before?"

"No, every one of them is different."

"There's forty eight pounds worth of different jokes?"

"Yeah, of course, I mean I guess. I don't know we haven't made our way through the forty eight pounds yet. Gimme another one."

Ebony unwrapped another and laughed when he aggressively bit into it, taking out his frustrations on the candy. He joined her and things felt good. She had some notes to put on her therapy homework.

"One more interview left," he said.

"I THOUGHT decompressing should look a little different this time," Malcolm said while leaning down and giving his mom a kiss on the cheek.

"And I happened to be coming by for my glasses," Miss Mabeline said. "No, not glasses. What did I come here for? Glasses. Gas. Gumbo! That's the word," she said as she snapped her fingers. "Oh, I *hate* that. The brain fog is the worst part of this."

"It's okay, Ma, you got there in the end," Malcolm said, smiling at her.

"So I did," she said a little sadly. "Well, I'm going to head home and leave you young people to do your thing. Ebony, congratulations on your series. Noel sent me some of the comments, and I've been reading along the series for myself. When you get a chance, I want you to bring by those semen beads. I've got to see that."

"MA!"

Miss Mabeline waved Malcolm away. "It reminds me of the time Jet and I taught at an artist commune in Colorado. That was a time. How do you store them?"

Ebony, with eyebrows to the ceiling, bit her lip to hold back a laugh. "Right now? In a little sack."

Miss Mabeline hooted. "Makes perfect sense!"

MALCOLM'S IDEA FOR EBONY TO DECOMPRESS, SURROUNDED BY HER favorite cousins, in her favorite place, eating her favorite food, was exactly what she needed. It hadn't been fifteen minutes since Miss Mabeline left them in stitches, and she was already feeling better.

No shower needed.

Jordan's casual cruelty and web of manipulation no longer touched her. She had gone through the fire, survived, went back to survey the damage, and came out the other side, stronger and grounded in the reality of what life looks like outside of a charismatic, handsome, green-eyed narcissist's field.

Even as she was eating her tiramisu and listening to Pumpkin talk about how their Aunt Evie already had Baby Nicky matching recyclables and composting, she was mentally piecing together her notes and starting the lede for her feature. She was ninety percent sure that the fifth interview wouldn't happen.

And she had made peace with it. Her 'almost forever love' wasn't the kind of man who sought fame. He also didn't believe in wasted movement. His life now didn't have room for shenanigans the likes of which Ebony would bring.

She turned her attention to Malcolm, now behind the bar helping a shorthanded Armello get customers served. He had rolled up his sleeves, showing off those fantastic arms of his and surprisingly made drinks like a pro. She was curious how he learned to bartend, and she couldn't wait to have a non-date, according to her worksheet, to get to know more about that.

As if he could feel her eyes on him, he looked her way and tossed her a quick wink that set her on fire.

"So when you gonna to stop playing around with that," Faith asked.

"I'm not playing. I'm doing the work. I'm going through my sheet."

"What sheet?" Pumpkin asked.

"This sheet her therapist gave her," January said. "If there was any time to blow off the rules of engagement for a relationship, this would be the time, E. He adores you."

Ebony shook her head, and before she could answer, Joy piped up.

"I think it's a good thing E's taking time to figure out who and what she wants; and not rushing in, dreaming about the future while ignoring the present. I wish I had done that."

January reached out and put her hand on top of her twin's.

"But you're here now," Pumpkin said.

"I'm here now."

Ebony and the girls ordered a second round, when she felt a familiar heat at her side and looked up, way up, to Malcolm, balancing their drinks perfectly on a tray and commanding the gazes of all the available and some unavailable women in the restaurant. No doubt several had recognized him from the viral series, as quite a few phones were suspiciously, casually pointing at them.

Ebony's phone buzzed, and she almost ignored it, but something told her to flip it over.

"X, HI. THANK YOU FOR RETURNING MY CALL."

Ebony turned away from Malcolm, unwilling to expose herself taking this call in front of him. It felt too raw and almost dishonest, which was ridiculous. This was her ex, yes, but Malcolm and she were... They were just...

Anyway.

"Of course, how are you?"

The smooth, deep timbre of his voice interrupted her warring thoughts and was like a straight shot of his favorite bourbon to Ebony's chest. A shock of smooth burn that made her eyes water.

Shit, pull it together, E. Answer the question.

"Good, I'm good." *Why do I sound like a chipmunk?!*

She adjusted the high pitch of her voice down to a hopefully normal range with a hard swallow as she stepped out of the restaurant onto the busy sidewalk. "How's your family?"

Okay. You sound relatively normal. Good job.

"Everyone is well. Thank you for asking."

They were so stiff with each other now. Slipping into formality was something she was used to him doing when he was uncomfortable. Swallowing again, she tried to sound relaxed and professional.

"Did you get the opportunity to—"

"I got the information you sent and I—"

They talked over each other, then laughed. His chuckle soothed her nerves.

"You first," she said, smiling.

"I'd love to see you again, E, but I have some concerns."

"Oh?"

"My wife's privacy and safety are my biggest concerns."

His wife.

Even though she knew he was now married, there was something in the way he said 'my wife' that rattled her. A possessive reverence that she'd never heard in his voice before. At least she'd never heard it when it came to her.

Stop it, Ebony. It's been over. Fact-finding mission only.

But... It still hurt.

She stepped to the side to let people pass her on the sidewalk, and ducked under the awning of the shop next door to the restaurant. Sucking in a deep breath, she refocused. "We work pretty hard to keep the identities under wraps."

"Yes, but this is huge," he pressed. "Every update from you leads to speculation, hundreds of articles, and internet detectives digging. If it were just me, that would be one thing, but... Why are you doing this, E? This isn't your style."

"My desires for the life I want haven't changed X, I'm getting out of my own way and trying something different."

"By turning your life into a reality TV show?" he growled out, and instantly her hackles rose along with her voice.

"If that's what you got from what I've been doing—"

"No, Ebony, I'm sorry, darlin'. I'm sorry," he backtracked quickly. "I'm just... worried about you. We may not be together, but I still care deeply about you. I don't like people judging you or misconstruing what you're doing." He let out a deep sigh, and they were both quiet for a moment. "I don't want my family caught up in anything, and I don't like seeing you so... exposed. I hate seeing, reading, how that sweet heart of yours has been broken."

"Thus, doing something different," she replied quietly.

"And you think this will actually help? Rehashin'...us?" His voice was soft, his formal mask slipping.

"All of this has been helping me to this point," she admitted. "I'm learning more about who I am, who I'm not, and trying to break patterns. We are a piece of that puzzle."

She imagined the look on his face, the crease between his

brow that he always got when he was deep in a mood or thought.

"Ok darlin'. The jet will meet you at the airport tomorrow morning. I'll send over the addendum to the NDA by then."

She blew out a deeply held breath, and her belly flip flopped.

Shit. Now I have to do this... she thought, but like a functioning adult she said out loud, "Thank you."

"Don't thank me, E. I broke your heart too."

"ARE YOU SURE YOU WANT TO DO THIS, EBONY? WHEN I TOLD YOU the man was getting married, you locked yourself in *my* room for two days blasting *Congratulations* by Vesta on repeat," Faith sat on her bed watching her hastily toss essentials in her travel bag.

"Ooh, that's right, it was bad," January agreed, and she took out, rolled and replaced Ebony's socks in her bag. "You could do a Zoom call..."

Ebony stopped long enough to level a look that made Jan smack her lips and refocus her attention on Ebony's haphazard suitcase. "This is my job. If I can deal with Jordan, I can deal with this."

Faith took all of Ebony's clothes out of the suitcase with a look of confusion. "Is your plan to distract him so he'll confess his deepest secrets?"

"What? No! He's *married!*"

"Not in that way," January chimed in. "What in the world is up with these clothes?"

Ebony stopped long enough to look, really look at what she had packed. Not a single item matched or made sense. She had even shoved in two left shoes and a parka. "Oh hell."

"Sit," Joy finally said from the doorway. She shoved some tea into Ebony's hands and steered her to the chair at her vanity. Embarrassed Ebony focused on the amber liquid in her hands. The cup was as warm as her cheeks and ears. Without looking at anyone in the room, she whispered, "She's beautiful. His wife, I mean."

Sympathy oozed from her sisters as the weight of their eyes landed on her. She kept hers on the tea.

"She's beautiful, and she's the same size as me, so it wasn't that...she's richer than a god, but he has his own money so it couldn't be that...He's not the kind of man who makes that kind of commitment lightly, so what was it? What was it that made her the one instead of me?"

"Oh honey, you broke up with him, remember? It wasn't right, and you did what was best for you," Jan said, stooping next to her.

"What if I made a mistake?"

"That's what you're going to find out," Joy said. "I'd leave the edible panties at home tho'." She tossed the still-in-the-package-gift to January, who flung them at Faith, who ducked with a shout. Faith was still giggling as she packed Ebony's charger.

I'm a fucking mess. Maybe that's why...

"Is everything squared away with Ms. Mabeline? When do you need to get back?" Ebony asked Malcolm as he joined her on the luxury jet sitting on the tarmac.

He took a glance around the cabin before he answered. "Mom's fine. Dwayne is going to stop by and monitor today's treatment, and I'll make adjustments if this goes longer than

Monday. She says she can't wait until you bring by the cum beads by the way."

She smiled the first genuine smile since the phone call with her ex.

Ebony's heartbeat ratcheted up several notches as they passed under the familiar cedar entry arch marking the entrance to the ranch. It had been disorienting landing at the new private landing strip near the ranch instead of flying into Denver International Airport. She had the feeling it was the start of understanding how much things had changed.

At least this part was familiar.

The long road that wound through the ranch always showed it off well. This time it showed off all its late-summer glory. Wildflowers and horses, the creek that she never had time to see, the lake just beyond her field of vision...the big ol' Colorado sky...

"This is beautiful," Malcolm said begrudgingly. His mood had shifted the moment they took off from the airport, and she honestly couldn't put her brain to understand why or work to bring him out of it. She was applying all of her brainpower not to "Nope" right back home.

All too soon for her nerves, they slowed down in front of the ranch's main house.

Malcolm's heavy hand landed on top of her own, stopping her from cracking the rest of her knuckles. "Any time you are uncomfortable, or need me to get you out of here, you have the signal. Okay?"

She nodded without looking at him. His hand moved from her hands to her chin, turning him to her. "Say the words, Ebony."

"If I'm uncomfortable or need to get out of here, you've got me."

He nodded as he looked her over, never taking his hand from her chin; he leaned in. "You are the remarkable Ebony Jones, accomplished and brilliant, brave and kind, champion of the Holiday Sisters. You're building the future you desire and deserve, and this is all in your hands. You've got this."

Ebony could've kissed him in that moment. Instead, *"all in too soon"* galloped through her mind, knocking all thoughts of kisses over in its wake.

Luckily for her, the driver opened the door at that moment, and she thought she saw a flicker of something cross Malcolm's face, but the bright Colorado sun replaced whatever she thought she saw. One moment she was staring into Malcolm's reassuring eyes, the next she was locked onto her ex's cautious ones.

"Xavier Alexander. It's been a while."

the almost forever love.

"EBONY, SWEETHEART, HOW ARE YOU?"

Xavier held open his arms and Ebony walked into them like she'd done countless times before, but this time, she stopped short of pressing her body into his. His arms folded around her like they'd done countless times before, but this time his arms stopped a safe distance from her lower back where his hand used to rest, slightly cupping her bottom. And instead of burying his nose in her neck and kissing it, he kissed the top of her head like a favorite cousin.

The hug ended quickly, and his arms dropped back to his sides instead of resting around her because, if nothing else, Xavier Alexander was unfailingly polite and appropriate on his worst days. It made her happy for his new wife... and for him.

"Xavier, this is my — this is Malcolm Knight, celebrated photojournalist. He creates the visual content for the series, which is far beneath him and his expertise."

Malcolm frowned at her briefly, his eyes intense. "You're beneath no one, and it's an honor to work with you."

Her belly flopped over as he held her eyes a moment longer before finally meeting Xavier's outstretched hand with his own. She missed their interaction because she was wrapped in a familiar bear hug from behind that made her breath catch in her chest. Her favorite almost brother-in-law was in town, apparently.

She laughed as James swung her around like she were a doll. "James, I'm gonna puke, stop!"

"You're going to squeeze her to death! Put that girl down so I can get my hug."

Ebony was placed carefully in front of Alma, her favorite almost mother-in-law with a laugh. "Mama Alma, hi."

Alma hugged her tight with a slight rock, and Ebony let herself sink into her warmth. Alma, with her waist-length, salt and pepper locs and flowy green dress, was all art, love, and light. "It's been too long, little Miss. Just because you're not dating my son anymore doesn't mean you can abandon us."

"I needed time, then it seemed like too much time and too many weddings had passed to come back," Ebony admitted quietly.

Alma squeezed her tighter. "It's love, not pie Ebony, we've got plenty of it. You are always welcome here, but I understand. Your aura looks amazing."

Alma continued to fuss over Ebony in the best ways as James introduced himself to Malcolm. A chime went off on Xavier's watch, and the shift in his mood quieted them without him saying a word.

"I need to go check on Shay," he said to his mother before turning his focus briefly on her. "My wife is ill, so our talk will have to happen tomorrow, darlin'. I'm glad you and the fam will have time to catch up. Dad should be back anytime now."

He nodded once to Malcolm and rushed up the path toward his house, which was close to the main house where his parents stayed.

"Did we come at a bad time?"

"You know my son," a deep voice with humor dancing underneath said from behind. "Intense is an understatement. Shay will be right as rain after the rain. Change in pressure sometimes gives the poor girl migraines."

Ebony squeaked and wrapped her arms around Pop Alexander.

"Now what's this I hear about some man without a pot to piss in or a winda' to throw it out of tryin' to move into that house of yours?"

"I'M GOING TO GO FOR A WALK," SHE SAID TO MALCOLM AS SHE passed his cabin. He sat on the steps reading and chewing a cherry Chuckle Taffy.

Such a thief.

They'd had snacks and lemonade with the Alexanders - minus Xavier and his wife - where Alma engaged Malcolm about his work. They were both animated as they discussed various locations and his equipment, and Ebony was content to listen. It captivated her when people spoke about their passions. Seeing the light in their eyes, their uninhibited, reflexive movements - it was divinely human.

Now the Alexanders were off doing the things one does to shut a sprawling ranch down for the night, and she was filled with... everything. Thoughts, feelings, energy... and she needed to process while her body moved.

"This is really good, Ebee."

"What is it? Wait did you print out my book?"

"How else was I supposed to read it?"

"On an eReader?"

"Nah, I like to feel the pages."

"But it's not a proper book yet."

"Of course it is."

"It's not even bound!"

"It's in a binder; it's a book. Anyway," he waved her protest away like a fly. "Three witches trying to prove their dad didn't kill their mother? It's like Charmed meets The Flash. It's really, really good. I suspect the dad did it, though." He squinted at her, looking for a hint of confirmation.

That made her feel especially gooey inside. "You're going to have to read it to find out."

He closed the binder. "You want me to come along?"

"Nah. I was out here almost every weekend for months. I'll be back soon." She snatched a piece of candy he had sitting next to him and kept moving.

"What's a top you cannot wear?"

She laughed and pretended to think for a moment.

"A tube top because I hate taping my boobs and there is not a strapless bra that can handle these." She did a lil shimmy as she walked away.

"A laptop. Come on, you didn't even try," he called after her. His eyes narrowed at the sky. "It looks like it's going to rain."

"Good! I love the rain."

TOO MUCH OF SOMETHING YOU LOVE CAN BE A TERRIBLE THING. STORY of my life.

Ebony thought a quiet walk during a summer drizzle would be a perfect way to ground herself and think through her feelings. Now she was stuck under a tree while the heavens tossed mop buckets full of water down around her. She would have to get a move on back to the guest cabins soon if she wanted to make it there before dark. As she hyped herself up to move out of her damp shelter, she heard a small meow. At least it sounded like a meow. It was faint; the rain was loud, and she was having trouble picking it up. She pulled out her phone and realized her battery was low.

That's right, this area of the ranch has dead spots. My phone must be draining faster.

The pleading meow caught her attention again. Ebony turned off her phone to save battery life, took a deep breath, and dashed out into the rain toward the sound.

After fifteen minutes Ebony was freezing, soaked, pissed, and still chasing the meow in a field of mud. It was the kind of mud that sucks your shoes right off your feet. Seriously. She had no idea where her sneakers were now.

With a mind on her lost shoes and a burning in her thighs from her slow, heavy plods through the muck, she made a misstep, turned her ankle, and down she went. Face to the sky, getting waterboarded by Mother Nature, one foot firmly ensconced in the ankle deep muck, the other throbbing, Ebony decided to let the Earth absorb her because she was too tired to do anything else, but lay there - filthy, wet, and cold.

"It's my own fault for waking up today," she said to the sky. "Yeah sure, let's fly out to Colorado to ask one of the world's sexiest cowboys why he couldn't be bothered to shift his busy schedule to spend Christmas with me but dropped everything to marry someone else who conveniently has a migraine that makes it impossible to do anything else because he has to tend to her with the fastidiousness of a Tibetan Monk while I go roam the Colorado mountainside in torrential rain Jesus Ebony what are you doing?"

"Meow?"

Turning her head to the left, she came face to face with golden eyes glowing in the dwindling light. It sounded like a cat, but the more she squinted, the more it resembled an enormous drowned rat. And the poor thing was caught in some kind of tubing and netting that looked like it was maybe for pipe drains or something.

"Poor baby. How did you end up in this mess?" Mustering all of her will, she pulled her stuck foot out of the mud and flipped herself over like a drunk turtle. Ebony spread her body mass out by laying flat because that's what all the old TV shows said about quicksand. This had to be a close fucking cousin.

"Meoooooow."

"Oh really? And then what happened?" Ebony bear crawled closer and rubbed its little paw. Something beneath it squeaked and twitched.

Ebony let out her own yelp. "Murder Mittens. You were hunting? I get that a kitty has to do what they do, but at this point, doll, you're gonna have to let it go."

"Meooow meoow, meoww."

"Well, now you're just being stubborn." Ebony carefully lifted one paw, firmly gripping it behind its claws of death. Then the other. The cat let out a mournful yowl of deep disagreement. The mouse? Vole? The kitty's lunch, for its part, stayed still.

"Dude, now's your chance."

But it was too much for the poor mouse. It was exhausted, covered in mud, and possibly hurt. She nudged it with her knuckle, and it squeaked, wiggled, then stopped. She took both of Murder Mittens' paws into her one hand, held her breath, and scooped up the tiny ranch land creature with the other.

Chanting, "Please don't have rabies, please don't have bubonic plague," she dropped the wretched thing into the side pocket of her sweater. It made no attempt to leave, and she tried not to be squigged out about carrying around a possibly dying, or, at a minimum, deeply traumatized mouse in her pocket.

It was getting darker by the second, so she pulled the sleeves of her sweater over her hands to protect them from the sharp edging around the plastic tubing and tried to untangle the hapless hunter. Several moments and a few cut fingers later, she pulled the kitty by its collar out of the drain, through the mud to her. It wiggled up her chest and shoved its wet face directly against her cheek, purring like a motorbike.

"Awww, well, we all get in over our heads sometimes. You are very welcome, but we need to get back, dry out, and figure out if you belong to the Alexanders or find your person."

With Murder Mittens tucked deep into her shirt and Lunch, the prairie prey, either dead or passed out in her pocket, Ebony buttoned her sweater up tight and crawled to the tree line where it was less wet. Free of the squelching mud she tested out her ankle... and it hurt like fuck.

"Okay, we are going to have to get help, Mittens," she cooed before sneezing twice. "Malcolm is rubbing off on me."

Powering up her phone, messages came flooding in. Swiping them away quickly, she was excited to have a signal, but with her phone at one percent, she had to get a message out before it died.

"Oh my god, Momma, stop posting one sentence at a time in the group chat!" Swiping to a new message, she quickly typed.

Malcolm knocked on the house's door. He banged again almost immediately. Xavier snatched open the door like he was ready to cuss out whomever was on the other side until he saw him.

"Ebee's been gone too long, especially with it raining like this. Her phone goes directly to voicemail, and I can't pick up her location. I need an ATV to go look for her."

Xavier nodded, reaching out to grab his hat off the hook. The woman Malcolm assumed was his wife, Shayla, appeared behind him in pajamas and looked a little ashen. "Oh no, I'll call up to the main house. James and the hands will meet you. Where was she headed?"

"She said just a walk, maybe check out the lake and headed east."

"Aww shit. The lake is west," Xavier said, running his hand over his beard. "Ebony has a terrible sense of direction, especially out here."

"I'll call some fellas from town too," Shayla said, swiping through her phone. "We can form a couple of parties and search in a grid. She might be pretty far out if she thought she was headed in the right direction." She moved to leave the room when Xavier stopped her.

"YOU stay here, Sweetness. You shouldn't be out in this weather."

"But—"

"Sweetness."

Shayla looked like she wanted to protest more, but hmmphed and shrugged. "Fine. At least let me go up to the main house. Momma Alma and I can look through security film together and see if we can pick her up on the trail cams."

This entire exchange was taking too long. "Bruh, ATV? Y'all can catch up; I need to be out there looking for her."

Xavier's eyebrow raised, but he didn't say more, motioning him out the door.

Ping!

help

i've pulled a regency heroine

E where are you?

E

He tried calling her, but it went to voicemail again.

"Pulled a Regency heroine?" Xavier asked.

"Regency… Oh! She must've twisted her ankle in the rain, or she's sick and needs to be bled by leeches," Shayla blurted.

Malcolm didn't know which one made him panic more, but the idea of Ebony out there hurt or ill in the dark sent a fear through him like he hadn't felt since Justin. His friend's cold dead eyes flashed before him before being replaced by Ebony's eyes crinkled in laughter.

"This way," Xavier motioned as he followed behind Malcolm.

Redirecting his body, he hadn't realized he was already out of the house. He didn't register the rain, the cold, nothing but a deep, driving need to find her.

THE SOUND OF A MOTOR CAUGHT HER ATTENTION AS MURDER Mittens shifted against her. Lunch still hadn't moved.

Eww.

She waved when the lights from a vehicle landed on her and tried to get up.

"Stay there," Malcolm barked as he hopped off and ran around the wide, long fence, avoiding the deep mud that was now her nemesis. He was hauling ass, and she didn't blame him. The cold, driving rain was unforgiving. At least the treeline shielded her from the brunt of it. In fact, as happy as she was that he'd found her, she wasn't looking forward to being out in all that again. Before her mind could mentally prepare for the weather, Malcolm arrived, barely breathing hard, which was impressive for the length and speed he'd run.

"Ebee, baby, are you okay?" He was on his knees in front of her, pushing her wet, floppy, and fro'd up hair back off her face so gently. His warm hand was a comfort, and she leaned into it ever so slightly.

"I'm fine, except I turned my ankle, and it's a long, wet walk back. I'm sorry you have to be out in it. That rain had you flying around that fence."

His eyes dropped to her ankle, and he pulled out a bottle from somewhere in one of the million pockets he had in his pants. "I don't give a fuck about the rain."

He sure acted like he gave a fuck about it.

He glanced back up at her, and she stopped breathing, struck by the intensity of his gaze. "Blink for me, Ebee."

I kept asking him to blink for me.

She blinked three times slowly.

Nodding, his shoulders relaxed, and he looked back down at her ankle. "This is going to be cold," he warned before he used the water to clean off her foot and ankle to get a better look at it.

While he examined the swelling, a second ATV pulled up, then three more. She couldn't make out all the large figures, but she felt bad about causing so much drama.

Wasn't this what Xavier was worried about?

Before too long, giant and objectively handsome mountain men surrounded her: Xavier and James, their cousin Caine, another man who identified himself as Fox, a play cousin and firefighter, and Mal still crouched down with her.

"Dear Playgirl, I never thought it would happen to me..."

The men chuckled, and Malcolm shook his head at her. Fox did a second check of her ankle, nodding to Malcolm.

"You're right, just a sprain. I'll wrap it here to keep it stabilized for travel, then redo it when you've showered. Where's your shoes, darlin'?"

Ebony sighed and rolled her eyes. "The Earth reclaimed them, and I let her."

"The mud?" Caine said, flashing his flashlight toward the field.

"Sucked them right off my feet like a freak with a foot fetish in a strip club. At this point, don't even bother. I can walk without—."

The last of her sentence died in her throat when Malcolm picked her up in his arms. "I got you."

"I've got to be heavy, Mal," she whispered as he took the long way back to the ATV. Besides her wet body, she was now wearing a big rain parka, James' cowboy hat, and an additional heavy blanket that was getting wetter by the moment.

He looked down at her and quirked up a grin, doing a couple of bicep curls with her as he walked. "I got you. And it's not the first time, remember?"

He really did. Have her that is. He didn't stumble or shake with the exertion. He just...had her. And she remembered that hot summer day in a darkened garage and how he folded her like a letter and dropper her on his beautifully pierced... *Damn.*

There was a shift in her she didn't have words for, but as she dealt with that internal shift, another occurred inside her shirt.

"Oh shit. Murder Mittens. Xavier, can you help? Malcolm can't—"

"I said I fuckin' got you, Ebee," Malcolm actually growled and clenched her to him more which would've set her cat on fire, the sexual one, but she was seized with worry over Malcolm's allergies because of the actual cat she'd acquired.

"I have a cat in my sweater. And a mouse in my pocket."

Murder Mittens popped its little head up and said hello and Malcolm sneezed.

"Anyone got an EpiPen?!"

Malcolm carried a freshly showered and two-strand twisted Ebony to a chair in the living room of her cabin. Momma Alma brought by a shower chair and a manicure kit, and still it had taken her a while to get clean and wash her hair. She'd had mud in almost every nook and cranny. And her hair? Even with Malcolm's help, it had taken an hour just to get it rinsed, cleaned, conditioned, and twisted up.

He was quiet and focused when he came in, freshly showered himself, to wash her hair; and gentle when he used the nail brush on her hands and feet. The air between them was heavy, charged with so many things unsaid.

She wished they were alone because the intimacy of her pressed against him made her feel more exposed than if she was back out in the elements. It felt like decades since she was last been in his arms.

"Are you *sure* you're okay with Miss Pussy being here?" Shayla, Xavier's wife asked, cuddling the hilariously named cat close.

"I won't be petting her anytime soon, but I'm okay. Over here." He grinned at her. "I've been getting allergy shots and meds for a few weeks now," Malcolm said as he tucked a blanket around Ebony.

Ebony waited for him to make eye contact with her, and Malcolm studiously avoided her gaze.

Hmmm...

She looked up to Shayla, who watched them with a hint of a smile. "Thank you again for saving Miss Pussy. She's a city kitty who likes to play mountain lion out here and gets herself into trouble. Mostly just scaring me with the dead mice she likes to gift. She's my girl." Shayla nuzzled the now clean and very floofy scamp.

"I'm usually the one getting into scrapes; I'm glad I found her. She's absolutely beautiful even when she's covered in mud. Is Lunch..." Ebony made a swiping motion across her throat.

Fox, the firefighting play cousin, laughed. "Little thing is just tired. Momma Alma cleaned it up and is going to give him or her the night to recover before 'releasing it to its destiny.'"

After Fox examined her ankle, applied fresh wrappings and a couple of bandages to the cuts on her hands, everyone who had crowded into her little cabin to make sure she was okay said their goodnights and shuffled out. Shayla profusely thanked her again.

Malcolm closed the door and leaned against it. [1]

"She is actually really nice, and she looks under the weather. I hope that doesn't happen with every storm."

He said nothing. He just watched her. Scanning her like he did when he found her under the tree. In the safety and warmth of the well-lit cabin, his gaze was intense, and she squirmed under the heat, looking everywhere but at him.

"That kitty sure is cute," she said to her lap. "When did you start taking shots for your allergy?"

He still didn't say a word.

Instead he pushed off the door and walked toward her, never taking his eyes off of her face. When he finally stood next to her, she wasn't brave enough to look at him. It wasn't until his hand gently grabbed her chin and nudged her head back that she looked at him.

---

1. If Only for One Night - Luther Vandross

"Blink those pretty brown eyes for me."

Oh.

Instantly, her eyes grew moist, and she happily blinked away, for her own heart and for his. She gave him that reassurance without hesitation.

"I'm fine."

"My mind knows that, but my… I needed to know."

He swept his thumb across her bottom lip, then bent himself nearly in half to reach her lips as she sat in the chair. He gave her the kind of kiss that made her ears tingle and her heart warm.

The kind of kiss that makes your heart ache because it's so tender. A kiss born of connection beyond passion, that leads to love beyond reason.

And it scared the shit out of her.

Was *that* stupid as hell, given she was on this whole quest? Yes. But it was because of this project that she was terrified. Was she in her pattern or was it more? Fall first. Fall hard. Give everything and end up with nothing, except acknowledgement that you're a good fuck and dependable. And this time the pain would be…

She started pulling back in all the ways she could, rescuing her lips from his soft full ones, rescuing her heart from what he might be saying with his. Shutting down.

"I'm tired," she whispered.

He crouched down beside her, his face level with hers. After a few moments he sighed a bit. "Alright Ebee, let's go to bed."

Ok it wasn't an invitation…

But she couldn't bring herself to kick him out. She tried to get up the courage when he turned down the bed.

She was channeling her no-nonsense ancestors when he lifted and carried her to the bed, placing pillows under her ankle to keep it elevated.

She was *just* about to open her mouth and tell him to go back to his own cabin when he took off his clothes, *DAMN,* and climbed into the bed behind her, his back against the headboard. He pulled her into his chest, wrapping his arms around her.

And… as she lay there snuggled deep in his arms, feeling the rise and fall of his chest, the warmth of him against her, she folded.

"No matter what happens tomorrow," his voice rumbled low and quiet. "You are loved, safe, and you are enough. The men that fumbled you, it was their loss, their mistake, their misaligned priorities."

Correction: she folded like a flat sheet in a bed-making contest.

"You're doing so well working on yourself, but understand, you, as you are, are enough. And you're never too much."

Fuck it, she was a flat sheet folded in a bed-making contest with hospital corners that they shrink wrapped. It made little sense, but suffice it to say a sistah was PRESSED.

He kissed the top of her head, grabbed her bonnet off the nightstand and put it on her.

"Goodnight Ebee."

"Good…goodnight Mal."

tender parts

The way every compliment Jordan gave had a knife hidden inside it 🔪 💀 "You always had potential." "You don't go deep enough anymore." Sir pick a manipulation style and stick with it 🤡

"Your beard lace is lifting." I'm crying because THAT'S what broke him 😭 not the NDA, not the rejection. The beard lace.

"And I've always wanted you to succeed in your little writing endeavors." oh he would've had to die actually.

That ending wrecked me because Ebony realized she could no longer find the humanity in him.

And for somebody who always sees the tender parts in people? That's not hatred. That's grief.

What got me is Ebony realizing she spent YEARS defending herself instead of studying HIM.

That's what narcissists do. They keep you so busy proving your reality that you never stop to ask why they need you confused in the first place.

"WHEN YOUR COUSIN moved in with her cat."

The sun wasn't quite up, but the birds were already sharing their daily gossip. Fresh Colorado mountain air lifted and fluttered white curtains from the cracked window, and Ebony woke to lips pressed against the side of her neck. His words barely registered because the heat of his touch short-circuited her brain wiring.

"Mmm...cat?"

He chuckled against her skin, sending delicious vibrations rolling through her upper body. [1]

"Last night." He kissed her behind her ear. "You asked me when I started taking allergy shots." His hands slipped down the front of her, deftly opening her satin PJs one button at a time. Her back arched slightly each time his fingers brushed against her skin. "The day after I left the hospital."

"That's...that's great. Proactive about...mmm...health."

He nibbled on her ear, and Ebony really didn't give a shit about cousins and cats at the moment.

---

1. Floating (featuring Hope Tala) by Raveena

Because in that moment, her mind was solely dedicated to reveling in the way the soft and slick material felt as Malcolm slid it the rest of the way off. The way he massaged her breasts equally mesmerized her, alternately tugging and flicking her sensitive nipples.

Even more interesting was the way he licked her from the tip of one shoulder across her back to the other. He returned to her neck, sucking at the soft hollow there while slipping his hand into her pajama bottoms and caressing her belly. He gave the generous flesh there a good, gripping squeeze, pinched her nipple, and growled in satisfaction into her neck.

Her head fell back onto his shoulder; the pleasure moving through her made her both weak and wanton. Her grip on his muscular thighs increased as she sought relief from the heat building at her core.

"I'm proactive about you," he whispered.

Malcolm inched his hands down her legs, and he didn't have to tell her to spread; her legs had a mind of their own, and she agreed. She tossed one leg over his thick, muscular thigh as she went to move the other; he placed a firm hand on her, stopping her.

"Careful, baby," he said as he lifted her leg and gently repositioned it so that her ankle was safe.

He returned to caressing the outsides of her thighs, then towards the back of her thighs, and finally he slid his fingers inside her pants, back to her core, spreading her open and using his index finger to trace a long, slow, sleek circle around her clit. Her hips writhing, swirling into the heat building within her, he continued to exploit her clit.

"I wish you could see yourself, baby, you're so fucking beautiful," he paused, making her whine in protest. "You're the *most* beautiful thing; stay right here.

Malcolm got up and walked to the other side of the

bedroom and grabbed the old-fashioned standing mirror. Situating the mirror leaning on its side, at just the right angle, he looked at her and smiled, then disappeared again, coming back with his camera bag.

Ebony's lips quirked up in a wry grin. "You brought your camera here last night? Did you plan this?"

He shook his head. Malcolm unfurled a tripod, then slipped off his boxer briefs, unfurling his dick. He hung heavy, erect with a dot of pre-cum on his tip. Ebony bit her lip to keep her moan in and watched him hungrily, like prey to her predator, as he moved the camera into place. Between the curved muscles of his ass and his thick, heavy dick, she was having trouble.

"I don't have the words; that's your area of expertise. But I have this."

When he was ready for her, he stood in front of her, his face heated, his erection bold. She licked her lips.

"Ebee, you look like you want to swallow me whole."

"I do."

He grabbed her chin firmly, smiling down at her as he jacked himself. "Open."

She did.

And he fed her the tip of him.

"Now suck. Just the tip."

She gave a moan of disappointment and tried to take more of him into her mouth. Slight pressure on her chin from his hand stopped her.

"Ebee. Be good. Just the tip or none at all." His eyebrow raised, and moisture flooded her panties. He was so sexy when he was firm with her. It made her want to do exactly what he asked. And as she sucked, he rewarded her with gentle strokes along the side of her face and long caresses down the sides of her neck.

"Baby, your mouth feels so good. FUCK. If I let you take me all, I'll be comin' down your throat in no time. And I want to show you. Will you let me show you what I see?"

He lightly pressed his thumb against her chin for her to open.

"Yes."

His smile made her chest ache, her pussy ache, her nipples ache. She was one big ball of nerves, need and emotion.

Malcolm slowly pulled her pajamas bottoms down her legs, followed by her panties and as he slid them down her body, he kissed her thighs, each inch along the way, he kissed her instep; he kissed the top of her foot, the very tips of her toes... Malcolm kissed every inch he touched. It wasn't rushed; it was worship, and she felt divine in his eyes, under his lips.

Lying behind her, he wrapped his arms around her, propped himself up on his elbow, and held her face between his fingers. She watched his face in the mirror with curiosity and quite a few nerves. Lifting her injured leg on top of his, he met her eyes in the mirror.

"Look at you." He rubbed his face in her twists. The heat of his breath made her neck tingle. "Beautiful, thick, dark hair, your twists make you look like a queen. Your cheekbones and eyes glimmer in the sun, these lips... soft as feathers, gracing a smile as shiny as copper," he smoothed his hands down her neck and across her chest, "rich, brown skin, gorgeous breasts with plum-tipped nipples..."

He tugged on them, eliciting a deep cry from her. "You look like a fucking painting. Ripe and free, in ecstasy."

Reaching between them, he positioned himself at her opening, his piercing slightly cooler than the man attached to it. Spreading her lips apart again, his fingers circled her clit igniting her body in waves of heat.

"Watch my hands. See how good they look holding you, teasing you, making you moan?"

"Yes."

"Watch me touch deep inside you."

With panting breaths, his hand holding her face, the other holding her thigh high and carefully, she watched, felt, and was shattered by the way he gave her inch by inch of himself until he was full seated in her.

She felt full, flushed, and claimed. Stretched so tightly around him, Ebony was overcome with need.

"Please."

"You never have to beg me, baby." He slid out. "You. Never. Have. To beg. For anything you deserve, and you. Deserve. My. Dick."

His words were punctuated by his long, slow thrusts, and her cries grew louder with each one.

"We are a work of art, baby, look."

They were.

Her body soft where he was hard.

Their skin, slick with moisture from their exertion, shone under beams of light from a rising sun.

The passion in their embrace - his arms locking her leg and face in place, owning her, and her hands grasping him back just as tightly. It was a claiming in deed and of heart.

It was carnal; the evidence of her arousal coating him.

It was beautiful; the white bedding draped, wrapped, and crumpled around them, contrasting with their dark skin.

It was perfect. Their eyes locked together, hearts beating wildly as one.

Her orgasm built and shattered over and through her, taking both of them by surprise and triggering Malcolm's. His arms instinctively locked around her chest as he buried his face in her neck and rocked his dick deep within her, filling her to the brim. She held onto his arms as the waves of euphoric joy activated, crashed, and reset her nervous system.

"I LOVE YOU. "

She didn't know how long it took for her to come down from what she had just experienced, but Mal stayed with her the whole time: covering her with a blanket and his own body to shield her damp skin from the cool, early morning air; cleansing her and holding her; and gently massaging her scalp.

When she finally came back to herself, she showered and got dressed while he did the same. She stood in front of the same mirror that had been the intense reflection of their lovemaking, now set to rights, fluffing out her twists when she heard him.

I love you too.

But she didn't say it. She just stood there, one hand in her hair, the other paused in midair, her eyes on his reflection in the bathroom doorway. Ebony's heart beat wildly in her chest, hope unfurled deep in her belly then doubt's punk ass came crashing through all of it like an 80s wrestler through a folding table. Loud, destructive, and predictable.

Same pattern E. Do you want to be sitting across from him in two years, interviewing him?

Still frozen, the thoughts running through her mind had stretched the moment past shock, zipped past uncomfortable, and were in a downhill skid to pensive embarrassment.

A quick knock on the door broke through Ebony's thoughts, and she escaped. Gingerly moving to the door, she opened it to a beaming Shayla.

"Hey! I wanted to check in on you and see if you were up

for brunch before you and X have your interview. We can grab Malcolm on the way—."

"No need," Malcolm said as the heat of his body pressed against Ebony's back. "I was just leaving; please send Mrs. Alma my apologies."

Malcolm excused himself, gently guided Ebony to the side, gave Shayla a nod, and walked off the porch and up the path without a backward glance.

And he took her heart with him, even if he didn't know it.

one

"WHAT MOMENTS in our relationship do you remember as the happiest or most meaningful?"

Brunch had been an exercise in acting. Ebony played the role of a relaxed woman delighted to meet Shayla's friends and her younger brother, who'd all appeared "on a whim" to check out Xavier's ex-girlfriend.

And she'd given an Oscar-winning performance.

Inside, she was dying.

Inside, she wanted to run from the curious, warm smiles and find Malcolm. She wanted to tell him she loved him and apologize for freezing and beg him to tell her he loved her again.

Outside? Well, outside they all connected on being from the Central Ohio area and cross-referenced who they knew and schools attended. Fox's wife - Selene - had been cooking in Momma Alma's kitchen all morning, and Ebony knew the food had to be delicious because, once everyone served themselves, it was total silence. She could've been a method actor because she ate like everyone else, showered praise on Selene while the food turned to ash in her mouth.

She'd even asked for a small to go serving. *For Malcolm.*

She'd gotten his name out without a sob, and someone, somewhere, should clap.

Now, she was standing opposite Xavier, doing the only thing that felt solid: work. She could lose herself in the mechanics of her job and not think about how Malcolm managed to mic her and test without touching or looking at her once.

Nope, she wasn't thinking about it at all.

Xavier, for his part, was uncomfortably aware of his microphone. He kept glancing down at it and adjusting his shirt. She pretended not to notice, letting him find his peace with it. And the question. [1]

"The early part," he said with a smile. "We had the same drive. It felt like we understood each other without having to explain it. Being with you felt... aligned. There was our work, then our lives together."

"What do you think I did well as a partner?"

"You were always honest, you didn't say what I wanted to hear, you gave it to me straight, no chaser."

"Were there ways I supported you that felt especially helpful?"

"You understood what I was trying to build with my family's ranch, and you weren't put off by my focus at first. That really mattered. And your laugh. Darlin', when you laugh, it's beautiful, like the sun through a prism - it colors everything in light. It would get me out of my head. If only for a moment. You didn't laugh much at the end."

She threw a rock into the water. "I didn't think you noticed."

He nodded and skipped another rock. "I noticed."

---

1. I Love You, I'm Sorry by Gracie Abrams

She plunked another rock not too far off from the shore.

"What do you think were the major sources of conflict between us?

"You needed me to shift—to make space for you in a way I wasn't prepared to. Tending to my family's business and resolving the conflicts had a ticking clock in my head."

"And I didn't."

He shook his head. "I thought I had more time. We would argue about it and my stupid ass thought when we stopped you were okay with waiting for me."

His next rock skipped four times. Hers dropped straight down.

These rocks are rigged.

"Did I ever do or say things that frustrated or hurt you repeatedly?"

"Ebony darlin', no. You were clear. You told me what you needed. I just... couldn't, wouldn't meet you there. I needed to be whole first, and to be whole, I *thought,* meant putting the business, this land, first. I was bad at putting anything into perspective. About as bad as you are at skipping rocks. Damn girl, are you even trying?"

Ebony's mouth dropped open dramatically at his audacity before a slow giggle crept out. "Jerk. I wasn't trying." She carefully positioned her hand. "Count the skips out and then tell me why you did all the things for Shayla you couldn't do for me." She flicked her wrist.

Plop.

They watched the ripple spread wider as the sun danced across the surface of the water.

"One."

Ebony glared at him out the corner of her eye. Xavier gave her a smirk. She felt her mouth twitch, and his grin grew. A snort escaped her, and before she knew it, she was laughing full out, with him joining in. It was silly. And not even that funny, but it broke the tension like her rock through the surface of water. In that moment, their laughter was the ripple effect of a love from another lifetime.

Clutching a growing stitch in her side and mindful of her ankle, Ebony plopped down in the grass. A big Colorado sky stretched over her; bird songs and a gentle wind were all around her.

Xavier sat down next to her with a grunt, still chuckling. "Like a prism," he said, looking at her with a fondness that felt... comfortably platonic. "You deserve to sparkle like that every day God gives you with someone who doesn't make you compete with their priorities."

Ebony's thoughts went to Malcolm and how she felt sparkly all the time with him. The heartache returned. She lay back in the grass, leg bent, thinking. She forced herself to recalibrate her brain back to the conversation when Xavier started talking.

"I could give Sweetness what she needed because I gave *me* what I needed first - forgiveness. I looked up and almost every relationship I had was strained or severed, and I knew I needed to make a different choice."

They sat in comfortable silence for a while.

"I thought you'd come back eventually," she admitted. "But this kind of peace and happiness looks good on you. I'm genuinely happy for you."

And she was. That knowledge settled deep in the core of her, shifting things in her that felt damn near spiritual.

"I'm sorry I hurt you, darlin'," he looked over at her with regret etched in his face, from the stress wrinkle he got in his brow to the downturn of his mouth. "I've wanted to tell you that for a long, long time."

"Why didn't you?"

"Because coming back to you wasn't an option," his eyes held hers. "You love quickly and so openly—"

She looked down, "Too quickly."

"It's a gift," he said, a hard edge tinging his voice for the first time.

Her eyes snapped back up to him.

"Don't let assholes who don't appreciate it make you think it's anything less than that," he leveled a stern gaze on her that dissolved into something sadder. "Darlin', you also cut completely. You withdraw into your shell, disappearing from everyone and everything associated with someone who hurt you. Part of it was me being a coward, but it also didn't feel right making you open up just to remind you I broke your heart with no real solutions."

They stared at each other for a moment.

"Am allowed to ask you questions?"

"Of course, this is a conversation more than anything."

He broke eye contact with her and looked out over the lake. "What did you do after you left here the last time?"

Shit. Shit. Shit.

Ebony listened for shutter clicks. And when she didn't hear any, she looked around for him. They had their usual arrangement even without Anika. She and the subject were mic'd the whole time. Malcolm listened in mainly for safety, but also to anticipate shots. If she told the truth, he'd know, and she wasn't sure how that would land. If she lied, no one would know, but she would.

Doggone integrity.

"I... turned down an offer to present at a media conference in Cabo to be with you, and when I left here, I reached out. Turned out they were happy to have me still. I tried to outwork the pain," she cleared her throat. "And when that didn't work, I spent the weekend after the conference working through the pain in other...ways."

"Ah." Then he snorted. "What did Faith say? Best way to get over one is to get under another?"

Ebony laughed. "I can't believe you remember her saying that."

"It's how she introduced herself! You don't forget that shit." He chuckled and glanced over at her. "Good for you."

"It was," she laughed.

He shook his head at her, a wry smile on his face. "Are you happy, darlin'?"

"A few weeks ago I would've said no. Now... even though things have never been crazier and I can't remember ever being this much of a mess, I can honestly say I'm getting there. "

"What changed?"

"I went on a really bad date."

i'm glad it was you

"IF I HAD to get under someone to get over someone, I'm glad that someone was you."

Their departure from the Alexanders' had been silent and tense, but she needed the time.

Ebony hugged the family, promising to stay in touch. Mama Alma held Ebony at arm's length, taking her in. "Be brave," she said, dipping her head to look at her. "Trust yourself, and everything else will work out."

Now, on the jet heading back to Columbus, she finally spoke to him, and she couldn't believe she said that to him, but it was true.

"I remember what I did to make you block me after Cabo, and I understand it a lot more now."

She lifted her head in shock; not only had they never talked about it, it seemed such a minor item compared to what they'd experienced together.

"I told you I'd call you, and I didn't. At the time, I thought it was no big deal, and I'd get to it. Then things got hard. I lost Dad and Justin, and I didn't bother contacting anybody for a long time. But that's no excuse. You were in a place of deep pain, and I became another man who didn't follow through. I'm sorry."

He was apologizing to *her* after she practically one-legged hopped out of the room when he told her he loved her.

"I'm such an ass. You shouldn't be apologizing to me after this morning. It was probably best you didn't call after Cabo."

He looked at her, bracing, for what she wasn't sure.

"I was in no headspace for a relationship. You said it yourself, I was different then. In all likelihood, I'd probably be sitting across from you, interviewing you as my ex. Instead of sitting across from you afraid that will happen if I don't do this right."

"Doing it right needs to include not leaving me like you did this morning." Malcolm said. His voice was raw; his gaze? Stern. "I love you. Have loved you for a while now and I wrestled with that. You aren't the only one who struggles with connection and loss, Ebee. You're on a journey, and I am committed to supporting you. This morning we detoured from what you said you needed: time. But that doesn't mean you can treat me like an emotional support dick. I started it, trying to get you to see how we could be... That's on me, but you running out on me like a fucking pirate..." He shook his head.

"I hurt you, I am so sorry."

"I wasn't expecting you to say it back. I..." he looked down at his hands. "I expected it, me, to matter."

"You're in love with him and he is in love with you," her mom said.

Ebony nodded. "I just want to *know* that this time... This time I'll end up like you two."

"Ebony, we started off young, with fewer relationship

resources, and it's not always been roses," her dad said. "What you see now is forty years of showing up for each other, of getting on each others nerves, of choosing each other every day and forgiving each other and ourselves on days that we don't. There's no way to know if it's going to work out—"

"But no matter what happens," her mother interrupted. "You'll survive it, Lil Bit."

THERE WASN'T A PUZZLE INVENTED THAT COULD KEEP HIS ATTENTION. Not a single dish from Armello's that tempted him.

"Maybe I should've just left it be," Malcolm shook his head. "I called her a pirate."

His mom chuckled a bit. "Malcolm, love isn't abandoning yourself to keep them. That's what Ebony is learning right now. Loving each other is being accountable to each other. That's where trust is built. That is what it takes to *last*."

"I thought it would be easier with the right one."

His mother laughed harder after that. "Who told you that?!"

"JOY, YOU OKAY IN THERE?" THERE WAS SOME SHIFTING AND movement behind the door before Joy opened up the guest bedroom door and attempted to smile.

"I'm good E. Just tired."

"Okay. Have you eaten?"

She nodded. "I am going for a walk later."

"Awesome."

"I'm not lost, you know. I'm just deconstructing ten years

of marriage and reorienting my world. Thank you for letting me stay."

"Stay as long as you need honey, I love you."

"You okay?"

"No. Not in the slightest, but I'm trying. I miss him."

Joy nodded. "Don't let what I've been through keep you from your forever love." Joy hugged Ebony tightly.

"Hey, E, I know it might be awkward, but I'd like to see you."

group therapy

Kinda sad this series is ending because Ebony feels less like a character now and more like that one homegirl you desperately want to stop self-sabotaging while also rooting for her happiness with your whole chest.

This series changed tone so quietly. It started with "let's interview the exes" and ended with all of us examining the ways we love, sacrifice ourselves, forgive people, and move forward. The feature better hurt me even worse.

I'm going to miss the comment section debates after every episode. We really built a tiny support group around Ebony making catastrophic romantic decisions and healing in real time.

I cannot believe The Five Loves of Ebony Jones is almost over. These interviews started as drama and somehow turned into group therapy for everybody watching. I'm not ready to let these people go yet. 😭

THE BAR WAS QUIETER than Ebony expected for a Friday night in Columbus.

Old school R&B drifted through the speakers; the lighting was low, and people minded their business. It was the kind of place where people actually talked instead of yelling over the bass. It didn't have a VIP section; the food was good, but no one bothered taking photos of it, and you'd get cussed out for recording someone.

She'd picked it on purpose. Quiet, neutral territory. She and Isaiah sat across from each other, their drinks and a basket of fries taking up most of the small table.

Isaiah adjusted in his seat and leaned in. "Keisha thought I was boring too," he said after the small talk had piddled out into nothing.

"I never called you boring."

He gave her a look. "You heavily implied it."

"I said there wasn't enough spark."

"That's just a nice way of saying boring." Isaiah shook his head, but he was smiling.

She smiled into her drink.

God, he was easy to be around.

That had always been the problem. Not chemistry exactly. Just... ease so steady it eventually flattened into roommate-level comfort.

Still, Ebony understood and appreciated all the reasons she'd loved him: his kindness, patience, steadiness.

"You know what I mean, though," he said quietly. "I think I stopped pushing myself."

Ebony tilted her head slightly.

"And now?"

He shrugged. "Now I'm thirty-six and realize I can predict almost every day of my life before it happens."

"Sounds like a personal hell."

"It kind of is, and life is short." Isaiah glanced at her again, something tentative creeping into his expression now. "I need your help."

She blinked, mentally rearranging her current load. *Wait. Put your own mask on first.* Cautiously she asked, "With what?"

"To help me be less boring."

She barked out a laugh loud enough that two people at the bar turned briefly.

"I'm serious."

"You are so not serious."

"I am." He grinned despite himself. "You always had ideas. You made me do things I never would've done on my own."

She shook her head. "Isaiah, you think adventure is some huge, life-changing thing," she told him. "Half the time it's just saying yes before you overthink it."

Isaiah considered, then nodded slowly. "Okay."

"Okay, what?"

"Teach me."

She narrowed her eyes immediately. "You sound like the

lead in a 90s Cinderella remake, complete with a makeover montage."

He laughed. "Does it involve pretending to learn how to be cool? And a bet for a dollar?"

She laughed at the thought. He watched her for a second with that same soft expression he'd always had around her. Like he genuinely enjoyed making her laugh.

"I'm asking my ex-girlfriend for personality help."

"That's worse."

He chuckled.

Damn. It would've been simpler if he'd ever hurt her. Instead, he'd just... failed to ignite something she chased from man to man for years. She thought about Malcolm, and that same ache tore at her. *That* was ignition. And Ebony ruthlessly shoved it down to the deep, dark place where she stacked all the other hurts she'd powered through.

That spark was nothing but pain. Maybe...safety, consistency, and warmth were enough.

"You busy right now?" she asked suddenly.

Isaiah blinked. "No?"

"Good. Come on."

He frowned as she slid out of her seat.

"Where are we going?"

"You said you wanted help."

"Girl, right now??"

"Yes, Isaiah. Let's go."

He looked like he was rethinking his request, but like a champ he dropped money for their order and a generous tip on the table and followed her out into the sticky August night.

"You know," he called after her as they walked down the sidewalk in German Village, "most people would start with a book recommendation."

"You don't need a book. You need exposure therapy."

"Exposure therapy," he repeated skeptically.

"Correct."

Five minutes later, they were inside a tiny late-night karaoke bar wedged between a bookstore and a pizza place.

Isaiah stopped dead near the entrance.

"No."

"Oh, absolutely yes."

"Ebony."

"You wanted growth."

"I didn't mean public humiliation."

She was already laughing.

"Don't be scared."

"I'm not scared. I just think this establishment deserves better than whatever's about to happen."

She grabbed his wrist before he could retreat. "You're doing one song."

"One."

"Yes, and you'll survive."

That familiar look crossed his face again—that reluctant amusement that always appeared right before he gave in to one of her ideas. She saw it click over in his head. The exact moment he decided.

Twenty minutes later, Isaiah was standing beside her under the twirling, rotating rainbow light someone had plugged in a decade ago, singing a decent rendition of a Boyz II Men song while she smiled hard and encouraged him.

He committed himself to his off-key harmonizing, and the way he kept laughing at himself instead of shutting down gave her an immense sense of pride.

When the song ended, they cheered on several more singers before they called it a night. He followed her back home to make sure she got in okay, and before she climbed up the steps, Isaiah stopped her.

"Thank you. That was great."

"That's a lie."

He looked down at her, still laughing. "Man, that was terrible. I'd rather fight a bear. I ain't gone lie. But that means we are on the right track, right? So, what's next, Coach?"

The streetlights highlighted his sharp features in a warm gold. He really was a handsome, sweet man.

Not every relationship has a head over heels love, with yearning and breathing for the next moment with them kind of love. Maybe safe and mutual respect is just as good. Different, but good enough to be a forever kind of love.

Isaiah stepped close. "You always made life feel bigger," he admitted quietly.

His eyes dropped briefly to her mouth before lifting back to hers, giving her every chance to step away.

She didn't. And so he kissed her. Soft and careful. And she searched herself for budding, blooming feelings.

A camera shutter click interrupted her inward search.

Ebony pulled back immediately and, to her horror, sitting on her steps was Malcolm. He slowly lowered his camera.

Isaiah followed her eyes, confused at first, then his energy shifted.

Malcolm's expression barely changed, but his eyes stayed on Ebony, and an incredibly long second passed. Then he glanced at Isaiah once before looking back at her.

"Good shot," he said evenly, lifting his camera.

EBONY DIDN'T SLEEP THE ENTIRE NIGHT. HER MIND KEPT REPLAYING everything over on a loop. She relived the kiss, the karaoke, the finality in Malcolm's tone. The way he just walked away without a backward glance.

At six a.m., a text came in. Still wide awake, Ebony reached a listless arm over and snagged her phone off its charger.

"Beautiful."

It was from Malcolm. Her stomach dropped and hope bloomed. Her fingers fumbled trying to get the message open, and when it finally did, she was physically ill.

She threw up everything she could've thrown up and cried because she knew, she fucking knew that she had made the worst mistake of her life, and she had a long list.

When Pumpkin found her, she had managed to wash her face and brush her teeth. That's it. Ebony sat on the floor of her office, a set of papers clutched in her hands, reliving everything, every interaction. Big and small.

Every precious moment she and Malcolm created and shared was gone, and it was her stupid fucking fault.

"She's been like this for hours," Pumpkin whispered. January took off her apron and sat next to Ebony. Slipping the papers out of her hand, she gasped and passed them to Joy. Each cousin read and made a small sound.

The Questions to Ask worksheet was full of all the ways she and Malcolm had built something real. For the Facts vs. Fantasy list, the facts wrapped around the page.

"Ok honey, this is good," Faith said. "Why do you look so..."

"Devastated," Joy said.

"I let Isaiah kiss me. I could've stopped him. But I...he's so steady and caring and sweet... It didn't feel like I'd lose the world if I lost him, and I stood there just to see. To make sure and..." More tears leaked as she handed them her phone.

"Wow. You two look beautiful," Pumpkin said.

"Like the end of Love Jones with the fog and the lamplight," January agreed.

"Wait, who took the — fuck." Faith showed them the phone again.

"Damn."

Isaiah sat next to Ebony, his hands clasped tightly together. She sat on the far end of the couch, almost tucked into a little ball.

Finally, after stilted small talk, she just had to get it out. Turning to him, she tried to let him down as easily as she could.

"Listen, Isaiah, about last night," she wrapped and unwrapped the tie of her robe around her finger.

"I'm in love with Keisha," Isaiah blurted out. "Kissing you, I knew. Keisha's the one for me."

"Ouch, and also I'm so glad, because kissing you was like kissing a shoe. Only man I want to kiss is Malcolm." Ebony blew out a breath, happy she didn't have to break his heart a second time.

"There was nothing there."

"There was nothing there."

They spoke together and chuckled.

"I think that's the danger of memory lane," Isaiah said. "You can mistake the comfort of memories for something real."

Ebony nodded, sniffing deeply. "I just wanted to be sure. I didn't want... it doesn't matter. He sent me this." She showed Isaiah the text, and he let out a deep whistle.

"It looks like a movie poster."

"Yeah. He's never going to forgive me after this."

"You don't know that. If you explain to him, hell, I'll explain to him."

Ebony shook her head. "He's had to hear me talk about and talk with all of these men in my life, as he ached for me. He told me he loved me, and I ran. Literally hopped out the door."

She stood and paced.

And when I told him I needed time to make sure that I was doing this right, that I wouldn't be sitting across from him in two years trying to figure out where we went wrong, he said he would wait for me.

"And then he sees this. I have no right to ask him to forgive me."

Ebony ran the sleeve of her robe under her nose. "I was so afraid to get everything I ever wanted. I threw it away on a shoe."

"Okay, it wasn't that bad."

Ebony looked Isaiah dead in the eye. "Old sneaker. You smell like leather, man."

"That's a new cologne. I'm trying out *Leather and Marble*."

"Leather. And. Marble. Oh my god!" Ebony gave him the first hint of a smile she'd had. It was wet and snotty, but genuine for her... Friend.

"So what did you tell Keisha?"

"I haven't told her anything yet. I was coming here to tell you. And hope that you didn't have hard feelings."

"I don't."

"Yeah, I got that. Thanks."

They laughed together. He took her hands in his. "I thought about walking up to her, looking her in the eyes and saying, 'Keisha, will you marry me in six to twelve months?'"

Ebony double blinked. "Why six to twelve months?"

"To give her time to plan," he said proudly.

"Oh my god. You really are bad at this."

"What? I thought I was endearing."

"You said she thought you were boring. What did she say exactly?"

"She said I was too measured and refused to be spontaneous."

"And you think asking her to marry you in three to five business days, like a bank transaction, is going to change her mind about that?"

"Right, right."

"I already know I want to spend the rest of my life with you. Why wait when we can have forever right now? Or something like that."

"Oh, that's good. Can I write that down?"

"You need a Grand Gesture," January said.

"She needs to go say sorry, listen to his feelings, then ride that man like the rent's due," Faith said.

"He's not returning her calls," Joy said. "Pull the work chain and get him to where he has to listen."

"And add a Grand Gesture!"

"A small gift. To show what he means to you. Something handmade," Pumpkin said.

"Lure him under false pretenses, apologize, and give him a potholder. Or a mixtape."

"No." Pumpkin rolled her eyes. "Well, yes, to the false pretenses, but there must be something that you can give or make that reminds him just how good you two are together."

Ebony had one thing. "Does Aunt Easter still have that craft machine?"

"Yep. Just make sure you back it up on him after you get finished giving him your Valentine."

Xavier admitting Ebony stopped laughing near the end of their relationship and her saying, "I didn't think you noticed" just gutted me a little. Sometimes the deepest heartbreak isn't screaming matches. It's realizing someone saw your sadness and still couldn't meet you where you needed them.

Xavier and Ebony laughing over her terrible rock skipping while discussing heartbreak felt so painfully real. 🐶 🪨 That's what old love looks like sometimes—not passion, not bitterness, just two people finally honest enough to stop bleeding on each other. 🩶

"Count the skips out and then tell me why you did all

the things for [redacted] you couldn't do for me." Ebony said answer this question but entertain me first. 😵

____

____

The way this interview shifted from closure to therapy to stand-up comedy... 😅

____

ARMELLO'S WAS ALMOST empty except for a couple talking quietly near the back and a skeleton crew of staff. Mello kept sending concerned glances their way, but Ebony, as she sat across from him with her recorder, didn't seem to notice. [1]

She was nervous... No, deeply uncomfortable, and whether it was because of him or because of who they were supposed to meet, it pissed him off.

He checked his watch again, jaw tight. "He's forty minutes late."

"Yeah."

"And you still think he's coming? Who is this dude and why didn't you send me a dossier on him? What's with the last-minute add, Ebony?"

She didn't answer immediately, eyes fixed on the condensation sliding down her water glass.

He leaned back against his chair with a humorless laugh. "Unbelievable."

"Malcolm—"

---

1. We Can't Be Friends (with RL) by Deborah Cox

"No, it's fine." He dragged a hand across his face. "Actually, no. It's not fine."

The sharpness in his voice made Armello glance over again.

"Keep your voice down."

"When are you going to stop caring about what other people think?"

Her expression hardened instantly. "That's unfair."

"Is it?" he asked. "Because from where I'm sitting, you dragged me out here for another interview with another 'great love' who hurt you while I—" He stopped himself, shaking his head once. "You know what? Forget it."

Ebony's shoulders stiffened. "You said you wanted to finish this assignment professionally."

"I did." He looked at her directly now. "I just didn't realize professional meant watching you choose someone else."

She stilled.

"That's not what this is."

"Then what is it?" he asked quietly.

"A Grand Gesture."

What the fuck is a grand gesture? Is that like a magnanimous goodbye? Classy and given with gentle, encouraging words?

Silence stretched between them. Outside, headlights flashed in the restaurant's windows, highlighting the rivulets of raindrops racing down the window into oblivion.

Ebony looked down at the recorder sitting between them. Then she reached forward and clicked it on.

Malcolm frowned immediately. "What are you doing?"

"The interview."

"Your mystery man is not here."

"Yeah..."

His eyes narrowed slightly. "Ebony."

"State your name for the record."

He stared at her for a long second. "Seriously?"

"Humor me."

"No."

"Malcolm."

He let out a short laugh under his breath, disbelieving. "You cannot be doing this right now."

"Please."

Something in her voice softened the edge of his irritation just enough for him to sigh.

"...Malcolm Knight."

"Occupation?"

"Photojournalist. Love-starved idiot, apparently."

"Specialty?"

"Humans." His eyes flicked toward her. "Bad timing."

She smiled softly, and it killed him.

Killed him.

He knew his heart still beat because the of the pain, but as far as he was concerned his life had stilled and slowed down.

Ebony glanced down at her notes.

"What was your first impression of Ebony Jones?"

He blinked once. "Absolutely not."

"Answer the question."

"No, because this is insane. Are you — are you making fun of me?"

"No." she shook her head, eyes overly bright. Ebony sat still, waiting him out.

He looked at her for another beat before exhaling sharply through his nose. "My first impression," he muttered, "was that you were amazing. You had me hanging on your every word. And, you were intimidating."

Her brow lifted slightly. "Intimidating?"

"That's wrong," he frowned, unable to not spill his guts around her. "I was intimidated. I knew I'd have to step my game up to talk to you. Yet, I was compelled to throw myself out in front of you."

She swallowed and nodded slowly.

"And after that?" she asked quietly.

He looked away toward the window. "After that, I realized you were funny and easy to talk to. Which was inconvenient."

"Inconvenient how?"

His jaw flexed. "Ebony."

"Please."

He looked back at her then, frustration and hurt sitting openly on his face now.

"Inconvenient because I liked you more than I was supposed to. And loved you before I should have."

The air between them shifted, and like it always did, the room narrowed, and it was just them. This time, instead of new friends, or reacquainted lovers, it was a fool in love with a woman who was looking for more.

"When did you realize that?"

"When I liked you or loved you?"

"Yes."

He gave her a long look. "I thought I really liked you after that first drink in Cabo. I absolutely adored you after that first phone call with the slug. "

Her breath caught slightly.

"You were serious, but honest and vulnerable. You hadn't been like that in Cabo," he said. "I understand why now. That first phone call you were not as nice, but you were vastly more interesting."

Despite everything, a small smile tugged at her mouth.

Malcolm looked away. He couldn't afford to enjoy her smile anymore. It was costing him everything just to sit across from her like this and not beg or cajole his way into her heart because, despite everything, he loved her too much to pressure her. She'd made the safe choice.

She clicked her pen once. "What do you think I'm afraid of?"

He sighed, exhausted and more than a little sad. Maybe that's why he didn't censor himself. "You think you're afraid to disappoint others, and maybe that's part of it, but you're more afraid to disappoint yourself."

Her eyes widened.

"You feel you let yourself down, loved too quickly and too hard, and left yourself unprotected. You are afraid if you love someone again, as completely as you've always done, that you'll let yourself down again. You're so afraid of letting yourself down again that you'll settle for the good man you know, rather than the love you really need from a man you're still learnin.'"

Ebony's fingers tightened around the pen.

Armello stopped by the table. "Everything okay?" He directed the question more to Ebony than to him.

Ain't this 'bout a bitch.

Ebony nodded her head.

He'd had enough. "No, it's not," Malcolm said immediately. He looked at the entrance again and checked his watch one last time. "He's not coming."

"I know."

"Then what are we still doing here?"

Ebony stared at him for a moment too long. "I'm messing this up. You really don't get it yet," she murmured.

His expression tightened immediately. "No, Ebony, I don't." He heard the hurt in his own voice through the anger.

"I believed in this work with you, but I don't get the additional mystery man, and I definitely don't get why you're interviewing me like I'm just another chapter in this story."

Her eyes softened then. "I'm messing this up... You were never just another chapter."

Malcolm stood, checking his phone. *Shit.*

Mom: Mal, I need help

on my way

He grabbed his jacket. "I gotta go."

"Mal, wait."

He paused reluctantly.

She reached into the large leather tote beside her and pulled out a rectangular box wrapped in dark paper.

His brow furrowed. "What's this?"

"You love puzzles."

"That doesn't answer my question."

The door to Armello's opened, and in walked Isaiah, all smiles.

This mutha...

"Ebony, guess what?! Oh, hey man, you two finished—"

Malcolm pulled his wallet out, threw cash onto the table, and tucked the box under his arm.

"Have a good night."

EBONY SAT AT THE TABLE, STARING OUT THE WINDOW AT THE SPOT where Malcolm had disappeared into the night.

"I am so sorry, Ebony," Isaiah said. "I have the worst fucking timing. I should have just blurted it out, but I didn't want to ruin your moment, and then he was gone."

Ebony shook her head. "It's been a long time since I've been that intimidated. Things with Malcolm are always so easy, even when we had tension, and tonight... I couldn't, I couldn't form the words. I knew what to say. I had it written down, and I tried to go through the grand gesture and I just... I didn't know how to say it."

A coffee cup was placed before her. She looked up and Armello's kind face stared down at her. He pulled out a chair and turned it around, sitting backward.

"He was so angry. I don't blame him at all, not one bit." She shook her head. "And before I knew it, things had gotten out of control, and then he was gone. I felt like I was losing him in real time. He's so hurt, and I did that. It paralyzed me."

Isaiah and Armello sat with Ebony silently, offering their support until her cousins burst through the door. Armello and Isaiah gave them the breakdown; Ebony, for once, had no desire or energy to tell the story.

"Okay, honey, well you gave him the puzzle," Pumpkin said. "Maybe he needs a few days to cool off, and then he'll reach for the puzzle to work through it. Grand Gesture still intact, just...delayed. Right, Mello?"

Mello shrugged. "Maybe?"

"You're not helping," January said.

"I don't want to lie to the girl. He's been really messed up. I almost banned you from the restaurant."

"Oh my god, Mello, really?!" January exclaimed. "After all that, you think she'd just toss him to the side like that?"

"She was kissing this dude."

"Well, technically. He kissed her; she just stood there," Faith said, adjusting her glasses. "She and Malcolm weren't together."

"In my heart, we were," Ebony said.

"Oh, Sweetie..." Faith sat next to her and took her hand. "And why are you here anyway, New Balance?"

"New Balance?"

"Because kissing you was like kissing a shoe," Faith shooed him away.

"Nah, I'm not accepting that nickname," he protested.

"You smelled like leather. Accept it," she argued back.

Armello laughed his ass off. "I bet you're saved in her phone under that."

Isaiah, fully distracted, called Ebony, and they all waited. His face popped up, and underneath?

"New Balance calling…"

Everyone at the table fell out laughing, well, except for Ebony and Isaiah.

"E!"

She shrugged. "It was funny," she said sadly, still looking out the window.

"Argh. ANYWAY, I came here because Keisha was craving some cinnamon rolls and grits, with a steak on top. Then I saw you and wanted to tell you I proposed to Keisha and she said yes, and I stepped in it."

"And tracked all over the restaurant," Faith said, rolling her eyes.

"This is on me and only on me," Ebony said quietly. "I'm happy for you, Isaiah." She finally looked from the window to him. "Did you do it the way we rehearsed it?"

"I tried, but I was so nervous, and she was so beautiful and sweaty—she had just got out of teaching her Big Body'd Yoga class. I just dropped to both knees," he got down to the side of the table to demonstrate in front of Ebony, "and said: 'I'm predictable, but you'll always know who I am and how much I love you. I'm reluctant to try new things, but I have no hesitation about starting a new life with you. I'm going to be braver, more flexible, and put you through the mattress every day we are together for the rest of our lives if you marry me. I love you.'"

The group blinked collectively for a second, then broke out in applause and accolades.

"Ok I see you, New Balance!"

"I liked the predictable line."

"Bars."

"Put you through the mattress is always a winner."

Isaiah blushed four shades of red. "Was it really that good?" he asked Ebony.

She took his hand in hers, nodding. "I loved it. Way better than what I came up with, and it's more you."

He got back onto his seat.

"Aye, Dog, that was so good, I'm going to make your shrimp and steak on the house. I have one cinnamon roll left. I was holding it for someone, but they'll be alright. Be right back."

Armello disappeared into the kitchen, and Ebony turned back to the window.

"That's an interesting combination," Pumpkin said. "It sounds like a pregnancy craving."

Isaiah grinned bigger, and Ebony took her eyes off the window again.

"It's early," he said shyly. "I didn't know until after I proposed."

Another round of quiet celebration erupted.

As she offered her congratulations, Ebony wondered how she could be bleeding out, dying in a room full of people and no one notice. Did it not seep from her soul into their shoes? Smell of metal, reek of despair? She turned back to the window. Waiting, watching, hoping for him. She had no right to hope, but still...

I thought he'd fight harder for me. [2]

---

2. What Am I Gonna Do On Sundays? by Olivia Dean

What's the word for when you have a word
that sounds like the sound it's describing?

Malcolm stopped pulling out of the parking spot.

Is this what you needed help with?

Yes. It's driving me crazy.

"Fuck, Ma…" He took a breath. It wasn't her fault. Brain fog was a part of both her disease and treatment.

I think you are looking for onomatopoeia.

That's it! Thank you son. This brain fog is a
son of a bitch.

Malcolm dropped his head back against his seat. He should go back in there. He'd already broken the first rule: come together, leave together. Instead, she asked him to meet her there and he went along with it.

Clearly, dude, whoever he was, wasn't coming.

But what if he did and Malcolm was gone? She'd need the visuals for the piece.

"Grrr… fuck!" He reached for his gear in the back seat and brushed against her gift. Warring with himself, he recognized he needed a moment. He needed to take a walk and calm down.

"What the fuck am I doing?!" Malcolm asked himself, stopping in the middle of the sidewalk.

Malcolm stared at the lights in the lamp store that never seemed to have any customers. He'd walked blocks reliving every single precious moment of their time together; giving up his soul the further he got away from her.

He turned around, half expected to see his own blood leaving a trail, because that's what he felt like.

Each step back to her was plodding,

then faster,

and faster,

until he was sprinting the last few blocks to her. As he waited for a car to pass so he could cross the street, he watched her through the big picture window of Armello's.

This time he didn't reach for his camera. His breath seized in his chest, his arms, heavy dead weights, hung limp at his sides as he watched her, surrounded by her sisters.

She focused on Isaiah as he dropped to both knees, passionately speaking to her. They erupted in celebration. Then Ebony, with a small, non-copper smile, took his hands in hers and nodded. Through the rain, through the darkness, through the window she mouthed the words he had prayed to hear from her lips: *"I love..."*

I can't do it.

He'd stood witness, recorded the moments of humans around the world, in the best of circumstances, in the worst... witnessed their lives beginning, ending, and almost all the parts in between, and survived. Scarred, but still living.

He couldn't survive witnessing this.

He turned into the darkest part of the street, and with practiced movements, became a shadow. As he navigated the darkness, the same thought pounded through his skull.

I thought she'd fight harder for me.

EBONY ALTERNATED FROM SITTING TO STANDING TO PACING AND BACK again in the waiting room of the hospital. In this wing, athletes, weekend warriors, and kids in casts moved about in various stages of injury and recovery. She kept glancing at the surgical board for updates, even though she knew it was too early for her mom's hip surgery to be finished.

On her third round of pacing, she looked up at a familiar face. It had to be a mirage.

Malcolm.

He strode to her tall, Black and beautiful. She stood there, frozen in place, eyes locked on his. Not believing it was him. Not believing how beautiful he was. Not believing how busted she looked. Not believing she had a second shot at clearing the air. Maybe?

"Um. What are you—?"

"How's your mom?"

"How'd you know?"

"Mom mentioned it."

She sighed, nodded, and shrugged. "We don't know. She was scheduled for a replacement later this month, but she slipped in the bathroom and broke it. The repair is going to be complex, but they said they didn't know how bad until they were in there. She's still in surgery, and we haven't had any updates, so I'm taking that as good news. We're not due to hear anything for another hour."

They stood there awkwardly, and Ebony's stomach churned. "You came to check on my mom?"

"Yes, and I was already here with Mom."

"Oh no! Is she all right?"

"Yeah, yeah, she had trouble taking herself off the machine and lost a good amount of blood."

"Oh, my God!" Her hand flew to her mouth, and her stomach lurched.

"No, she's okay, but she used a tourniquet. After that, they wanted to make sure she's okay, give her a pint of blood, and keep her overnight for observation."

"Malcolm, I'm so sorry to hear that. What floor is she on? I'll go down after Mom is settled in her room."

"She'd like that. She still wants to see those beads."

Ebony's eyes widened in amusement, and she almost smiled. He noticed it, too, and looked away. After that they stood around again looking everywhere but at each other.

Do it, Ebony. Just say I'm sorry, I love you.

"Have you had a chance to look at your gift?"

Girl what?

"At your parting gift? Nah."

"That's not what it is, Mal."

"That's what it feels like, and I've got a lot on my mind. This is really not the most appropriate time."

"No, no, no, you're right. You're right."

That was so self-centered; why did you ask him that?!

She used to feel so bright and shiny next to him. And now. She was dull. Tarnished.

"I'm sorry for everything."

"Ebony," he said low and frustrated.

She held up her hands. "No, that's. That's all I was going to say."

"I'm sorry that sounded—"

Malcolm touched her arm for the first time in what felt like years. And his touch burned. Destroying the flimsy string holding her together.

"Lil Bit."

Ebony's head snapped around at the tremor in her dad's voice. Rushing to where a nurse was standing with him, she looked from her dad to the nurse and back.

"She's going to be just fine," his voice trembled.

"OH, Ebony looks beautiful. I love it when a bride does something unexpected," his mother said casually, as if he wasn't on the verge of throwing up because she did look beautiful in the bridal white pantsuit, jacket nipping in at her waist, accentuating her curves. She smiled big and wide, just like a bride should, and he was just fucking sick.

"How you let her go, I'll never figure out."

"I didn't let her do anything. I told her how I felt; she asked me to wait and take it slow, then she was kissing Isaiah and he proposed. Everywhere I go, that dude is fucking there," Malcolm said, thinking back to the restaurant, the hospital where he showed up to check in on Ebony's mom, claiming he was there because his kid broke her wrist. He was like a bad penny.

He turned back to stocking the supply cabinet for his mother.

"I just don't understand why she would say that, when Noel told me she gave you her heart.

"She gave me a puzzle, but that's not the heart of Ebony Jones. Now, she's settling."

The doorbell saved him from having to explain what he couldn't really explain. He *knew* she loved him, but if she couldn't trust herself, they would keep up this thing that was getting unhealthy for both of them. They were hurt and chafed raw, and instead of being a balm for each other; they caused each other more damage and pain.

"Man, put together the damn puzzle and let's go," Mello yelled without preamble as he walked into the house. "Hey Auntie Bell, I brought this for you." He stooped down a little to kiss her cheek.

"Ooh, cabbage!" She said excitedly as peeked into the container.

"And potatoes, double-boiled so it won't mess with your potassium."

She patted his cheek. "Thank you, nephew!"

Mello preened for a minute, then turned back to Malcolm. "Puzzle. Now."

"What the hell, man? Fine, I'll open the fucking puzzle."

Malcolm had been carrying it around like a child with a blanket, hesitant to put it together, reluctant to put it away. If he couldn't have Ebony close, he'd keep her last gift to him next to him.

The box and the puzzle looked homemade, but it was a standard jigsaw. He started as he always did, separating the edge pieces, but instead of the picture getting clearer, the pieces got blurrier.

"She's in Vegas with him."

"I know." Mello said, arranging sections of color together.

"What does the note say?" Mabeline asked, reaching for a small slip of paper he hadn't seen. "The Six Loves of Ebony Jones. Open after puzzle complete."

"Six?" His ears must have been as clogged as his eyes. His

heart wouldn't believe it until he saw it himself. [1]

"Lock in," Mello urged.

Malcolm nodded, stood, and locked the fuck in. His focus narrowed as he moved pieces into place. With no photo to go off of, he had to zoom in on shapes, and for the first time in weeks he had a clarity that came from extreme purpose. Blinking his eyes clear, he moved until the picture materialized. It was he and Ebony in the cabin. Their reflection in the mirror.

Her breasts. His arms. Her perfect, rounded belly and thighs. Their faces pressed together. Legs intertwined, a small bandage around Ebony's ankle the only thing marring her beautiful body, her curved line. Their bodies and souls joined. They were fucking art.

"That is beautiful," his mother whispered.

"Auntie, don't look," Mello admonished. "It is beautiful tho'."

"Reminds me of me and Jet."

"Eww Auntie."

Malcolm tuned them out and opened up note, his breaths coming fast and hot like he'd run six miles for an evacuation.

---

1.   open by Joy Rhodes

<u>The Six Loves of Ebony Jones</u>
~~1. The first love.~~
~~2. The crazy love.~~
~~3. The safe love.~~
~~4. The love that almost broke me.~~
~~5. The almost forever love.~~
6. The unexpected Love. 🤍

"To the unexpected Malcolm Knight: I never imagined a bad date would bring the best love, the realest love I've ever known.

Love I didn't have to chase, because it welcomed me. Love I didn't have to change for, because it accepted me as I am.

Love so sweet and pure, it scared me. So passionate I suspected it was fantasy, so patient I feared it would break me if I lost it. Lost you.

Please forgive me. It was like kissing a shoe.

Forever and always,
The No Longer Elusive Ebony Jones

"Mello?"
"Yeah?"
"We need to get to Vegas."
"Mello, call Mom's center and have them set up a treatment out there for tomorrow."

"I get to come too?" his mom said in surprise. "I won't slow you down?"

"If you don't go pack your meds and drawers, you will."

His mother giggled and scampered off. Malcolm scrolled to a contact on his phone and hit the speaker. When it connected, he said without preamble: "I'mma be real ghetto with you, man. I need to borrow your plane right quick. I need to stop Ebony from marrying the Black Flat Stanley at some Elvis chapel in Vegas at midnight."

"When a brotha says call me if you need anything…This is exactly the type of carrying on I'm talking about. We just walked out of our niece's birthday party in Columbus, actually, so Shayla can fly us. Aye Sweetness, down for a Grand Gesture flight to Vegas?"

"Of course! Good thing you caught me before I got into the apple wine. Wheels up in thirty!"

This reminds me of your father's Grand Gestures."

"Seriously," Malcolm yelled as he wiped his face and carefully packed away Ebony's gifts. "What is a grand gesture?"

"I told Ebony you probably didn't have a clue. Gotta know your customer," Mello shook his head, swiping at his phone. "We're ready."

Malcolm looked at his mom. "Where's your luggage?"

"We'll buy panties in Vegas, son," she waved a small bag that kept her meds. "Let's go."

"I'M SORRY, MALCOLM. I HAVE TO WAIT FOR THE HABOOB TO PASS before I can land," Shayla, Xavier Alexander's wife, said over the intercom. "We're in a holding pattern until it does. Radar shows it shouldn't be long now."

Malcolm was losing it. First, they were delayed by a summer thunderstorm in Columbus. Now they were delayed by a haboob.

"What's a haboob?" Mello asked.

"Massive dust storm," his mother replied. "Listen, honey, if you don't stop the wedding, you can always seduce her, and she can get a quickie divorce."

"Ma!"

"I'm providing solutions. The woman said kissing that man was like kissing a shoe! No way she wants to live with that the rest of her life."

THE WEDDING CHAPEL LOOKED EXACTLY AS CHAOTIC IN PERSON AS IT had online when he'd looked it up. Tacky and lit up in pink lights with a cardboard Elvis near the entrance. Through the open chapel doors, Malcolm could hear music and cheering.

He checked his watch and stopped cold.

"Oh my God."

Even with the Alexanders chartering a helicopter to avoid traffic on the Strip, it still took a while to get to the venue. Inside, guests were gathered around the tiny altar while an Elvis impersonator officiated with far too much enthusiasm.

And there she was in her white pantsuit, standing beside Isaiah.

Malcolm snapped.

"EBONY!"

"Son, wait."

"We should've stopped him before now," Mello whispered.

Every head in the chapel turned. Elvis stopped mid-sentence. Isaiah blinked and Ebony froze, holding a fucking bouquet.

Malcolm marched down the aisle, breathing hard, his mother and Mello following slower.

"What are you doing?" Ebony hissed.

"What am *I* doing?" Malcolm repeated loudly.

Isaiah frowned. "Man, I'm getting married—"

"NOT TODAY BRUH!" Malcolm yelled. He stepped closer to Ebony, hand on his heart, not crowding her, just closing the distance gently.

"I put together the puzzle and read your note."

Her face softened. "I didn't know what a grand gesture was. I thought it was like a last goodbye."

"Oh no!" Ebony said, her hand reaching up and covering her mouth.

"Baby, I love you too. Everything about you. It's not just your beautiful body," he said, steady. "Or how you own every space you enter. And it's not how much you give to people before you even notice you're doing it, before they even ask. Or how you light up my entire day just with your smile. It's not just because you are brave in carving out the life you want."

He looked away, gathering his thoughts. "Your presence is sacred, Ebony. Your attention, divine. You see *me* and still love me. As a Black man, there are times I don't feel...human in other people's eyes. But I'm real in yours. You let me into your soft spaces and made room for me in a life that was already full."

He stepped closer. "I know what that cost you. I'm grateful," he said. He shook his head, still in awe. "You're the best person I've ever known. I've watched you, learned you. I've seen how your mind works, and brilliant doesn't even cover it."

His breath eased out slowly.

"I love you," he repeated, quieter now. "Baby, please don't marry this man. You can't spend your life kissing a shoe."

Another woman in white—standing directly on Isaiah's other side—looked offended.

"Ok now, I'm not gonna be too many more shoes," Isaiah said.

"You interrupt my wedding, and you say my man kisses like a shoe? Isaiah who is this clown?"

Malcolm paused.

Looked at the woman.

Looked at Ebony.

Looked back at the bride who was on the correct side in an American wedding.

"Oh."

The chapel went silent for exactly one second before Ebony doubled over laughing. Not polite laughing. Full-body, can't-breathe laughing. He saw nothing but shiny copper, and he filled his soul with it.

Isaiah started laughing too. The actual bride covered her mouth, anger gone.

Even Elvis looked amused.

Ebony was still laughing, wiping tears from under her eyes. "Why did you think Isaiah and I were getting married?!"

"He proposed to you in the restaurant! You're both wearing white!"

"What?!"

"Ok now look," Isaiah said with bass in his voice. "You seem like a good dude, but you've got one more time to upset my bride. Keisha, I practiced what I was going to say with Ebony, but in the end, I messed up what we rehearsed and went from the heart. I showed Ebony and her cousins what I did and said. That's all."

"Oh." Keisha smiled and gave him doe eyes. "It was a really good proposal."

"Also, Mal, everyone is wearing white," Ebony choked out.

Malcolm looked around wildly, and unfortunately, she was correct. The bride, bridesmaid, Isaiah, the guests...even Elvis had on a white rhinestone suit.

Keisha suddenly pointed between Malcolm and Ebony. "Wait. Is this the photographer who shot your series?"

Ebony's smile slightly. "Unfortunately."

"Oh, this is *good*," Keisha said, grinning wide. "You can shoot our after-party to make this up to me."

"Uh, sure."

Isaiah stepped forward, now grinning again. "For the record, I realized I was still in love with my ex."

The bride raised her hand, showing off her engagement ring proudly.

"And Ebony," Isaiah continued, "was nice enough to be my best man."

Malcolm zeroed in on Ebony.

"I thought I lost you."

Her expression softened instantly. "Never."

Around them the chapel erupted back into noise—guests talking again, Isaiah apologizing to literally everyone saying, "Sometimes you gotta be spontaneous."

But Malcolm only saw her, and that copper smile lit up brighter than he'd ever seen before.

And I get to see it for the rest of my life.

Elvis pointed directly at Malcolm from the altar. "SON, YOU GONNA KISS HER OR KEEP HOLDIN' UP THIS CEREMONY?"

The entire chapel burst into cheers.

Malcolm pulled her close, tucking one of her waist-length braids behind her ear, smiling for the first time in what felt like years.

"For someone who doesn't know what a Grand Gesture is, you sure know how to pull one off."

"Wait 'till you see what I do the rest of our lives," he said softly before he kissed her deep.

one year later

"OK SO HOW does this work again?" Ebony's mom asked as they sat in the stand wearing t-shirts with Malcolm's face on the front with "The Puzzler" underneath.

"Each solver in the individual category gets a five hundred piece sealed puzzle and the timer starts when they open it," Ebony said, adjusting her position on the hard seats. "The fastest one to complete wins. If there is no one finished by time, then the most complete puzzle wins."

"And this many people are into it?" Her dad asked bewildered.

"The stream of it online has fifty million views."

He looked impressed by that. "Well at least we don't have to wonder which one he is."

From the stands they could easily find the 6'3" Black man crouched over a table, hands flying.

"This is just the exhibition match, Malcolm isn't on the circuit, but since we knew we'd be in South Korea I signed him up. I thought he'd cartwheel."

Her mom laughed. "Pumpkin's meeting us at the bookstore right? How long do you have to stay?"

"By contract, two hours, by excitement? Until the doors close. By willpower? Maybe three. Once I navigated the time difference, I'm knocked out by ten p.m. Max."

Her mom laughed. "So much for partying your way through South Korea."

"We party! We just leave before it gets started or I fall asleep in the middle. It works."

Well, don't push yourself. You're looking a little flushed."

"Excuse me, are you Ebony Jones?"

Ebony looked up to see a young woman about twenty years old holding a copy of "*The Witches of Time*." "I couldn't get tickets for tonight, do you mind signing my copy?"

Ebony showed all thirty-two teeth in her mouth. "Of course!" She pulled out the pen she carried for just such an occasion.

"The U.S. needs to get hip," her dad grumbled.

Ebony snorted. The book was doing well in the States, but exploding in popularity overseas. Sales paid for upgrades to the house, and she did not mind traveling around the world with her favorite Vacation Boo for signings. Especially because their parents often joined them. It was the perks of being only children; they didn't have to share.

Tonight was a special edition release party, and the buzz was electric. South Korea really knew how to welcome a sistah. It didn't hurt that Pumpkin was making a special appearance cosplaying as one of the lead witches, Luna Simone. She almost broke the internet with her costumed announcement.

Ebony's journalism career still outpaced her bookish one, and she was okay with that. She had a renewed passion and focus. With an independent platform built on the success of the Six Loves series, Ebony had more opportunities to connect with people and a team willing to chase her around the world.

Now, did it help she and Malcolm worked together all the time? Probably.

They pushed, challenged, and encouraged each other. It was the icing on an already decadent carrot cake.

Her dad nudged her. "Here he goes, here he goes!"

She checked the time on the clock. "He's doing great, this is his best time ever!"

When Malcolm sat back, you would have thought he scored the winning touchdown, the way her dad flipped out.

"That's my boy!" His voice boomed. "He's as quick as Jet!"

Malcolm turned around to them and waved, grinning from ear to ear.

"Oh he's so proud of himself!" her mom laughed, beaming and waving back. "He did so well!"

"Oh my gosh! He's going to the next round!

"Are you okay?"

"Yep!" Ebony lied as another contraction rolled through her. She would not have this baby now. Her baby boy was high and chillin', no dilation. False contractions had them thinking he was going to show up early on Martin Luther King Day, prompting her dad to decide his grandson was going to be the next Black president.

"Did you have another contraction?" her mom whispered.

"Nope! It's just the kimchi."

AFTER SIGNING SEVERAL MORE COPIES OF HER BOOKS, TAKING PHOTOS, and waiting for the next round of puzzling, she was getting a little uncomfy. A little hot. She was already heavy because the kid was huge.

She shifted her focus to the next round when it hit her. An intense band of pain wrapped around her middle and concentrate in her back. She reached out and grabbed her mom.

"Oh boy, ok here we go."

"No, let Malcolm finish."

Watching him she glanced at her watch. When the next pain hit it felt like someone whopped her in the back with a hammer. Her whimper broke Randolph Jones. He hopped up and called, "It's go time!"

Malcolm's head whipped around and he was out of his seat racing toward her.

"Your puzzle!"

"I only care about one puzzle," he said as he picked her up and signaled the medics on duty.

"Remember how you almost didn't put it together?" she grunted out as he carried her to the ambulance.

"Never gonna let me forget it huh?" He smiled down at her. "I'll have you know I carried it around with because it was the last thing I'd have of you. Slept with it next to me."

Her heart grew almost past the pain.

Almost.

"Holy shhhhhhhh."

"He's coming fast," her mom said worried.

"Little one, you kicked your momma's ass getting here and you were still late. You missed Valentine's Day by how much mom?" Malcolm asked as Ebony recovered from an absolutely bananas delivery. Randolph Jet Holiday Knight came in like a running back and was the size of one. She blamed him.

"Four minutes," Noel laughed.

"Wait, Noel, your watch, don't you keep it five minutes fast?"

Noel's face told the story.

Ebony looked up from gazing at their son like he had been sent directly from Heaven and far as Malcolm was concerned, he had.

"What's happening?" She asked exhausted.

"When that baby decided to run here, it was a minute from midnight in the States," Noel said, awestruck. "Valentine's Day."

"Happy Birthday Valentine's Day Love," she whispered against his Jet's sweet smelling head.

"Happy Valentine's Day my love," Malcolm whispered against hers.

THE END.

Ready to see the Annual Juneteenth Games and Ebony's birthday shenanigans?

——> https://BookHip.com/FARZRXA or scan the code below.

THE CRAZY LOVE.
THE FIRST LOVE.
THE LOVE THAT ALMOST BROKE HER.
THE UNEXPECTED LOVE.
@TERREECE
THE ALMOST FOREVER LOVE.
THE SAFE LOVE.

acknowledgments

I would like to thank God, my family, especially my husband, David, who was always my first reader, my biggest champion. The one who made me feel like it was okay to be big and who delights in me every single day throughout the craziness that is being married to an author.

I also want to thank my children, who never allow me to shrink and who remind me of what I taught them: you are enough as you are. They help shape my perspective, and I'm forever grateful for that.

I also want to thank my friends, all of you contributed to this book, and every one that I've ever written and will write. Thank you for being my sounding board. Thank you for offering support and ideas.

Thank you to my readers who are amazing and supportive. This is the best job ever. Thank you for allowing me to be big.

A native of Columbus, Ohio by way of Toledo, bestselling author and journalist Terreece M. Clarke writes about smart women experiencing extraordinary love.

She is an advocate for those whose voices are often ignored has written for a variety of websites, magazines, newspapers, and organizations. Her work has garnered the attention of the New York Times, Disney.com, and Jezebel.com.

Terreece's debut novel, Heartbeat, became a #1 Amazon international bestseller in two categories and launched the bestselling Courageous Love Series.

When she's not juggling family, she's busting a move or reading in her bubble. Be sure to follow her on all the socials.

tiktok.com/@terreece

instagram.com/terreece

threads.com/@terreece